Praise for Mariah Stewart

LAST CHANCE MATINEE

"The combination of a quirky small-town setting, a family mystery, a gentle romance, and three estranged sisters is catnip for women's-fiction fans."

—*Booklist*

"A good read, with a nice blend of mystery, family drama, and romance. Readers will look forward to the next installment."

—*Library Journal*

THE CHESAPEAKE DIARIES

"The town and townspeople of St. Dennis, Maryland, come vividly to life under Stewart's skillful hands. The pace is gentle, but the emotions are complex."

—*RT Book Reviews*

"If a book is by Mariah Stewart, it has a subliminal message of 'wonderful' stamped on every page."

—*Reader to Reader Reviews*

"The characters seem like they could be a neighbor or friend or even co-worker, and it is because of that and Mariah Stewart's writing that I keep returning again and again to this series."

—*Heroes and Heartbreakers*

"Every book in this series is a gem."

—*The Best Reviews*

"Captivating and heartwarming."

—*Fresh Fiction*

A DIFFERENT LIGHT

"Warm, compassionate, and fulfilling. Great reading."

—*RT Book Reviews*

"This is an absolutely delicious book to curl up with . . . scrumptious . . . delightful."

—*Philadelphia Inquirer*

MOON DANCE

"Enchanting . . . a story filled with surprises!"

—*Philadelphia Inquirer*

"An enjoyable tale . . . packed with emotion."

—*Literary Times*

"Stewart hits a home run out of the ballpark . . . a delightful contemporary romance."

—*The Romance Reader*

WONDERFUL YOU

"*Wonderful You* is delightful—romance, laughter, suspense! Totally charming and enchanting."

—*Philadelphia Inquirer*

"Vastly entertaining . . . you can't help but be caught up in all the sorrows, joys, and passion of this unforgettable family."

—*RT Book Reviews*

DEVLIN'S LIGHT

"A magnificent story of mystery, love, and an enchanting town. Splendid!"

—*Bell, Book and Candle*

"With her special brand of rich emotional content and compelling drama, Mariah Stewart is certain to delight readers everywhere."

—*RT Book Reviews*

MARIAH STEWART

The Chesapeake Bride

POCKET BOOKS

New York   London   Toronto   Sydney   New Delhi

Pocket Books
An Imprint of Simon & Schuster, Inc.
1230 Avenue of the Americas
New York, NY 10020

First Pocket Books paperback edition September 2017

POCKET and colophon are registered trademarks of Simon & Schuster, Inc.

For information about special discounts for bulk purchases, please contact Simon & Schuster Special Sales at 1-866-506-1949 or business@simonandschuster.com.

The Simon & Schuster Speakers Bureau can bring authors to your live event. For more information or to book an event, contact the Simon & Schuster Speakers Bureau at 1-866-248-3049 or visit our website at www.simonspeakers.com.

Manufactured in the United States of America

10 9 8 7 6 5 4 3 2 1

ISBN 978-1-5011-5435-5
ISBN 978-1-5011-5438-6 (ebook)

For Robb, with much love.
Welcome to the family, baby boy!

The
Chesapeake
Bride

Diary~

I love the changing of the seasons—and I think summer into fall might be a favorite, being as how I relate to the whole "autumn of my years" thing. That's how I see myself, anyway. If sixty is the new forty, I believe seventy must be the new fifty, eighty the new sixty, and so on. Therefore, I fall into that third quadrant. Don't try to change my mind or confuse me with facts.

One of the reasons I love this time of the year: the steady influx of tourists into St. Dennis begins to wane. Not that I don't love our visitors. Why, without them, St. Dennis would have continued to languish and would never have become the Eastern Shore mecca it now is. But there's something sweet about having your hometown belong to you and yours again, even if it's just for a while. I know soon enough the holidays will be upon us and many will flock to town for all the beautiful festivities—the Christmas House Tour, the weekend of caroling, the tree lighting at the square on Old St. Mary's Church Road, Christmas at the Inn (a favorite of mine), and, oh, yes, the shopping! But this little respite between the beginning of September, when the families leave to return their offspring to school, and the holiday madness belongs to us, we old St. Dennis folk who like a little downtime.

Not to say there's nothing going on here! There are new babies to celebrate and a special wedding on the horizon, one that makes me especially weepy. My dear nephew, Alec, will be marrying his lovely Lisbeth in an event that will be the talk of both St. Dennis and Cannonball Island for a long time to come. I'm not privy to all the details, mind you, but since my daughter, Lucy, is planning the wedding, I've heard bits and squeaks of what she has in mind, and it will, no doubt, be perfectly wonderful.

When we were children, Mama told us that when good folks passed, they earned a star in the heavens where they could sit and shine down on all the goings-on here on earth. Our brothers scoffed, but we girls believed her, and so it is that I know my beloved sister, Carole, will be watching happily from her star as her son marries his bride out on the point in just a few more weeks.

Thinking about the point makes me think of all the changes that are coming to Cannonball Island soon. So much, it could make your head spin! For the first time in roughly two hundred years, new dwellings will be going up on what had once been barren land. I heard from one in the know that some of the older homesteads—mostly those that have fallen into ruin or have been abandoned—will be replaced with new versions more suitable to modern living. Some are up in arms about this, but frankly, it's about time. Those dilapidated old shells offer no shelter and, if anything, detract from the beauty of the island. My good friend Ruby Carter—the island's matriarch—has given her blessing, and that's good enough for me. Besides, Alec will be serving as the environmental consultant, so I feel confident that all will be well. The new homes are being designed with the island's history in mind, so the legacy of those early settlers will be well protected. The architect is a lovely young woman who is serious about this project, so I know, eventually, all will be well.

Of course I do.

I know, too, that a certain islander with a "rolling stone" reputation will be finding his rolling days coming to a halt before too long. It will be amusing, to say the least, to see him meet his match. Will he be bested?

The smart money's on the new girl. That's all I have to say about that.

And so much excitement over all the goings-on at the mouth of the river on the other side of Cannonball Island! Who knew such mysteries lay beneath the water, waiting to be discovered—and now that they have been, well, the flurry of activity these days has my poor old head spinning like an old-fashioned top. I cannot wait to see what they find, and I'm more than happy that one of the principal players is staying at the inn. Not that I'd pry, but if one overhears a snippet of conversation now and then . . . well, let's just say it's good to keep informed. Now, how all this is going to affect the construction that was slated to begin in November, well, I suppose everyone will have to wait and see. Could be there will be delays, which will keep the new girl around for a while longer and will keep the rolling stone on his toes.

My, what fun this will be~

Grace~

Chapter One

Owen Parker shortened the last leg of his morning run, going over instead of around the dune behind the Cannonball Island General Store. The calendar might say September, but the thermometer mimicked July. Even the slight breeze off the Chesapeake did little to cool him. Sweat caused his T-shirt to cling to his chest and his sunglasses to continually slide down the bridge of his nose. He'd had enough for one day.

His great-grandmother Ruby Carter stood on the back porch of the store and watched him approach, her hands on her hips. Her white hair was pulled back in a tidy bun at her nape, and she was dressed in one of her favorite uniforms: a white sleeveless blouse with a round collar and a cotton skirt that hit smack in the center of her calves. Today's skirt was light summer green. Her other favorites were cotton-candy pink and a shade of lavender that precisely matched the color of the lilacs that grew around the back of the store in spring. While her height had diminished somewhat over her one hundred years, her back was still relatively straight and her voice strong. Her mind was as sharp as the proverbial tack. In her, the old island still lived, through her stories and through the speech patterns peculiar to Cannonball Island.

"You get much more sun, boy, you'll be fried like a fritter 'fore too long," she said as he crossed the driveway. "There's sunscreen there on one of the shelves inside—use some once in a while."

He smiled and kissed her on the cheek as he came up the steps. "I think it's too late for sunscreen. I've been tan for months now. Since Costa Rica."

"Don't know why you have to be running off to foreign places all the time. Sun's just as good here as there."

"But it's not always summer here, Gigi."

"Summer be overrated. God made all four seasons for a reason."

"What reason was that?" he teased.

"Do I look like God?" Ruby frowned. "Not mine to know what he be thinking. He has his plan and it's not mine to question. Yours either."

"Your garden's still hanging in there." He nodded in the direction of the fenced-in plot where she grew vegetables and her favorite flowers. "All those tall things still look pretty good."

"Tall things be hollyhocks and dahlias." She turned to look at her pretties and admired them. "My Harold loved dahlias. Used to buy him one every year for Father's Day. Those sweet things you see growing out there—that big pink one and the smaller yellow ones—they be offshoots of offshoots of offshoots of the ones I bought him years ago. You know how to divide 'em, you can keep 'em forever." She turned back to him. "Least for as long as you be on this earth. Can't know for sure who you can count on to tend to such things after you be gone."

"I'll tend to your dahlias, Gigi. Just like you showed me. I'll dig them up before the frost and I'll wrap them in newspaper and put them in the shed, just like you do."

"Order to do that, you have to be around, boy. You saying you be staying on the island from now on? That you be back for good?"

"No," he said cautiously. "But I will plant your dahlias in the spring after the frost, and I'll dig them up in the fall before it gets cold. I don't have to be here full-time to do that."

She stared at him, and for a moment he thought she was going to say something, but the moment passed. When a car pulled into the driveway, she turned to go back into the store to see to her customer. "Folks need to know where they belong, boy. Just like I told your sister. See how she's heeded me."

"Lis is marrying a local boy. Up until she fell in love with Alec, she had no intentions of ever coming back here to live. No matter how much you bugged her about it. Why, if I didn't know better, I'd think you somehow made her fall in love with him."

"Just 'cause you can sometimes *know* don't mean you can make folks do your will." She smacked him on the arm as she turned and went into the store. "You be living proof of that."

Owen suppressed a smile and followed her. "I'm going to run upstairs and take a shower, Gigi."

"That be the best idea you had since you woke up today." She went into the front of the store, and he took the steps to the second floor, still smiling.

Until a year ago, Ruby lived over the store, which had been in her family for two hundred years. At one hundred years of age, though spry and lively, the time had come for her to eliminate taking that trip up and down the steps twice every day. The large storage area behind the store had been redesigned and renovated into her new living quarters—a sitting room, a modern kitchen, bath, and bedroom. Alec Jansen—engaged to Lis—had used his considerable carpentry skills to convert what had been empty, unused space into a comfortable, modern apartment.

The bedrooms on the second floor above the store were mostly unused, except for the room Ruby had shared with Harold, which Lis, an artist, had taken over for her studio. The room Owen occupied was the same one he'd slept in when he visited as a boy. He knew some might find it strange that at thirty-eight he was living with his great-grandmother, but he couldn't care less what anyone else thought about the arrangement. His masculinity was intact even though the old metal bed he slept in was still covered by the same white chenille spread from his childhood, and the walls remained painted in a light shade of blue. The upholstery on the chair that sat near the window was threadbare plaid, and the curtains hadn't changed since he was in his teens, but Owen liked the familiarity of it all. After long periods of living elsewhere, it always soothed his soul to come back to this room where he'd spent so many happy times. It never occurred to him to stay anywhere else.

Owen had only been back on Cannonball Island for a few months, having spent the past couple of years here and there like the rolling stone he'd always been. There'd been Alaska and the fishing boat he'd worked on before he flew a mail plane for a few months until he tired of the cold. Next he headed for Australia, where a friend owned a cattle ranch, but mending fences and chasing cattle bored him, so he retreated to Costa Rica and spent time diving off a sunken ship, rumored to have been loaded with gold from the California mines, that had gone down in a storm in 1853. Owen had joined up with an old friend, Jared Chandler, whose salvage company had bid on the wreck and won the right to excavate it. Owen had spent a few months there before something had told him it was time to go home to Cannonball Island. He'd assumed that inner voice had been prompted by his sister's reminder that Ruby had celebrated her one-hundredth birthday without him, and the terrifying thought that she might pass on before he'd spent time with her. Jared's offering Owen work on a ship that had sunk in his home waters had made the decision a no-brainer—that and his sister's impending marriage added up to Owen's being homeward bound.

He'd thought of stopping in Arizona to visit his mother, Kathleen, on his way to the island, but she'd

recently remarried—again—having found widow-
hood no more to her liking than her second husband
had been. Apparently the third time for her was the
charm, because she sounded happier than he could
remember. Owen'd checked in with her but her calendar was full, she'd told him, with her stepgrand-
children's events.

Who knew that stepbabies and toddlers trumped
your own grown children?

Owen hadn't minded, not really. His mom hadn't
had an easy time when his dad, Jack, was alive, and
she was entitled to a happy life. Owen would never
begrudge her that. He and his sister, Lisbeth—Lis—
knew how unpredictable and unpleasant their father
had been and the cloud they'd all lived under while
he was alive.

Showered and dressed, Owen made his way
downstairs, pausing on the landing to look out the
window. A stone's throw from the store on the opposite side of the road flowed the narrowest section
of the Waring River. A mile farther and it widened
where it reached the bay. He hadn't had cause to
think about its course until last week. Not until
Jared had started asking questions had the river,
its mouth, and its relationship to the bay become
relevant.

"This diving job is going to be more complicated
than I'd thought," Jared had told Owen by phone
late in the evening of the night before.

"Anytime you're diving in the Chesapeake,
it's complicated," Owen had replied. "Visibility is
always an issue because the water is dark pretty

much everywhere, plus it's a route on the way to Baltimore Harbor, and there are all those crab and oyster fishermen to be worried about. You're talking about diving off Cannonball Island in the bay waters, and—"

"That might be changing. Something's come up."

"Something like what?"

"Something like the Maryland Historical Society thinks there's something down there that they might not want disturbed."

"What are you talking about?" Owen had grown up on the island, and while old folks had been full of tales of the old days, he couldn't recall a story about something in that area of the bay, and he said so.

"Not the bay," Jared told him. "The Waring River. The mouth of the river in particular."

"Start from the beginning."

"As you know, a builder's bought up as much of the unused land on the island as he could. His plans include building a dock in the river where his buyers can tie up their boats. They're all ready to start dredging in the mouth of the river so it's deep enough to allow for all those pretty yachts. So in the meantime, the state EPA has done some testing to determine how many houses could be built, how development would affect the bay and its natural resources, waste water, drainage, that sort of thing."

"Right. All standard. My future brother-in-law is the environmental consultant for the builder, Deiter Construction."

"Well, in the process, they scanned the waters

around the island and apparently found evidence of something at the mouth of the river that had not been seen before."

"You mean a vessel of some sort?"

"Yeah. Maybe even more than one. They did some preliminary scanning, and it looks like there could be more than one. Like something sank at some point and landed on something else that was already down there. No telling what without diving and photographing, though, so that's what we're going to be doing."

"Huh. In the morning, I'll ask Ruby if she's ever heard about something sinking in the river."

"I guess if anyone local would know, she'd be the one. Is anyone on Cannonball Island older than Ruby?"

"Not that I know of."

"We'll be doing our first dive as soon as I can get one of our smaller boats up here. The one we brought is too big for the job we're going to be doing. It would have been fine for working out closer to the channel. I'll be taking this one back to my dad's place in South Carolina, and I'll bring back the *Juliana*. I should only be gone a few days. Call me if anything comes up that I should know about, and be ready for that first dive when I get back."

"I'm ready when you are."

Owen had hung up, but the implications of what Jared had told him kept him awake until after midnight. If a sunken vessel of any kind was found in the river, the builders' construction timetable could be delayed until the vessel and whatever else might be down there had been identified and properly recorded. Depending on what they found, the dredging for the new dock could be scrapped indefinitely. The permits for the first new construction on Cannonball Island in over a hundred years could be put on hold.

Owen was still thinking about the phone call when he awoke that morning, wondering how the builder, Brian Deiter, was taking the news of the delay, assuming he'd already been told. Specifically, Owen was wondering what the project's architect, the builder's daughter, Cass Logan, would think.

The builder's beautiful blond daughter had made it clear she was immune to Owen's charm and good looks. Oh, she'd always been friendly enough in the past whenever they would run into each other, but she'd never hesitated to let him know she had absolutely no interest in him. Since he was unaccustomed to women ignoring him, Cass occupied a special place in his thoughts. He'd never walked away from a challenge.

He was still thinking about her, wondering what it was going to take to change her mind about him, while he stood on the landing and watched the sun glint off the river. He went down the remaining steps and peeked into the store. Finding Ruby busy with a customer, he went out to the porch and back to his favorite rocking chair.

A few minutes later, the door behind him opened, and he heard Ruby's deliberate footfall as she stepped outside.

"You thinkin' on settin' all day?" Ruby Carter

walked to the edge of the porch, her eyes narrowing as she challenged him with her stare.

"Maybe." Owen flashed a smile and patted the arm of the chair next to his. "Sit with me for a bit?"

"Maybe for a bit." Ruby sat. "Something on your mind?"

"Did you ever hear about any vessels sinking in or around the mouth of the river over on the southwest side of the island?"

Ruby established what she called her rocking rhythm before she responded. "Many a something gone down out there over time."

"Like what?"

"Hard to know truth from tale, but it been said one of those merchant ships went down with some tea, back in the day. Before we came to the island."

"You mean before the War of 1812, when the loyalists in St. Dennis were forced to leave and sent here to the island?"

"Way before that. Course, no one be living on the island then, nothing here but shrub pine and salt marsh. Townsfolk forced some to pack up and leave, thinking they'd die out here." She smiled. "Showed them a thing or two."

Ruby's ancestors had been among those loyal to the crown of England when the War of 1812 broke out. When several of St. Dennis's patriot sons had been conscripted by British warships, angry townsmen had forced the loyalists onto the uninhabited island across the sound. Somehow the exiles had survived despite having to build their shelters out of the small pines that grew there and having to subsist on what they could catch from the bay and raise in hastily planted gardens. Over time, a little colony was established, and those who thrived were proud of their rebellious heritage of having defied the odds.

"What was the story you heard about the merchant ship?" Owen sat back in his chair and waited.

"Well, I heard tell about a man from over to Virginia, owned some of those big ships. Brought tea and pottery and such from England—indentured servants, too—took back tobacco and wheat and whatever. The folks over to Annapolis decided they didn't want English tea coming into Maryland—this was after the folks in Massachusetts threw all that tea up there into the water. When ships came in with tea, they sent them back to England. Some of the ships stayed in the harbor too long—they got burned with the cargo still aboard. 'Cept the indentured folks, a'course." Ruby rocked, her eyes on the bay. "Seems one of them ships owned by this Virginia fellow tried to make it up the river here to hide from the folks who wanted to burn it. Storm struck outta nowhere, smashed the ship on the shoals out there in the bay, near the mouth of the river. That big ship went down, everything with it, so they said."

Owen frowned. "Gigi, there aren't any shoals in the bay near the mouth of the river."

"Maybe not this day, but back then, there be shoals. That tea ship not the only one that broke up there."

Owen knew the changing currents in the bay had, over time, built up some sections and flattened others. Sand and silt pushed by one fierce storm might later have been redirected by another.

"What else had you heard?"

"I heard some tell of early people who had a settlement on the other side of the river, thereabouts, be lost when the land sank. Maybe be down there near that tea ship."

"You mean there was a Native American settlement on the shore across from the island?"

Ruby nodded. "Native of these parts for sure, been here long before our people."

"And you think it sank into the bay?" Owen thought about the stories he'd heard over the years, about how many islands in the bay had disappeared when the water rose.

"Lots of places be sunk. Whole islands downwind of here be lost, too. Houses, all went into the bay."

"But there were warnings, right? The water levels shifted gradually and the shoreline eroded." Owen recalled the stories of Chesapeake islands totally disappearing without a trace and knew they were true.

"Bit by bit the waters rose, ate away at the land, ate the ground right out from under trees and such, whole houses slid right on into the bay. Still, some folks ignored what was happening, barely had time to get their goods to dry land. Soon enough, whole islands where folks lived and worked and farmed were eaten alive by the bay, and that be the truth. Holland Island, Cockneys Island, Eastern Neck Island—all be gone. Others, too."

"Why do you suppose Cannonball Island has been able to remain intact?"

Ruby continued to rock. "No way to tell for sure, but we haven't had a direct hit by one of them big hurricanes since I was a girl. We get the rain, but it seems not the worst of the winds. No telling why. Last real big storm I remember hit hard took a few pines off the point, nothing more."

"You really think there could be the remains of a settlement down there?"

"All be down there at one time, not for me to say what still is or isn't. Folks say that was a summer village, early folks come to grow wheat and feed off the bay. Winter comes, they go elsewhere. I never did hear tell where. But like I said, water shifts things, moves things around as it pleases. No telling where things be now." She glanced at Owen over the top of her glasses. "Seems to me those new machines y'all have should be able to say."

A car pulled into the store's parking lot and drove around toward the back. Owen watched his sister's old sedan come to a stop.

"Hey, Gigi. Owen." Lis waved as she approached. "Break time?"

"We just sitting and chatting," Ruby told her. "You feel free to sit and chat, too, Lisbeth."

"I just stopped by to see if you needed any help unloading boxes in the store. I know today's delivery day." Lis sat on the top step and turned so she was facing her brother and great-grandmother. She was dark haired, like Owen, and slender. Their features were similar, both having inherited wide-set eyes the same shade of green, and dimpled cheeks.

"Already taken care of," Owen told her.

"Oh, my, aren't we the efficient one." Lis stretched out her legs. "So Alec tells me there's going to be a delay in building the dock."

"That's the word."

"So where does that leave your girlfriend? Think she'll stay around during the delay?" Lis smirked.

Owen scowled. "If you're referring to Cass Logan, she's not my girlfriend, and I have no idea what her plans are."

"Jared might know. They looked pretty cozy chatting in the lobby at the inn yesterday. I stopped in to see Grace about borrowing folding chairs for the wedding, and I just happened to walk through the lobby to Grace's office." Lis grinned. "Jared is such a stud. If I'd known you had such hunky friends, I might have learned to dive myself."

"Lisbeth, you just being a brat, tweaking your brother's nose like that." Ruby tried unsuccessfully to hold back a chuckle. "And you, Owen, if you have an interest in that girl, best you be man enough to speak up, before someone else has a mind to."

"Someone else might already have done so," Lis said.

"All right, that's enough. Yes, I admit I have *somewhat* of a casual interest in Cass." Owen nudged at Lis's outstretched leg with his foot. "She doesn't seem very interested in me."

"What? What did you say?" Lis cupped a hand up to her ear. "It almost sounded as if you admitted you'd met a woman who seems impervious to your legendary charm."

"I know. Hard to believe. But then, I suppose it was only a matter of time." He pretended to be crestfallen.

"Well, there's still that redhead who started to work at Steffie's ice cream shop a few weeks ago. Maybe a little young for you, though. Thirty-eight would be almost another generation to her."

"Yeah, but those were thirty-eight fun-filled, action-packed years." Owen stood, and Ruby shifted in her chair, about to stand as well. Both Lis and Owen moved to give her a hand.

"I'm able to stand and walk on my own, thank you both very much." Ruby straightened her back. "Time to be getting back inside, see what needs to be done. And I got a new book that came in the mail yesterday, not going to read itself."

"Another gory story of murder and mayhem? It kills me that you love those creepy stories." Lis pretended to shudder.

"They just be made-up, Lisbeth. That's why they call them fiction books."

"Whatever floats your boat," Lis conceded. "You need me to do anything, Gigi?"

"Owen took care of the shelves and swept up the floor. Filled the coolers and changed a lightbulb. No, I'm good for today." Ruby made her way into the store. "Tomorrow's another day, though, so stop back."

"She never fails to amaze me," Lis said after the door closed.

"Me, too. She's barely slowed down since we were kids."

"I hope I'm as hardy as she is when I'm one hundred. If I'm lucky enough to live that long."

"You've got a shot at it. Only the good die young."

Lis hopped down the two steps to the ground. "But seriously, about Cass? Just a little sisterly advice: if you're interested, speak up. I don't know what her story is, but Cass Logan is not a woman who's going to be alone for too long."

"How do you know she's not involved with someone, someplace else?"

Lis shrugged. "I don't know for sure, but she doesn't have a settled look about her. Of course, you're the one with the 'sight,' not me. I'm surprised you haven't already figured her out."

"You know I don't do that." Owen frowned.

"Ruby says it isn't something you 'do' or 'not do.' It's something you have or don't have. You and Ruby have it. I, on the other hand, do not. Which I never thought was fair, by the way." Lis started toward her car. "I never understood why you and not me."

"I'd gladly hand it off if I could." He stood on the porch, leaning on one of the posts. "It's not something I ever wanted."

"Ah, so you admit it." She stopped near the car's front fender and turned. "You admit you have the Carter eye."

"Maybe. But not for Cass."

"What do you mean, not for her?"

"I mean, maybe I have some kind of second sight, but it doesn't seem to apply to her. Not to anyone I'm close to. I never could read you or Ruby. I have no idea how it works." He shrugged and lowered his voice. "I can't read Cass."

"Aha! So you have tried."

He shook his head. "I never have to try. The knowing is always just there. But I admit, if I did, I might try to read her."

"Huh." Lis seemed to think this over for a moment. "How 'bout that?"

"What?"

"Nothing." She opened her car door. "'Cept Ruby always says she could never get a read on her Harold, either."

Lis got in and started the car, then backed out of the drive, pausing once to look back and raise a hand to wave. Owen waved back and stepped down onto the grass, walked aimlessly toward Ruby's garden. He knew all about how Ruby could never get a read on their great-grandfather, always referred to as Ruby's Harold or, less frequently, Grandpap. Ruby always said it was because they were too close, it would be like reading herself. But that sure as hell wasn't the case with him and Cass Logan, who made small talk with him but, other than that, never seemed too interested. He wished he knew how to change that because, yeah, much to his annoyance, his sister had been right about one thing.

If he could get a read on Cass, by any means, he'd take it.

Chapter Two

Cass Logan had booked a suite of rooms at the Inn at Sinclair's Point for a week that had so far stretched into two. She could have gone back to her condo in Baltimore while they awaited the permits for Deiter Construction's latest project, but she liked the accommodations and was enjoying herself so much she decided to extend her stay. She played tennis every morning, and every other day she went for a bike ride to explore the area. She'd set up her computer on the desk in the suite's sitting room and spread out her design plans on the coffee table, and though it was only a temporary office, the suite had everything she needed.

As the lead architect for her father's company, Cass had designed homes for several of his projects along Maryland's Chesapeake shores. But this project—Cannonball Island—was special.

The already-small population of Cannonball Island had been declining for years along with the number of watermen who called the island home.

Entire families simply left to seek employment and a life elsewhere, walking away from homes that had been battered by storms for a century or longer. As one former resident whose property was directly across the road from the Chesapeake had put it, "That roof was replaced every eight to ten years for the past fifty. Time to move on." As a result, the island was dotted with abandoned homes in various stages of disrepair. Deiter Construction had tracked down the owners and purchased the properties at fair market value for the structures and the land with an eye toward building houses that retained the design and flavor of the originals.

When Cass and her father met with environmental consultant Alec Jansen to discuss the feasibility of development of the island, she'd gotten her first look at those tiny, dilapidated two-hundred-year-old houses. She saw not the rot, but the charm and the serenity of the unspoiled island. She'd imagined expanded floor plans that incorporated reclaimed wood and brick in the new homes. She'd been able to convince her father that her vision was the one that would best sell, and to the surprise of just about everyone—except Cass—Brian had completely scrapped his original plans to build modern structures of glass and steel and gave his daughter the green light to design the project as she saw it.

Of course, if the houses didn't sell, she'd have more than a little egg on her face. Her dad was entrusting her with the multimillion-dollar development of valuable land. Cass knew and appreciated the stakes, and she recognized she had a lot to prove. The solution was to make sure no stone was left unturned in making the project as unique and attractive as possible. There were lots of places on the Eastern Shore where a bundle could be dropped on a new home. The Deiter Construction houses on Cannonball Island had to deliver something the others couldn't. She was still trying to put her finger on exactly what that might be. The use of whatever could be salvaged from each property was important, but there had to be more. She was positive she was on the verge of finding that elusive something.

This morning Cass had played her usual hour of tennis and returned to her room with a spring in her step. She brewed coffee in the small coffeemaker and poured a cup, then, still in her tennis whites, went through the open French doors onto her balcony. She liked to feel the cool breeze off the bay while she worked and often took her iPhone with her to sit on one of the comfortable chairs and read her email and make phone calls.

From her chair she could watch the other guests of the inn go about their activities, and she often did. There was always something to do for those who liked to keep moving, as the inn offered tennis, sailing, canoeing, kayaking, and biking. A library on the first floor had books for rainy days, and organized walking tours of the town were offered. The playground on the far side of the inn had been masterfully planned, and full-time former camp counselors were there to supervise the children should the parents want to spend their time doing something other than watching their kids on the play equipment. The

Inn at Sinclair's Point had more going for it than Cass's quiet, empty apartment, so there was no mystery in her deciding to stay on while the project was getting under way. Not that Cass disliked her condo, but she'd been alone for months since her divorce became final, and she'd found that too much peace and quiet left her feeling restless. Spending some time at the inn was the perfect antidote.

She finished reading her email and responding to those requiring a prompt reply, then went to the railing and leaned over to watch a young family cross the lawn on their way to the parking lot. The mother had a child on each hand, and the father carried a third. Something in the man's stride reminded her of her now-ex-husband, and she felt the slightest pang of regret—not for the divorce, but for the sorry way their marriage had ended.

The day Bruce Logan walked into Cass's English lit class sophomore year at Penn State, she knew he was the guy for her. He was tall and lean and had that rugged look about him that always turned Cass's head. He was on an ROTC scholarship, so Cass knew he'd owe the military a year of service for every year of college. Back then, it hadn't seemed like a bad idea. They were married the day after graduation, and the plan was for Cass to get her architect's degree, after which she'd work for her father while Bruce served out his obligations. She'd save as much money as she could so that when his required term of service was completed, they would be able to buy a house and start a family. Unfortunately, neither of them could foresee that Bruce would fall totally in love with the military. When his time was up, when he should have been preparing to leave, he was volunteering for another tour of combat—and after that, another. It hadn't taken Cass long to realize that the plans they'd made were never going to happen.

"I'm sorry," Bruce had told her. "I love you, Cassie, I do. But what I'm finding out about myself is that I was meant to be a career soldier. It's who I am. I'll go wherever they send me and I'll stay as long as they tell me to stay, do whatever I'm told. I know it's not what we planned, but I think all my life I've been looking for something bigger than myself, and this is it."

Why that *something* hadn't been the love they'd shared and the life they'd planned together, Cass would never know. But clearly, where he needed the challenge of the next deployment, she needed the stability of a home. Cass didn't judge him, but she couldn't live that life. She suggested the divorce, and he had quickly—a little too quickly, she'd thought—agreed.

Their parting had been bittersweet, but she'd let him go and set about making a life for herself. She'd been unsure where she'd land until she set foot on Cannonball Island that first time. Something here had spoken to her in a way she couldn't define, but she knew she was meant to be here, meant to be the one to help set the island on a new course, just as Bruce knew where he belonged.

This was her path now, and she was determined to follow to see where it might lead.

A ping from her phone reminded her she'd reserved a bike for a late-morning ride. She went back inside and turned off her computer. It was a beautiful sunny day in a perfect little bay town, and she was determined to get out to enjoy it. She changed into bike shorts and a matching tank, tied on her sneakers, tucked her short blond hair behind her ears, and, after grabbing her room key and sunglasses from the desk, set out for the kiosk behind the inn. She picked up the bike she'd reserved and the required helmet, along with a bottle of water from the cooler. Soon she was pedaling leisurely along the inn's long winding driveway toward Charles Street, the main road that ran from the highway through St. Dennis and straight out to the bridge that separated the town from Cannonball Island.

At the end of the driveway, she paused. A ride through the side streets of the town or to the island? She weighed the choices. She'd just gone on a walking tour of the oldest section of St. Dennis's historic district two days ago, so clearly, the island was the way to go today. She'd get a better workout if she rode all the way around and came full circle back to the bridge. It would give her a chance to once again look over the available home sites so she could finally decide where she wanted to build her own house, because she was determined that one of the houses would be hers. By the time she'd circumvented the entire island, she'd probably have polished off the single bottle of water she'd brought with her, so she could stop at the general store and buy another.

If she happened to run into her friend Ruby, that would be a plus. Of course, it was just as likely she'd run into Ruby's great-grandson Owen Parker, who was tall, dark, ruggedly handsome, and oh so easy on the eyes. Not that she was the least bit interested.

Cass had Owen Parker figured out the first time she met him. *Too good-looking for his own good* had been her first thought, but something else about him made it hard to look away. His artist sister had been exhibiting some of her paintings at the art center in St. Dennis, and on a whim, Cass had decided to go. It had taken just one conversation with Owen to know he was also charming and funny, a man with many interests and a scattered background. This scattering of places and things had set off her alarms. It seemed that over the past few years, he hadn't stayed long in any one place. Cass wasn't about to give a second look to any guy who followed a wandering star. She'd been there and done that. The ink was barely dry on her divorce papers.

Still, she couldn't deny that the last time she'd met someone who drew her eyes the way Owen did was the day she'd met her ex. *And look how that had turned out*, she'd cautioned herself. Best to ignore the man even while she fell in love with the island.

She pedaled along the road that ran the entire way around the island in a loop, the bay on one side, the dunes and wetlands on the other. Where the marshes had receded, small houses battered by time, wind, and water, abandoned by the families that had built them, stood facing the bay. Deiter Construction had bought every one of them. Cass still couldn't decide which of the sites to purchase for herself. She had it narrowed down to three possibilities. Today she'd ride past all three.

The first was on the eastern side of the island, and with that destination in mind, she pedaled a little faster. Two lots past the oldest chapel on the island—itself long since abandoned by its congregation—she came to a stop. Straddling the bike seat, she scanned the site from one red-painted lot marker to the others.

Two hundred years ago, the ancestors of Tom Mullan had built this small house from the scrub pine they found on the island and some oak that a relative had smuggled to them by boat from the mainland. It had three of the smallest bedrooms Cass had ever seen and a great room that boasted a brick fireplace. The Mullan place had been the first structure on the island Cass had entered, and she'd immediately been struck by the possibilities of what could be done there. For that reason, and because the property had a clear view straight across the bay four seasons of the year, Cass had developed a liking for the location.

She put the kickstand down and moved her sunglasses to the top of her head as she walked the driveway that had been created by innumerable cars parking on the same spot of grass over the years. A pair of red-winged blackbirds watched her warily from reeds that grew on a nearby dune. It was so quiet she could hear their wings beating when they took off. She reached the walk in front of the house and studied the structure.

The design was so charming, so elegant in its

simplicity, the windows small but well placed, the door set back just a bit under a little arched over-hang. As an architect, she appreciated all its lines and curves. She hated the idea of this house being a teardown, but really, it was so small, it was just enough for one person.

The thought was like a thunderclap inside her head. It was so simple, it was genius.

Why couldn't they renovate a few of these little houses—the ones that were salvageable—and sell them to singles who wanted a private getaway spot all their own?

Mentally she walked through the interior once again. Kitchen, living room, dining room, mostly one space. A fireplace. Three tiny bedrooms, but two could be combined into one to give a decent-size room, closet, and bath. The other bedroom could be a study, or an artist's studio, or a guest room. The hall bath could be expanded through a small addition to the back of the house. They'd have to gut the inside, but that was okay, certainly better than taking the entire house down, and they'd reuse all the old materials they could.

Window boxes on those front windows, she thought as she walked around to the back, and out here, a patio big enough to entertain if that's what the owner felt like doing. A cobbled walk, maybe, and a place out front for a few chairs where one could watch the bay.

She felt like patting herself on the back. She was already planning what she'd tell the marketing people to stress in their ads.

Maybe just a handful of these little places, just enough to give those who were interested in such things the feeling of a community. The area from St. Dennis to Rock Hall offered so much in the way of activities and cultural events that one would be hard-pressed not to find a dozen fun things to do on the weekends. Not everyone has children or a significant other. How nice to have a place that understands the needs of singles.

Would it be best to sprinkle such places throughout the island, or to build a sort of colony? She'd have to think about that and study the houses they'd already purchased to see if others would be suitable.

She was still writing ad copy in her head when she heard the pounding of feet on the macadam. She looked to her right just as the runner passed her bike, gradually slowed, then stopped.

"Hey, Cass." Owen Parker stood at the foot of the driveway in running shorts, sunglasses, and that was about all. The shirt he'd apparently been wearing when he first set out hung around his neck. He was breathing hard, and sweat dripped down his face as well as his bare chest.

It was tough to look away from such manly beauty, but she forced herself to ignore the gloriousity that was Owen Parker. *There be folly*.

"Hey, Owen. Nice day for a run." She affected a neutral tone and strolled casually to the road.

"It was when I first started out, but since the clouds have moved out, man, it's hot. Almost as hot as yesterday, and yesterday was a beast. I didn't even get my full run in. At least today, I got one full loop around the island." He used the shirt to wipe the sweat from his face. She tried to ignore that one slow stream that slid down his chest to the waistband of his shorts. It took all her willpower not to reach out and run her finger along its path.

He swiped at it and it disappeared.

Cass cleared her throat. "It has warmed up. Still nice, though."

"Yeah, my mom always said a hot day on the island was better than any other day anywhere else." He shrugged. "Of course, she moved to Arizona first chance she got, so I guess we should take that with a grain of salt." He glanced up the driveway to the house. "I heard you bought the place. Your dad's company, that is. This place and a bunch of others."

"That's right."

"Knocking 'em all down?" She could see his eyes narrowing even behind the dark lenses of his glasses.

"That hasn't been decided yet." She crossed her arms over her chest.

"Oh? I'd heard that was the plan."

"There is no final plan." She slid her glasses from the top of her head to her face.

"You still thinking about building a place for yourself?"

"Where'd you hear that?"

"Alec mentioned it over dinner one night last week. You know he's engaged to my sister, right?"

She nodded.

"So the question was . . ."

"A nosy one. I heard you. I'm not sure what I want to do." She stared at him for a moment.

"Sorry. I guess Alec got it wrong. I was under the impression you liked it here."

"I do like it here. It's peaceful." She turned and looked back at the old Mullan house. "I like that my designs for the homes are all touched by the history of the island. It's a place where you can hear yourself think and you can . . . Well, you get the idea."

"I do. Lived here a good part of my life."

"But not recently."

"No. Not recently."

"Why's that? If you love it here so much, why have you been just about everywhere in the world but here?" Turnabout was fair play, she decided. He asked a personal question, wasn't she entitled to do the same?

"I guess, for a long time, there wasn't much to keep me here. Now Jared's got this gig going, and I'll have work to keep me busy." Owen smiled. "I do love a good dive."

"Are you a professional diver?"

"Yeah, but I only take on jobs I want to do. All dives aren't created equal." He looked to the bay. "I love to dive here because I can't resist the opportunity to see what the bay's been hiding from me all my life. Besides, it's home. But I've enjoyed warm-water dives, too—Florida, Mexico, the coast of South America, parts of the Mediterranean. But I always come back to the island." He swabbed the back of his neck with the shirt. "In between dives, I do other things."

"I seem to recall you telling me that. Bush pilot. Fisherman. Ranch hand. Did I miss anything?"

"That'll do. I guess the diving we're going to be doing here has thrown a monkey wrench into your plans. I'll do what I can to keep things moving so we don't delay you too much."

"What are you talking about?" she snapped.

"You know, the ship . . ." He stared at her.

"What ship?"

"The ship over in . . ." He ran a hand through his hair. "Oh, hell. Didn't anyone tell you?"

"Tell me what?" She felt like grabbing him by the neck and shaking it out of him.

"The Maryland Historical Society suspects there's a sunken ship in the mouth of the Waring and they've put a hold on the permits until we figure out what's down there and if—"

"Who is *we*?"

"The salvage company they called in to explore the site. Chandler and Associates. Well, actually, I've been hired to do some of the diving, and—"

"The salvage company . . . you mean Chandler? Jared's company?"

Owen nodded. "Well, his family's company, but yeah, I'm going to be working with him."

"I met him at the inn. He never mentioned any of this." Cass felt bewildered.

"Does he know you work for Deiter Construction?"

"We never really got into that. It was just a conversation in the lobby. Dan Sinclair introduced us and we just had a brief conversation. He said he was here to dive on a wreck in the bay. He never said anything about the river. About our dock."

"Probably because he didn't realize it was something you should know about."

"How long is this going to take? Why can't we begin construction while you're diving? Why weren't we notified?"

Owen held up one hand and counted off on his fingers to answer her questions. "One, no way of knowing right now because it hasn't been determined what's down there. Two, if the ship is where it's believed to be, the dock you wanted to build at the mouth of the river will have to be relocated. You're going to have to find another place somewhere around the island where the water is deep enough so the dredging will be kept to a minimum because there are oyster farms in the bay. You're going to have to locate them and steer clear." He held up the third finger. "I imagine the state has already sent a letter."

"To my father? Oh, crap." Brian Deiter was not going to take this well. He hated delays, and if he received a letter out of the blue telling him his newest project was being put on hold, he wouldn't care if the *Titanic* was found at the bottom of the Waring River. "I'm going to have to call him and tell him. What's this ship they think is there?"

"Ruby thinks it's a pre–Revolutionary War merchant ship."

"Oh, crap. That'll hold things up forever." She was in hot water and she knew it. Her father had already sunk a lot of money into this project. She cringed at the thought of the phone call she was going to have to make.

"Maybe it won't be too bad," Owen said as if trying to soften the news. "Maybe it's something that can be dealt with quickly."

"What are the chances of that? A Revolutionary-era merchant ship," she repeated aloud. "Swell. I guess I better make that call."

"Hey, sorry for giving you a bad day."

She nodded absently and turned away as she took her phone from her pocket and speed-dialed her father's number, her heart in her throat. She walked up the driveway to the house, no longer thinking about the plans she'd drawn up for its revival. It pained her to realize the renovations here might be further in the future than she'd planned.

And her father might pull the plug on the entire project if he got his back up, and that would be a disaster. She had put so much of herself into the planning, plus it could tarnish her personal reputation, damage her credibility. Everyone in the company knew this was her baby. She was starting to wish she'd held off making the call when her father picked up.

"How's my favorite girl?" He sounded as if he was in a good mood. Cass's heart sank, knowing she was about to ruin it.

"Dad, I'm sorry to have to make this call, but—"

"Cassie, you all right? Something happen there?" His voice went full-on concerned dad.

"Oh, no, no. I'm fine."

"You don't sound fine. You sound upset."

"I am upset. I just got some news that . . ." Oh,

why beat around the bush? Might as well put it out there. Cass took a deep breath. "Dad, you're going to be getting a letter from the Maryland Historical Society. They're going to be putting a temporary halt to the dock on the island. They think there's—"

"What?" Cass could see her father rising from his chair, his face turning red as he loomed over his desk. "What the hell are you talking about?"

She explained the best she could with the few facts she had.

"How long is this going to go on? What kind of delay are we talking about here? If I can't offer a dock to the potential buyers who want to be able to come and go on their boats, I got a problem. The dock has to be convenient to the houses. No one's going to walk clear around the island to get to their damned boat."

"You're assuming there's a place to build a dock on the bay side, Dad. That hasn't been established yet. I'll find out what I can, and I'll let you know as soon as I hear something. I wanted to get to you before you heard from the state."

"There *was* a letter from the state somewhere," he mumbled. Cass could hear him rustling papers on his desk. "Must have misplaced it somehow. Tell me again why moving the dock has stopped the entire project. Why can't we just move the dock and get on with it?"

"Because in the construction phase, we need to transport material to the island by boat, remember? The one bridge onto the island wasn't built to carry heavy loads."

"Why don't we just build a bigger damned bridge?"

"It's a historic site, Dad. Back in 1814—"

"Eighteen fourteen," he grumbled. "It's 2017. So how long's this gonna take, Cassie? I got contractors lined up, I got supplies on order, equipment on hold. I can't expect everyone to wait around until I get the all clear."

"I spoke with one of the divers who's going to explore the site and determine if in fact it's going to merit historic designation. He said he's determined to get this under way as soon as possible, and he'll let me know as soon as he knows what's down there." Owen hadn't exactly said all that, but it sounded good, and if it placated her father for now, she'd go with it. "We're just going to have to be patient and hope for the best, but in the meantime, you might want to think about moving some of the subs to the Carmen Hills project."

"I hate to . . ." Her father sighed deeply. "But you're right. As soon as you hear, though . . ."

"You will know as soon as I know."

"I want to put up a spec house as soon as possible." Cass could hear in his voice that he was starting to calm down. "I've been thinking maybe one of those lots that face the bay."

"We might be able to start clearing the lots. I don't see the harm in that, but I'll talk to Alec and see what he thinks. Without the materials, though, we have nothing to build with. I can ask if he thinks there's another option for the dock. I think we need to be proactive and get ahead of this thing. If we could move the dock to, say, the bay side, that's where you'd offer the houses to the buyers who have boats."

"Just what I was thinking, Cassie. You took the words right out of my mouth. Talk to whoever you have to. Tell him we're ready to put up a spec, one of those really great designs of yours. Keep this project on track. I hate delays. Time is money. And you know if this thing drags on too long, I'm going to have to bail on the entire thing." He sighed deeply. "So you coming back to Baltimore while this is being hashed out or what?"

"I think I'm going to hang around St. Dennis for a while. I haven't had a vacation in forever and I'm overdue." Cass paused. "I like it here. I have a lovely suite of rooms at that beautiful old inn where they treat me like a princess and feed me very well three times a day—sometimes four, if you count afternoon tea, which I've come to adore. Why would I come back to Baltimore?"

"Well, your mother worries, you know, that maybe you're spending too much time by yourself. Like, maybe you're depressed since the divorce, and—"

"Tell Mom I am happier now than I have been in a long time. As for being alone, I've met some interesting people here and I'm busy every day. I've been playing tennis in the morning and I joined a group to bike with sometimes in the afternoon. I've gone on walking tours and garden tours and to an art exhibit."

"Really? All that?" Cass could hear the frown in her father's voice. No one in his experience had been happy about being divorced. She knew both he and her mother had been harboring this image of her being crushed after hers became final. They were having a hard time believing she was actually happy on her own.

"Really. Besides, I've been finishing up the designs for the houses we'll build once we get the green light. We have twenty-two lots to sell, and I want every house to be different yet still reflect the island's heritage. That's the promise we made to Alec and to Ruby Carter, and I very much want to honor that. I can't think of any project I've worked on I've enjoyed more."

"Well, you're the architect. Make me proud I gave you free rein for this project."

"I always make you proud, and you know it." Cass knew it was true. Her father had been delighted with every home and every commercial building she'd designed for his clients. "We will keep this on schedule, and when these houses are completed, visitors to the island will be hard-pressed to know which of the houses are two hundred years old, and which are brand-new. At least, from the exterior."

"That was the plan and that's what's going to sell out this project. So, call your mother once in a while. And keep me in the loop. Let me know what you hear."

"Will do, Dad."

That hadn't gone so badly, Cass mused after she disconnected the call. Other than his initial blowup, he'd been rational. That was a plus. Now she was going to have to do what she could to keep things moving forward.

She put in a call to Alec and left a voice mail outlining her father's concerns and asking for Alec's advice. She walked around to the back of the house, where she'd envisioned a patio made from the brick they'd remove from the crumbling fireplace. She wondered if she could find someone local who made bricks by hand so they could re-build the chimney. There was no way she would ever give up on this project. She was just going to have to make certain things moved quickly here. If her father started losing money due to the delay, he might decide to cut his losses and sell what he'd already bought here. She could not allow that to happen.

A ping on her phone alerted her to an incoming text from Alec.

Looking into it. Will get back to you.

Asked and answered. She called her father and let him know the situation was being addressed.

She'd just gotten back onto her bike and was about to put on her helmet when Owen made his second pass.

"Aren't you dying from the heat?" she asked when he slowed down.

"Yeah. I was just thinking I was done for the day, but I'm too stubborn to quit. Thanks for giving me a reason to stop."

"Don't let me hold you."

"I'll take any excuse I can get." He wiped his forehead with his forearm.

She wondered what happened to his shirt but didn't ask because she didn't want him to know she'd noticed and remembered. "Tell me a little more about this ship that you're diving on."

"All I know is what Ruby told me. She thinks it's a ship that was carrying tea when the colonists had decided they didn't want English tea. She said she'd heard a story about a shipowner from Virginia trying to hide one of his vessels that had been refused at Annapolis, but a storm had come up and the ship went down where it anchored, which, according to her story, was in or near the mouth of the river. She also thought there could be one of the bay's sunken islands down there, but that will require a lot more research, depending on what we find and where we find it."

"A sunken island?" Cass raised an eyebrow.

Owen explained how the winds and waters of the bay had eroded so many islands over the years and had relocated some of the sunken ships from where they'd landed when they first went down, to where they now lay.

"You mean islands were here one day and gone the next?" She pondered how that might happen.

"In most cases, it took a little longer than that."

"But you mean small islands where no one lives, like Goat Island, right?"

"No. A lot of the islands that disappeared had whole communities, a lot like here. Houses, businesses, farms—all gone."

"What did people do?" Cass wondered aloud, fascinated by the idea of towns, of farms, just, poof! Gone! "How could that happen?"

"That's a story in itself." He smiled. "I could tell

you all about it over dinner. What are you doing on Saturday night?"

She shouldn't. Really, she shouldn't. But she was drawn to the story. Not, she told herself, to the man who was telling it. But it would be better to keep him in her corner, wouldn't it?

"Just dinner?" she debated.

"That's the offer."

"Nothing else?"

"What else would there be?" he asked, all innocent charm.

"You make it really hard for me to say no."

"Why would you want to say no?" He flashed a disarming smile.

"All right. Just dinner." *And information,* she thought. Maybe by then he'd have an update on the ship. If they were going to have to move the dock, maybe he'd have some thoughts on that as well.

"You still at the inn?"

"I am."

"I'll pick you up at seven, if that's a good time?"

"Perfect."

"See you then." He turned to jog away.

"Hey, Parker," she called after him.

He turned and glanced over his shoulder.

"Bring your stories."

Without breaking stride, Owen waved to acknowledge he'd heard.

That was dumb, her little voice scolded. *You should have said no. He's a player.*

Yes, Cass admitted. *But he's a player with some really great stories, stories I can build on when we begin to advertise and market this project. And he's a direct hotline to the ship that's mucking up my plans.*

Besides, it took two to play, and she had no interest in playing.

CASS HAD JUST enough time to return to the inn, check in her bike, and take a quick shower before joining Grace Sinclair, the inn's owner, on the terrace for tea at four. From the doorway, she could see Grace at the large round table under the pergola where they met every afternoon. Dressed in a simple pale yellow sundress, her white hair pinned loosely at the top of her head, Grace appeared to be holding court. Cass was a little disappointed to find most of the seats already taken. She'd enjoyed the conversations she and Grace had had. Of course, some of the others at the table might be thinking the same thing when they saw *her* approach the table. *Touché*, Cass told herself as she slipped into an empty seat.

"Cass, I was hoping you'd join us today." Grace briefly introduced the newcomers at the table.

Cass wasn't sure she'd remember anyone's name. "Nice to meet you all. And for the record, I wouldn't miss afternoon tea. I'm becoming addicted." Cass nodded when the server offered her a cup and waited for Cass to make her choice of several teas. She'd had Earl Grey three times in the past week and wanted something a little different—but not *too* different. She didn't care for green tea and, at this time of the day, needed a little more caffeine than some of the herbal teas offered. "I'll try Prince of Wales, thank you."

Her tea was served and a plate of sandwiches passed her way. She helped herself to a ham and mustard, a salmon and cream cheese, and a watercress, her new favorite.

"Before you arrived, we were talking about the rumor going around town that there may be a sunken ship at the bottom of the river over near Cannonball Island, and word is that it may have been a merchant ship carrying tea during Revolutionary times," Grace said.

"We thought it apropos to discuss while having tea." A woman with blond hair that resembled straw and who apparently thought herself quite clever added, "Get it? Because we're drinking *tea*?"

"Yes, I get it." Cass took a nibble of salmon and ignored an urge to roll her eyes.

"The owner of the company that's been hired to locate the ship will be staying here at the inn while the diving is going on. I can't wait to talk to him. I think it's all very exciting." Grace sipped her tea from a pretty china cup that she'd once told Cass had belonged to her grandmother. All the cups they used for tea had belonged to someone in Grace's family, and why, Grace had asked rhetorically, should they remain unused in the cupboard?

"Actually, I spoke with one of the divers a little while ago," Cass said. "Apparently the diving will start soon. He did say something about ships having gone down somewhere else but drifting into the river." At least, she thought that was what Owen had meant.

"Oh, yes. We have wicked storms here on the

Chesapeake," Grace explained. "Winds blow the waters about, currents change and shift. It's no secret things underwater and above get moved from time to time. Why, whole islands have disappeared."

Cass had her cup raised to her lips, but it remained there when she heard Grace's comment. It was almost as if she'd known the lost islands had been a topic of conversation barely an hour ago. Cass knew Grace and Ruby were close friends. Had Ruby mentioned to Grace her theory that there could be a lost island at the bottom of the bay near where it met the river?

"Whole islands disappeared?" one of the women at the table asked. "You mean, real landmasses, gone?"

"Oh, yes," Grace assured her. "It's happened many times. The storms flood the land and eat away at the sand. Why, some years back, Hurricane Isabel caused a number of islands to completely flood. Tangier and Smith Islands were totally underwater. The damage was in the millions of dollars."

"Smith Island?" Another women perked up. "Where those fabulous cakes are baked? *That* Smith Island?"

Grace nodded. "The point being, it isn't unusual a ship on the bottom might drift or be pushed by currents to someplace other than where it sank." She turned to Cass. "I hope this development won't hold up your project, with the state being involved."

"Actually, we are experiencing a delay right now because of the possibility that we might have to look for another place to build the dock to bring in equipment and building supplies. Lumber and such. Plus, eventually, the dock will be offered to buyers for their own use. It's getting complicated."

"What kind of project are you working on, Cass?" asked the blond with the strawlike hair. Julie? Joanna? Cass wasn't sure.

"We're going to be building a few—a very few—small houses on Cannonball Island."

When the woman looked at her blankly, Cass told her, "It's at the end of Charles Street, right over the bridge."

"Oh, and the island has a wonderful history," Grace exclaimed, then told how the British loyalists were forced to leave St. Dennis during the War of 1812 and were banished to the island. "There's no place like it, Joanna. It's one of the Chesapeake's true unspoiled treasures."

"And you're building there? Are you a builder?" Joanna pressed.

"I'm an architect. My father is a builder. His company has developed up and down the Chesapeake over the past twenty years."

"I have it on good authority the homes you're designing for the island will be unlike anything else . . . well, anything anywhere." Grace turned to the others. "Cass is basing her designs on the original architecture of the island, some very unique places, I assure you. She's using the actual materials used to build the original structures wherever possible in her new homes." Grace beamed at Cass. "I love the idea of using the same hardwood from the original floors in the new houses. The old window glass, the old brick . . . every house will be unique and will carry the spirit of the one that once stood on that same land. Imagine—walking on the same floors as the first inhabitants of the island. I think it's so romantic and quite clever of you."

"I'd be interested in seeing your designs," the man sitting across from Joanna said. "I've been thinking about buying a small place on the bay for weekend getaways."

"I'm afraid none of the houses will be grand, and most of them will be modest in size. Some will even be quite small," Cass told him. Might as well get that out there. "We're trying to have as little impact on the environment as possible."

"So much the better. I don't need much space, and it would be nice to have some time to myself, maybe one guest once in a while." The man smiled broadly. "There's something to be said about a vacation place that no one expects to be invited to, and I applaud your efforts to respect the history. In my spare time, I write poetry. Not very good poetry, but I enjoy it nonetheless. I'd love to have a getaway to sit and write whenever I please." He smiled as he reached into his pocket and pulled out his wallet, took out a business card, and passed it to Cass. "Who knows? Maybe such a place could inspire me to write something that's less than dreadful. Give me a call when you're ready to start selling. I'd like to take a look."

"Me, too." Joanna dug into her bag, came out with a small pad upon which she wrote her name and phone number. She passed it to Cass. "I'd love to have a place of my own. Well, *our* own. It's just my husband and me, since our kids have grown up and taken off. We don't need a lot of space, and we're both interested in the environment and in history, so it sounds like the type of thing we'd like."

"I'll be happy to get back to you"—Cass glanced at the names—"Todd . . . and Joanna. As long as you're not looking for a splashy luxury home with an excess of space, you might find something you like among our designs."

"Scones, dear?" Grace held up a plate. "Or would you rather have one of these lovely little cakes today?"

Cass went for a lemon scone, a small smile turning up one corner of her mouth. Grace had fully intended to bring the development of the island into the conversation all along. She must have known both Todd and Joanna were looking for something to buy or build on the bay. How nice of her to bring up Cass's project.

She bit into her scone, her eyes meeting Grace's, and Grace winked. At that moment, Cass knew if she hadn't learned one other thing since she arrived in St. Dennis, she'd learned to never underestimate Grace Sinclair.

Chapter Three

～

Cass opened the door of her hotel closet and went through the contents. The week of scheduled casual business activities had morphed into what she was now considering a working vacation. She'd brought one business-suitable dress, a dark blue navy sheath she could wear in the event her father called her to a meeting at the last minute, but other than that, the closet held mostly sundresses, two pairs of linen pants, and a denim skirt.

What to wear for dinner with Owen Parker?

She rejected every one of the sundresses as being either too low, too short, or both. She was sure Owen would like nothing more than to see as much skin as possible. Well, she wasn't interested in giving him anything to look at. She'd agreed to go to dinner because he'd enticed her with stories about the island that she might somehow use in marketing her project, and as an added bonus, she might get clued in to any updates regarding the proposed dock. That she'd agreed to go didn't mean that she distrusted him any less or that she'd forgotten that, in her world, his middle name was Player.

The denim skirt would do nicely. It came to just below her knee. With it she'd wear a white button-down shirt. The sleeves were long, but she could roll them to her elbows. She zipped up the skirt and buttoned the shirt to one button above cleavage. She frowned when she looked at her reflection in the mirror, then undid the top button. She was going for that *friend only* vibe, not *last stop on my way to the convent*. Wide hoop earrings of hammered silver and a gathering of silver bangles for her wrist, a pair of strappy sandals, and she was almost, but not quite, ready when the desk called to tell her she had a visitor. She feathered her blond bangs, dabbed on a tiny bit of plum eyeliner that always brought out the green of her eyes, swiped on a little more mascara, dabbed lip gloss onto her full lips, hung her sunglasses from the V in the front of her shirt, and left her room.

Cass was halfway down the stairwell when she saw Owen waiting at the bottom, watching as she took every step. The look on his face made her so self-conscious that not until she got to the last step did she notice what he was wearing. Blue jeans. A white buttoned-down shirt, dark glasses hanging from the neck.

She stared at him for almost as long as he stared at her.

"What?" he asked.

"We look like the Bobbsey twins."

"Who?"

"The Bobbsey twins. You know, Nan? Bert?"

Owen shrugged. "I don't know them."

"Seriously? You never read the *Bobbsey Twins* books when you were a kid?"

"I didn't read much of anything when I was a kid."

"Wow. You're the first person I ever met who actually admitted they didn't read." She wrinkled her nose to show her disdain.

"I said I didn't read when I was a *kid*, not that I don't read now. I read a lot now. So forgive me if I don't get the Bobbsey thing."

"I just meant that we're dressed alike. White shirt on top. Dark denim on the bottom."

"Looks better on you. You ready?"

"As I'll ever be." She smiled and headed toward the door.

Owen caught up in one stride. "We have one stop to make before we get to where we're going," he told her as he opened the car door for her.

Well, he does have manners, I'll give him that, Cass thought as she buckled her seat belt. "Where are we stopping? And where are we going?"

"You'll see." He started the engine.

Was there anything more annoying than a cryptic man?

At the end of the drive, he made a right. She'd assumed he'd be turning left, toward town, where the restaurants were located. Even a newcomer to St. Dennis such as her knew that no restaurants were on the other side of town.

As they approached the bridge over the sound, she raised her eyebrows. "Cannonball Island?"

"Mmm-hmmm." Owen nodded.

"There are no restaurants on Cannonball Island."

"Says you." He paused on the other side of the bridge and craned his neck as if looking for traffic, right before he made a turn to the left.

"I thought this road was one-way." Cass frowned.

"Unofficially. It's custom, not law. But there's nothing coming the other way, and I don't feel like driving all the way around the island to go five hundred feet to the general store." He whipped around the curve, then made a quick right into the store's parking lot.

"Why are we going to the store?"

"I need to make a pickup."

"What are you up to, Owen? You promised me stories."

"I'm going one better." He got out of the car. "I'm bringing you a master storyteller." He slammed the car door and took the steps leading to the door of the store two at a time.

The storyteller. Ruby Carter, of course. Cass could have kicked herself. She could have simply spent an afternoon at the general store and forgone the dinner with Owen.

The door opened, and Owen came out onto the porch holding Ruby's arm, and a smile spread across Cass's face.

Cass was delighted to see Ruby. They'd met several times, and Cass adored her. If anyone knew the island's stories, it was this woman. And if anyone could take the edge off Cass's actually spending the next few hours with Owen, it would be Ruby.

Hmmmm. Interesting move on his part.

"Miz Carter, I'm so happy to see you." Cass turned in her seat to greet the old woman.

"Be happy to see you, too, Cass. Owen said you be needing some talk about the island folk and so on." As usual, Ruby got straight to the point. Owen helped her into the car and snapped her seat belt for her before closing the door. "I suppose I know something there."

"I'm sure you know everything there is to tell," Cass said.

"Maybe not everything. Some be knowing more, maybe. But I know a bit. Can't live one hundred years in the same place and not learn a thing or two, what is and what's been. What people be saying and what they be thinking."

"Well, I can't wait to hear what you remember," Cass said over her shoulder, then turned back to face the front of the car.

"Not a whole lot wrong with my memory," Ruby told her.

"Well done," Cass said softly to Owen.

"Thank you." He was obviously pleased with himself.

They'd driven around the island—Owen, no doubt fearing Ruby's rebuke, decided not to drive contrary to local custom. About two-thirds of the way around, Owen pulled into the driveway of one of the island's only two-story houses and turned off the car. Cass studied the house before her. She hadn't seen it before due to the thick stand of pines and cypress trees that grew across the entire front of the property. White clapboard, with a wraparound porch and lots of gingerbread trim, it was clearly Victorian in style, an anomaly on Cannonball Island.

Were they picking up yet another storyteller?

"Gigi, hand me that bag there on the floor next to your feet, please." Owen had gotten out of the car and helped Ruby out. Cass had opened her own door, and Owen held it while she stepped down from the Jeep.

"What is this place?" Cass asked.

"Emily Hart's."

"Is this a restaurant?"

"Of sorts."

"What does that mean?"

"It means it's a restaurant when Mrs. Hart serves folks at her dining-room table and you pay her for the meal. You pay her when you make the reservations, and if you don't show up, you don't get a refund. You eat whatever it is she cooked that night, information you should try to obtain before you ante up the cash, 'cause if you don't like what she serves, it's too bad. Like I said, no refunds. Got all that?"

"Yeah. Clear as mud. Do you know what she's serving tonight?"

"She hadn't made up her mind when I stopped by. But it doesn't matter to me. Everything she makes is terrific. Now, would you please close Ruby's door? I want to give her a hand here since the ground is a little uneven."

Cass closed the back door and, equally confused

and intrigued, followed Ruby and Owen up the steps. She'd never heard of Emily Hart, and there was no sign out front to identify the place as a restaurant.

The wraparound porch was wide enough to host a row of rocking chairs and was framed by a railing that could use a new coat of paint in the near future. The front door was painted black, the top half stained glass, and stood half-open. Rather than knock, Owen pushed it all the way into the foyer, held Ruby's elbow as she stepped inside, then motioned for Cass to follow. Still uncertain as to what was going on, Cass complied, her curiosity piqued.

"There you be, Ruby. I been watching for you. Owen be good enough to stop over this morning to see if I had room for y'all. I told him there was always room at my table for Ruby Carter and her kin." A short woman in her late seventies, Emily Hart was whip thin, had white hair piled atop her head, and was dressed in bright blue polyester pants and a matching top. Taking Ruby's hand, she said, "Nothing like seein' an old friend to make your heart feel good. Come on in, now. Owen, you go 'head and close that door behind you. The table be full now."

Emily turned to Cass. "And who you be, girl?"

"Mrs. Hart, this is a friend, Cass Logan," Owen said.

Emily studied Cass's face for a moment. "She be a pretty one, Owen Parker."

Owen laughed. "Just a friend, Mrs. Hart."

A twinkle in her eye, Emily nodded. "That would make her smart as well as pretty. Now, y'all go on in and find your places. Dinner be ready in just a few."

"What's on the menu tonight?" Owen placed a hand in the middle of Cass's back and ushered her to the end of the hall, then into a room on the left.

"Oysters to start. I know you be liking them. Always did, if I recall," Emily replied.

"Best oysters in the world come from the Chesapeake," Owen said.

"You be right as rain 'bout that, son." Emily patted Owen on the back.

Owen stepped aside so that Ruby and Cass could enter the dining room. He held the chair at the head of the long table for Ruby, seated her, then held a chair for Cass.

Still just a bit confused, Cass smiled at the others who were already seated at the table, which accommodated ten. At the opposite foot sat a woman of around fifty, her brown hair streaked with gray, and next to her on either side were two men in their twenties. The others at the table were a man and woman who sat with their heads together as they whispered to each other, and a young couple who studied the others as if mentally taking notes.

"Now, just so's you know, this be Mrs. Janet Hagen and her sons, Tim and Joe. They be from Pennsylvania. Ruby, you remember Tom Hagen, Ida and Harry's son?"

"I do." Ruby nodded.

"Tom—Janet's husband, rest his soul—passed on last summer. Janet here brought their boys so they could see where their father growed up. We're pleased to offer them our hospitality." Emily leaned on the back of the closest chair. "Next to Tim there be Pat and Carl Wagner. Up from South Carolina."

"You be Carl the third," Ruby told him, her eyes narrowing.

"I am. Did you know my dad?"

"I knew your dad, but I knew your granddaddy better. He was a friend of my youngest girl, Hannah. You be the image of him."

"I never knew him. He died before I was born."

"Dredging for oysters in the bay, storm came from nowhere and churned up waves the likes of which we'd never seen. Carl and his brother, Allen, couldn't get their boat turned around. It went down in twenty minutes, I heard tell, all on board."

"I heard he'd drowned, but I never knew the details," the young man said.

"You stop over to the store tomorrow, I'll show you a picture of Carl and Al with my Harold, two days before their last."

"Ruby owns the general store there by the bridge to the mainland," Emily explained. "You be sure, now, to stop on up."

"I definitely will." Carl nodded.

Emily continued with her introductions. "Go far enough back, we all be related, one way or another. Now, these here young folks be Diane and Ed Jenkins. Diane's mama grew up on the island, left to go up to college, and never did come back." Emily turned to Ruby. "Know who her mama was?"

Ruby studied the woman's face for a long moment. "I be guessing one of the Pratt girls. Both be gone for a while now."

"My mother was Josie Pratt," the young woman told her.

Ruby nodded. "Josie be a friend of my granddaughter Kathleen, Owen's mama. Nice girl. Couldn't wait to see the world, that one. I heard she was one to travel after she finished her schooling."

"She did. She studied photography and worked for a magazine writing travel articles before I was born. She flew all over the world, taking pictures for them. She's not doing well. The doctors say she has about another three months." The woman's eyes filled with tears. "We made the arrangements for this trip back in May, when things looked a little better and she wanted to see the island one more time. By the end of August, she realized she wasn't strong enough to travel from New Hampshire to Maryland, but she wanted us to come and take pictures of different places on the island and in St. Dennis so she could see . . ." Diane swallowed hard. "Wanted to see the place where she grew up."

"You stop over to see me and I'll show you some pictures of Josie and Kathleen when they were just little things. And next time you talk to her, you tell her Ruby Carter said hello."

"You're Ruby Carter?" The woman's eyes widened. "I've heard of you. My fraternal grandmother, Rebecca Singer, talked about you."

"Your grandmother be buried right down the road. I expect you'll want to pay your respects while you're here," Ruby told her. "The Singer graveyard be in front of the second house to the right of the first chapel you come to when you leave here. Little white fence be around the stones. You'll find Becky Singer there."

"No end to who knows who here," Emily told them. To round out the table, she added, "This be Owen Parker, Ruby's great-grandson, and his pretty friend . . ." Emily shook her head. "I'm sorry. Who you be again?"

"Cass Logan."

"Right. So that's who you all are. Now I got to be back in the kitchen or you won't be eating until morning." Emily grinned as she left the room. "Not that I don't make as fine a breakfast as you'd get on the Eastern Shore. Folks been asking me, but I . . ." Her voice trailed away as she disappeared into the kitchen.

An awkward silence followed, but lasted no more than a moment.

"Mrs. Carter, what can you tell me about my grandfather?"

"How well did you know my great-grandmother, Mrs. Carter?"

"Do you remember my aunt Sherry, Mrs. Carter? My mother's older sister?"

Ruby smiled and pointed to the pitcher of water in front of Owen, who lifted it and filled her glass for her.

Cass picked up her glass and met Owen's eyes across the table. *Jelly-jar water glasses?* she mouthed.

"You get extra points if you can identify the brand, more if you know what flavor," he whispered across the table.

"Welch's," Cass whispered back. "Grape."

"Points for the brand, but it has to have been strawberry."

Cass frowned. "How would you know that?"

"Because strawberry is the only kind Emily ever buys at the store."

Ruby shot him a scowl. "You being disrespectful to Mrs. Hart?"

"No, ma'am. Just sharing a little island lore with Cass."

Ruby glanced down the table, her eyes settling on Carl Wagner. "Your great-uncle Allen was a waterman by trade, but he painted some mighty nice pictures. Some of them be hanging down at the new art center. A few others in the dining room at the inn there on Charles Street."

"You mean the Inn at Sinclair's Point?" Carl asked.

Ruby nodded. "He had the knack, all right. But his daddy saw no future in painting. The year we moved over the store—that be me and my Harold and the last of our children who still be home—Allen's daddy told him if he liked painting so much, he could paint the house for him." Ruby smiled. "Allen not be one to argue, so he spent the rest of that summer painting that house. Wasn't till the fall that his daddy realized he'd painted a picture of a whole slew of boats out on the bay on the side of that house."

Emily's granddaughters came in with plates of raw oysters. They placed one in front of each guest except for Diane Jenkins, who waved them away.

"That house is still standing," Owen said. "And

the painting is still there. It's faded and weathered, peeled off in places, but you can see a few of the boats. I used to take the long way home from fishing out on the point just to walk past it. I saw something different every time."

Cass studied the three plump oysters on her plate, then picked one up and slurped it down. She glanced across the table at Owen. In his hand, he held one of his oysters, but he seemed to be more interested in Cass's than his own. She smiled, picked up a second, raised it to her lips, and, still looking at him, tilted her head back and the oyster slid between her lips.

"Word was Allen's daddy wanted him to paint over it all, said if he wanted the bay in his backyard he'd have built a house on the beach. But Allen's mama wouldn't hear none of it. Said it made her smile to see all those boats up close like that. After that, Allen sent away for paints and such, small canvases that he had sent to the general store so his daddy wouldn't know he was still painting, and he'd pick them up on mail day." Ruby glanced at Owen. "Some of his work be hanging down there in the Enright mansion, same as your sister Lisbeth's."

"I had no idea we had an artist in the family," Carl was saying. "Where's this art center? We'll have to go there before we leave St. Dennis."

Ruby gave directions.

Cass downed her last oyster and licked her lips. Owen was still staring at her.

"Are you going to eat that?" Cass said, her eyes on the oyster he still held in his hand.

Owen turned his attention to his oysters as the servers returned to collect the oyster dishes.

"You're falling behind, Parker," Cass whispered from across the table.

He downed the second. "Some things need to be savored." He leaned closer to the table and whispered, "And sometimes you can't wait." He quickly popped the third oyster into his mouth and swallowed it in a flash.

A tiny smile crossed Cass's lips. She turned her attention back to the conversation around them.

"What year would that have been, Miz Carter?" Carl asked. "When my great-uncle was painting?"

Ruby thought about it for a moment. "I'm guessing maybe it be around 1948 or so, then on till he passed. That be sometime in the fifties, thereabouts."

Cass was busy making mental notes. *Just the sort of thing I wanted to hear. Some human interest for the marketing brochure: obscure artist spurned by his family paints in secret and creates images of the Chesapeake. I'll have to check out that house, maybe use a photo of that painted wall for the cover of the brochure.*

The main course was crab cakes, mashed potatoes swimming in butter, green beans served in a huge white pottery bowl, and fried green tomatoes served with a horseradish sauce—everything served family-style. When bowls were emptied, the girls appeared and refilled them.

Cass devoured her crab cake and one of the tomatoes, picked at the mashed potatoes, and could have eaten seconds and thirds of the green beans.

Everything was almost too delicious for words. While she ate, she listened to the conversation around the table, thinking how she might include this story or that in her marketing plans. From time to time she glanced across the table at Owen, and found he, too, was absorbed in the discussions. Surely he must be familiar with most of what was being talked about, having grown up on the island. Was it genuine interest in the stories or deference to Ruby that had him hanging on her every word? If Cass were to guess, she thought it might be a little of both, but she leaned heavily in favor of deference. From time to time throughout the meal, Cass'd observed his interactions with Ruby. There was no denying he adored her. Sweet, Cass thought. A man who wore his heart on his sleeve where his great-grandmother was concerned was a rare find. Didn't make him any less of a bad risk where other women were concerned, but it was nice that he was so devoted to Ruby.

Still a player, her little inner voice reminded her.

Owen turned suddenly and looked at Cass, and for a second she thought he'd been reading her mind. She turned toward the end of the table, where one of Janet's sons was asking a question about his grandparents and others about his father. Then Diane wanted to talk about her mother, Josie, and what Ruby remembered about her childhood. Throughout the meal, Ruby answered questions and told stories, all of which Cass silently vowed to remember so she could write them down the second she got back to her hotel room.

We could name the houses after the original owners, and for each house we could make up a little booklet. We'll have signs made up to identify the properties, such as Wagner House to commemorate Carl's family.

Marketing these houses with their unique histories would be so much fun, Cass thought. She could hardly wait to begin.

She tried to focus on what Ruby was saying and ignore feeling Owen's eyes on herself.

". . . Kathleen and Josie thought they be so clever, you see. They had their hiding places, so they'd set out for school just like always, then meet up down near the old chapel and sneak on out to the point, hide for a time in that old cottage of ours." Ruby turned to Cass. "That place you be helping Alec fix up for him and Lisbeth. Should be done next week, I hear. It best be, with the wedding so close now."

"Were they ever caught skipping school?" Diane asked. "My mom and your granddaughter?"

"Those two couldn't stay hid to save their souls. They'd get hungry, they'd get thirsty. They'd need the bathroom." Ruby chuckled. "They'd be slipping into the store, creep around to the cooler, and grab something to drink. Snatch a box of cookies or crackers off the shelves and slip on out again. Like I didn't know they were there. So of course someone would drive by, see the two of them heading over the dune with their snacks, like they thought they be invisible or something. Like they were the first on the island to think they could sneak out of school."

More questions, more stories. More for Cass to memorize.

We can take photos of the houses before we begin working on them and maybe get some pictures from Ruby, copy and frame them for the new owners. Like a family album of sorts, joining the new families with the old. Play that up in the advertising: Become a part of the Cannonball Island family. Cass began to repeat the stories over and over in her head: The Wagners were watermen and Allen was the painter whose father wanted him to dredge for oysters. Josie was the girl who skipped school with Kathleen Carter, and the two of them caught frogs and took them to Sunday school. Tom Hagen was sailing by the time he was five and joined the navy as soon as he was old enough.

Conversation was put on temporary hold when dessert was served, and everyone ended their feast with just-out-of-the-oven apple pie and homemade ice cream.

Glancing at Owen across the table, Cass said, "You're going to need a wheelbarrow to get me to the car. I don't think I have ever in my life eaten that much at one time." She leaned back in her chair, regretting her decision to wear the skirt with its tight waistband instead of one of the looser-fitting sundresses. "But the food was out of this world, and the stories were just as good. I don't know which I enjoyed more, or when I had a more interesting dinner."

"I don't know how many times I've heard those stories, but I get caught up in them every time."

Owen held up the bag he'd brought in with him. "So caught up I forgot about the wine. I'll save it for next time."

Cass didn't respond. It would seem unkind to tell him she didn't plan on a next time after he'd arranged for this truly enjoyable evening. This was Cannonball Island. This was the unspoiled, friendly, beautiful island that wasn't like anyplace else she'd ever been. Surely buyers would want to live here for all the same reasons she did.

Emily Hart entered the dining room to a round of applause, which she accepted as her due. Smiling as she saw each of her guests to the door, she made them all promise to come back soon, while the crabs were still plentiful and the rockfish were running.

OWEN PARKED HIS Jeep near the back door of the inn and left the motor running when he got out and walked around to Cass's side of the car, arriving just as she'd unhooked her seat belt. He opened the door and stood aside for her to get out, then closed the door behind her.

"I had a great time, Owen. Thanks so much for taking me to dinner at Mrs. Hart's and for bringing Ruby. She really is a treasure. You're so lucky to have her." They walked to the double doors that led into the lobby. "I want to go back to Emily's and take some photos. I'm surprised I didn't think of it while we were there, but it's a great draw for the project. This elderly woman, cooking incredible but simple meals in her home kitchen . . . I think it's going to be a huge selling point."

"Uh, no." Owen stepped aside for Cass to enter, his jaw suddenly set, his eyes narrowed, his tone of voice hardened. "No publicity about Emily. If I'd thought for one minute you'd use her to sell houses, I'd never have taken you there."

"Why not? People would love to hear about—"

"So would the state board of health. No. Nothing about Emily to anyone."

"What does the board of health have to do with it?" Cass kept up with him step for step across the lobby.

"I have to spell it out for you? Okay, here's the deal. Emily Hart has never applied for a business license, a restaurant license, or any other kind of license. She started out cooking for friends after her husband died because she needed the money. She only cooks for people she knows or their relatives. She's never advertised, and according to Ruby, no one's ever gotten sick eating at her table, but if she had to go through the state for a license, she'd have to shut down. She's just too old and set in her ways to change the way she does things, and as Ruby says, 'No one be needing a license to cook in their own kitchen and serve at their own table.' You are perfectly free to debate the whole *paying customers* thing with Ruby, but don't say I didn't warn you."

They stopped at the bottom of the stairwell.

"So you're saying I can't mention Emily's spectacular dinners in the marketing. Even if it would bring other people to her door and she'd make a lot more money." Cass folded her arms over her chest.

"She serves dinner on Tuesday, Friday, and Saturday only. Ten people at a time. She's close to eighty years old and she can't handle more than three days a week. And she wouldn't be making more money. She'd be making no money because the board of health would be all over her."

"But her granddaughters could—"

"You don't get it. It's Emily's table that people come back to over and over. Publicize what she's doing and you will be responsible for shutting her down." His eyes were angry. "Frankly, around these parts, I wouldn't want to be the person who shuts down Emily Hart."

It took less than ten seconds for the message to get through to Cass. "Okay. I do get it. No mention of Emily to anyone, not in the advertisements, not even to prospective buyers."

"Thank you. I'd hate to see anything happen to that woman. She's like Ruby: a Cannonball Island treasure."

Cass nodded, then took a step backward and used her business voice lest he think this was anything more than what it was: a casual dinner.

"So, thanks again for a fun evening." She took another step back.

"Hey, glad you enjoyed it. I know Ruby sure did." He touched an index finger to his forehead as if saluting. "See you around."

Owen turned his back to her and walked across the lobby, pausing only briefly to say something to the girl on the reception desk before going back out through the double doors to the parking lot.

As Cass started to climb the steps to the second

floor, it occurred to her that Owen hadn't offered to see her to her room—an offer she'd have soundly rejected, of course, but one she'd totally expected him to make—nor had he even tried to kiss her good-night. Not that she wanted him to. Not that she'd have let him. But still . . . he hadn't even made the attempt.

Not that she was disappointed, but it made her wonder what he was up to, because she knew he wanted to kiss her—she knew the look—knew he'd wanted to since the night they met at Lis's exhibit at the new art center. They'd flirted lightly, but she'd dismissed him as nothing other than an accomplished flirt. Had he finally accepted that she wasn't interested?

That would be totally out of character for a man such as Owen, who knew exactly how good-looking he was, how funny, how charming he could be, how clever. Some might say irresistible. Though not Cass. Hadn't she successfully resisted him for almost two months now, which in his world was probably a record?

Methinks you protest too much, her inner voice taunted.

Her growled "Shut up!" earned her a startled look from the couple passing her in the hall as she slipped her room key into the lock. Red-faced, she ducked inside and as quietly as possible closed the door behind her.

Chapter Four

Owen stood on the beach and rolled up his pant legs to his knees before stepping into the cool waters of the Chesapeake. Less than a foot from shore, the slimy tentacles of sea grass reached out to embrace his calves, and he flinched. As many times as he'd been in the bay, he'd never gotten used to that first tickle, which made him think of eels and octopuses slithering around his legs, of mean-spirited crabs with their sharp claws just waiting to grab on to an ankle or a toe. He knew all this was unlikely to happen—well, the crabs were a definite possibility, but as far as he knew, there were no octopuses in the bay. Eels, maybe, but they, like most sea creatures this close to shore, tended to flee rather than fight.

There was just something cringe-worthy about stepping into water that was so dense with vegetation you couldn't see what lurked there. That was true of much of the Chesapeake, where the waters were dark with grasses in some places, and just plain dark in others. He tried to remember if he'd ever seen clear to the bottom anywhere around Cannonball Island and had to admit he had not. If such a spot existed, he'd not found it.

Yet here he was, wading in blindly to see how far one could walk before hitting the shelf where the bottom dropped off. He seemed to recall from his younger days that the drop was about ten or twelve feet from shore. A few more steps and he'd reach it. Mindful that he was close to the edge, he dug his feet in, which meant the sea grass caught between his toes—another sensation he particularly disliked. But he was a man on a mission and determined to find the ledge. Besides, it bothered him that he, big strong Owen Parker—adventurer, man of mystery, love-'em-and-leave-'em Owen Parker—had to fight the urge to scream like a girl when that first tentacle of slimy grass wrapped itself around his calf and reached for his knee.

"Scream like a girl's a little harsh," he muttered before taking another step forward, ever mindful of the crabs. It was still their mating season, after all.

His left foot found the spot he was searching for before his right foot, and he paused momentarily to avoid sliding down the uneven slope. He stood six feet three inches tall, and the water was just below his knees where drop-off began. But he knew from past experience the drop could be anywhere from fifteen to thirty or forty feet below the surface of the water, something he wasn't prepared to look into at that moment. For one thing, he wasn't dressed for swimming. For another, his purpose today was to try to determine how much the drop—and therefore the depth—had shifted since the last time he'd been here.

Was it his imagination, or did the drop-off begin farther from the shore? He knew that here, at the exact point where the river joined the Chesapeake, the depth had changed over time. The width of the river had changed as well, as had the shoreline. He'd long ago learned that the only thing constant about the bay was that it was ever changing.

He tried to recall just how long it had been since he'd waded into these waters. The best he could come up with was a range of three to five years.

Could that be right? He scratched his head and turned toward the shore. There was no denying he'd enjoyed the time he'd spent in the exotic—and not-so-exotic—places he'd been to since his last trip home, but it was good to be back on the island. It felt good to wake up in the old store every morning and to go downstairs and have coffee with Ruby and talk over whatever was on her mind that day. Sometimes it was something mundane, such as how Jolene Baker's nephew had gotten her car stuck in the mudflats when he foolishly tried to take a shortcut across the island, and they had to get someone to tow it. Other times it was something profoundly beautiful, such as the story of how her Harold had wooed her by bringing part of his catch every day to her family's back door when her father was ill and unable to work on the bay. Harold would quietly leave his offerings right next to the door where they couldn't be missed, and he never missed a day in the entire six weeks of her father's illness. Not until after her dad'd recovered did Harold ask to court her, coming to the front door with a handful of daisies for her mother, and a fistful of cornflowers for Ruby.

"I can still see him standing there, right outside the door," Ruby'd told Owen. "Daisies for my mama, and a bunch of those sweet blue cornflowers for me. How he knew I favored them, I never knew and he never said. But for all our life together, he never came into the house without a few of those pretty blue posies in his hand when they were in season. He was so tall and so handsome, I'd'a married him anyway, flowers or no. I never told him that. Guess maybe I should have."

She'd grown silent, and Owen had waited her out. He knew Ruby well enough to know that when she grew reflective, something else was always to come.

"It was winter when we lost our Annie to the influenza. My Harold had to dig through the frozen ground to bury her. There were no flowers for her until the spring. Soon as they were up a couple of inches, Harold dug some up and planted them on her grave. He almost never talked about her, but I know his heart was right down there with her every time he thought about her. Everyone grieves in their own way and that's a fact. He loved that little girl—she was eight when she left us—just like he loved the son we buried just a few hours after he was born. Seemed so unnatural to me, to have carried that baby all those months, then have nothing to carry in my arms."

Another short silence. "My Harold's buried down there with them, at that graveyard next to my poppy's old place. His kin wanted him buried over in the Carter plot, but he'd made me promise to lay him next to his babies, and that's where he is. That's where I'll go when the time comes." She'd looked up at Owen. "Might not be any room left for you or your sister, so you're going to have to find a place of your own."

Owen had smiled. "I don't care where they plant me. I'll probably die somewhere else and they'll just bury me in some obscure corner of some unknown churchyard."

Ruby's eyes had narrowed and she'd rolled up her newspaper and smacked him with it. "You'll be buried right here on the island where you belong, and you won't be giving me sass about it."

"Well then, I guess back there behind the store is as good a place as any. We can pull up a corner of your garden and they can bury me and Lis and Alec and their kids right there."

Ruby must have liked the idea because she didn't argue the point. "What about your kids? Where they gonna go?"

"You have to settle down before you have kids. You see me settling down, Ruby?"

"Humph. How much you know, boy," she'd said softly, that twinkle in her eye telling him she knew what he did not.

Damn, but he'd miss her when she was no longer around. He couldn't imagine life without her. She had been the one constant in his life. Wherever he was, however long he'd been gone, he'd always known Ruby would be there to welcome him home with a hug and a sly remark. His throat tightened at the thought of the unthinkable.

He hurried through the seaweed to reach the beach, which was a mixture of rough sand and pebbles. He put his flip-flops back on and headed back to the store. Passing Emily Hart's driveway made him think about the one person he hadn't wanted to think about today. Cass was dangerously close to getting under his skin, and he couldn't have that.

Last night he had tried to read Cass, but just couldn't get through, which annoyed him more than he'd like to admit. What was up with that?

He'd wanted to kiss her when he dropped her off. But he knew she was expecting him to, and he wanted to throw her off guard just a little. It remained to be seen if it would have the desired effect—making her wonder why he hadn't kissed her when he could maybe have at least made the effort.

He'd rather have her wondering why he hadn't tried than her feeling smug for having turned him down. Yes, it was a bit of a game, and ordinarily he wasn't a gamer. For all he played the field, he was always up-front with any woman he dated. But this was different. Cass was different. He wanted her to think about him, so he did the one thing he figured she didn't expect him to do.

He'd never had to work for someone, and he admitted that could be just a bit of Cass's allure. Well, that and her pretty face and her sweet little compact body. He'd always been a sucker for short women.

Of course, if he had any sense, he'd forget about Cass and go to the new roadhouse out on the highway on Monday night, maybe meet someone who'd be happy to spend some quality time with him.

He'd have to give that some thought.

In the meantime, while he waited to hear from Jared, he'd see what chores he could do for Ruby. Thinking about her had made him feel sad over something that hadn't even happened. Maybe he should plan to stick around for a while, help her while he still had her, let her know how much he appreciated having her in his life.

OWEN CAME IN through the side door of the store carrying an armful of dahlias he'd cut from Ruby's garden. He'd eyed the cornflowers but decided those were Harold's alone to give. He placed the flowers along with her favorite snips on the counter and paused on his way to the kitchen for a vase.

"What else can I do for you this morning, Gigi?"

"Tom be along sometime this morning with a delivery. Maybe you could unpack the boxes and restock the shelves." Ruby sat at the old round wooden table next to the window on the far right side of the store, her favorite place to read the newspaper or a magazine, or, if things were really slow that day, one of the crime novels she so loved. Today she was reading the latest issue of the *St. Dennis Gazette*.

Owen grabbed a cold bottle of water from the cooler and walked over to see what this week's hot topic was in the local newspaper. He peered over her shoulder and read the headline: "What Lies beneath the Dark Waters of the Waring River?"

"Wonder who Grace was talking to before she wrote that article?"

"Wonder all you want." Ruby's eyes never left the page. "You gonna put those pretties in water, or are you planning on letting them die right there on my counter?"

"Oh, right. I was going to get a vase and got distracted."

"What be distracting you?" Ruby finally looked up.

"I don't remember." The sad truth was he didn't remember why he hadn't followed through with the vase, filled it with water, and dunked in the dahlias. It was as if something was there, at the far edge of his mind, begging him to look. But try as he might, he couldn't bring it into focus.

He hated when that happened.

He made his way into the kitchen and opened the cabinet where Ruby kept her favorite vases. He picked a turquoise pottery pitcher he knew she especially liked, filled it at the sink, and took it into the front of the store. He knew Ruby always snipped the stems off a little before putting flowers in a vase, but didn't know how far to cut, so he left that part for her and plunked the dahlias into the water.

"Gigi, you want me to leave the vase here?" he called.

"Right over here on my table with me be fine, thank you, son."

Owen carried the vase along with the snips over to the table. Ruby looked over the arrangement and started to pull the stems out one by one and cut off the tips.

"What be on your mind?" she asked without looking at him.

"Just a little rammy, I guess." He leaned over the back of one of the chairs and watched her prepare the flowers for the vase.

"I don't know *rammy*."

"Just . . . I don't know, at loose ends, I guess. I'm getting bored waiting for this project to start. I don't seem to have any other purpose here."

"Tom be bringing stock later, seems you be having plenty of purpose then. And if you be all that bored, I can find plenty for you to do."

Owen smiled. No one could put him in his place like Ruby. As he started to ask what she had in mind, he heard footsteps on the porch. Seconds later, Cass was walking across the wooden floor with great purpose. Just his luck. If *rammy* and *antsy* were steering his mood, he had this woman to thank for it.

Seeing her now made it clear to him that his little plan had backfired. He was the one wondering why he hadn't kissed her when he might have had the chance.

Cass looked right past him as if he weren't there and went straight to Ruby. "Miz Carter, I just came from the—"

"Well, hello, Cass. How'd you enjoy your dinner last night?" Ruby looked up as she folded her newspaper. "If you ever had fresher oysters or a tastier crab cake, you're going to have to tell me where. Maybe even take me so I can judge for myself."

"No, Miz Carter, I never did. Best seafood ever. But just now—"

"Glad we agree. Now, was there something you be wanting to say? Take a breath now, girl."

Cass took a breath. "Last night you were talking about the graveyard by the chapel down the road from Mrs. Hart's place."

Ruby nodded. "Gave Josie's girl directions to find her grandmother's grave. Becky Singer be buried in that family plot."

"Which is so overgrown with weeds, she'll never find what she's looking for. The weeds are up past my knees."

"How'd you come to know that?"

"I was intrigued when you were talking about all those little private burying places. I remembered hearing something about them before, about how families buried their relatives right outside in their yard. So I thought I'd check out a few of them. I was thinking I'd need to figure out how to deal with them once we started marketing the houses we're going to build. So I went to the one you talked about last night to take a look for myself and found it a mess. Isn't anyone responsible for taking care of the graves on the island?"

"Time was, those little graveyards had white fences around them to set them off to themselves, kept the little ones from playing on 'em, kept the old folks from tripping over the stones. You see that white fence in someone's front yard, you knew their kin was right there with them, where they belonged. Once families leave the island, there be no one left to tend to them, I suppose. Hadn't much thought about it myself. Used to be preachers on the island, they'd get folks out to do some tending from time to time, but those were other days."

"If the others all look like this one"—Cass pointed down the road—"it's going to turn a lot of people off, not to mention the fact that it's disrespectful to the people who are buried there. Someone from the island should be concerned about the state of those little private cemeteries."

"And who do you think that might be? You know we don't have a mayor and such, like other places. Things needed to be done, folks just did. I guess with so many leaving, there be no one left to care about the ones who passed on." Owen didn't need to look up to know Ruby's eyes were on him. She took every possible opportunity to remind him that, as far as she was concerned, his place was on Cannonball Island, tending to its business, and nowhere else.

"I'll go take a look at the Singer place," he said. "I can mow the grass, if nothing else. It's a small plot, it won't take any time at all."

"You better have a big mower with really sharp blades," Cass told him. "I wasn't kidding about the grasses being over my knees."

"I'll take a sickle." He turned to Ruby. "There's still that old one out in your shed, right?"

"My Harold's tools are all still out there. Sickle be one of them. Don't forget to clean it when you're done with it, and put it back right where you found it, hear?"

"I'll treat it like it was my own."

"You'll treat it like it belonged to your great-granddaddy, because it did."

"All righty, then." Owen kissed Ruby on top of her head. "Tell Tom to leave whatever he brings out on the porch and I'll bring everything in when I get back."

THE SUN BLAZED down the way it sometimes did in late September around noon. After twenty minutes swinging his great-grandfather's sickle to cut down the high grass, Owen was covered with sweat. He took off his shirt and hung it over the fence surrounding the old graveyard.

Meanwhile, Cass made the rounds of the grave markers as he cleared them. "Look here. Isiah Singer. Born . . . I think it says 1814. Died 1881." Cass looked up at Owen. "Eighteen fourteen would have made him one of the first babies born on the island."

Owen nodded. "Maybe even the first."

"I wonder if there's any way to find out, short of checking every gravestone on the island. But even doing that wouldn't guarantee we'd know for sure. It could be that the first person born here died elsewhere and wasn't even buried here."

Owen stepped around her with the sickle.

She went on to another marker. "This one is totally illegible. And this one . . . I can make out Singer as the last name but not the first. Looks like it starts with an E. Born 1821. Died 184-something. I can't read the last number." She stood and went to the next. "This is like reading a book. A family saga."

She knelt down to read the next one in line. "This guy . . . Joshua Singer . . . he was a bit of a ladies' man. He's buried with three wives." She looked up at Owen and grinned. "Jealous?"

He laughed. "Nope. I don't envy any man who had three wives."

"Not all at the same time. The first one, Mary, died when she was . . . oh, my, seventeen. Must have been a child bride. Wife number two . . . Elizabeth, died when she was in her thirties. And the last one . . . ha! Ruth outlived him by eight years. Looks like she was another younger bride. She was twenty-two when she married him. Guess Joshua was a stud."

Cass stood next to the broken fence and watched him work. "What can I do to help?"

"If you really want to do something, you could rake up all this stuff I'm cutting down."

"Where do I get a rake?"

"Ruby has a couple in the shed." He stopped for a moment, wiped the sweat from his face with his forearm, then wiped his arm on his shirt.

"I can do that. I'll be back in a few."

"Hey, Cass," he called before she got too far up the road. "Ask Ruby for a couple of big bottles of water."

"Will do." She raised a hand and kept walking.

Cass hadn't been kidding about the height of the grass. How was it that no one had noticed before? Were all the old graveyards around the island as overgrown and neglected? He'd bet most of them were, except for those whose adjacent homes were still occupied.

And the ones where Ruby's kin were buried, he reminded himself. All of them. He knew this for a fact because she'd had him tend to them before he'd been back on the island for too long.

Gravekeeper. Cemetery attendant. Add those to my résumé.

If you wanted to live on Cannonball Island, you had to be a jack-of-all-trades. Not that he was planning on making the island his home again. This was temporary, only until this diving job for Jared was finished, however long that might be. Owen was certain that by then he'd be ready to be on the move again. Hopefully, by then, whatever had told him it was time to come home—that voice he heard inside his head, sometimes when he least wanted to— would have been satisfied. That voice—wherever it came from, whomever it belonged to—had been inside him for as long as he could remember. The only times in his life he'd really messed up had been the times he'd ignored it. Owen'd spent his life trying to ignore its implications, but he'd never been able to shake free of it. Ruby'd told him to just let it in, to hear what the voice had to say, but he'd never wanted anything to do with it.

"You be happy to have that voice someday," Ruby had admonished him.

"I doubt it," he'd shot back.

"Be careful what you wish for. You lose what you don't use, son."

"Good. Then anytime now it should be gone."

So far, that hadn't happened. At times he could stifle it, at times he could tune it out. Then the other night *it* tuned *him* out when he thought he'd try to read Cass.

Turn around.

Without thinking, he turned in time to see Cass headed toward him, pushing Ruby's rusty old wheelbarrow. The uneven front wheel caused it to wobble. The light behind her gave her an all-over aura that drew his eyes and held them. He had to force himself to look away.

"That must be a bear to push." He dropped the sickle and went to the road to help.

"I've got it." Cass was all but out of breath, but she pushed on.

He stopped the barrow's forward motion with one hand. "Here. You take the rake, and I'll take this beast."

He handed her the rake and grabbed the handles and started to push before she could object. It gave him something to do besides look at her. She was sweaty from pushing the barrow up the road, her short blond hair plastered to her now-shiny face. If she'd had makeup on, it had melted in the sun or it had been washed away by sweat. She was as sexy right then as she'd been in that black dress she'd worn the night he met her at the art show.

"Damn," he'd said under his breath.

"It is a little unwieldy. Thank you. I didn't want to complain, but—"

"What?" He tuned back in.

"The wheelbarrow. I agree, it's a tough push. I said thanks for taking it off my hands."

"Oh. Right."

They stopped at the edge of the fence, and Owen pushed the wheelbarrow across the sandy soil to the gate.

"I guess we should pick up the loose grass that I cut down and load it into the wheelbarrow. Then I'll come back later with the mower and cut it down to normal grass level, make it look neat."

"I think Diane's family would appreciate that." Cass stood with her hands on her hips. "I can rake it into piles and you can pick it up and toss it in here." She pointed to the wheelbarrow. "Oh, I almost forgot. Here's your water." She took the plastic bottle from the bottom of the wheelbarrow and handed it to him.

"Thanks. I bet I sweated off about eight pounds already today." He unscrewed the top and drank down half the bottle. When he finished, he looked skyward. "I had no idea it was going to get this hot today. You can get dehydrated pretty quickly working too long out here."

"Miz Carter sent up a couple of those. She said we'd probably need them." Cass opened a bottle and took a drink, then removed the others and set them on the ground in the shade from the fence. "She also sent sunscreen and said for you to use it." Cass dug the plastic bottle from her back pocket and handed it over. "She made me use it before I left the store."

"Thanks. For someone who has never in her life used the stuff, she is almost militant about everyone else slathering it on." Owen pulled off the cap and poured lotion on his arms and the back of his neck, then spread the remainder over his chest and face.

He was tempted to ask Cass to rub it on his back and shoulders but knew instinctively that would be a bad move. Her hands on his hot bare skin? Ah— no. A very bad idea.

"Well, if you're done cutting, I'll rake."

"I'm done. Go 'head and do your thing."

Owen leaned against the fence and tried not to watch. Cass was dressed in shorts and a T-shirt that, before long, began to stick to her in all those places he'd told himself not to focus on. He was grateful when there were piles of grass for him to pick up. By the time she finished raking, the wheelbarrow was full to almost overflowing. The grass that wouldn't fit into the wheelbarow was in a pile near the gate, and Cass looked as if she'd had enough raking to last a long time.

A car drove by, then stopped and backed up.

"Hey!" Lis had rolled down the driver's-side window. "What are you guys doing?"

"Cleaning up the Singer plot." Owen walked over to his sister's car.

"Kind of you to give the old man a hand, Cass," Lis said.

"Actually, I'm helping Cass. It was her idea."

"Nice." Lis nodded approvingly. "You're becoming a real islander, Cass. Before long, you'll be picking up your mail at the general store and sitting out on the old pier, catching your own crabs, just like the rest of us."

Cass laughed.

"Gotta run. Alec is waiting for me. We're going to look at some dining tables a woodworker over in

Ballard makes from old barn wood." Lis waved as she took off.

"Have you ever gone crabbing?" Owen asked as he walked back to the plot.

"No. I prefer my crabs caught and cooked by someone else." Cass leaned against the rake and rubbed one hand with the other.

"Let me see what's going on there," Owen said, noticing Cass rubbing her palms. He reached for her left hand and turned it over, then looked at the right. "You've got the beginnings of some nasty blisters. Why didn't you say something when it started to hurt?"

Cass shrugged. "I didn't think the raking would take as long as it did. I didn't realize how much grass there was, so I didn't think it was a big deal."

"It'll be a big deal if you don't put something on them. Come back to the store with me. Ruby has some stuff that will fix those right up." He finished one bottle of water and reached for a second. When it was empty, he turned the wheelbarrow toward the road. "Can you carry the rake and the sickle?"

"Sure." She put the empty water bottles in with the grass and walked along the shoulder of the road. "That little graveyard looks a lot better. It made me sad to think that Diane would travel all the way to get here, then not be able to find her grandmother's grave because the grass covered it. Thanks for helping me."

"Thanks for calling it to my attention. It never occurred to me to check in on those old places that have been abandoned. I guess if I'd been here when it started to overgrow, I'd have taken notice, but once the grass grows up like that, you can't even see the headstones." He slowed his step just a little. It was nice to have her all to himself for just a few minutes, to not have to share her attention. There always seemed to be someone else around. Of course, last night was his doing, but still . . .

"I should take a look around the island tomorrow and see which of the other home cemeteries need to be cleaned up," he said. "It is kind of embarrassing, especially knowing you're trying to sell some of those places. I don't know what people would think."

"They'd think the places were abandoned, which many of them were. It's sad for them, you know? The people who are buried there? It's like no one remembers their names. Who they were, what they did. Who they loved. Where they're buried."

"There are places like that all over the island. And you're right. It is sad. Maybe when you start building, you can hire someone to keep up with them."

"That would work for as long as there's building going on, but once the crews leave and the buyers move into their new houses, what then?"

"I don't know." They'd reached the parking lot in front of the store. Owen wheeled the barrow to the shed and stopped in front of it. He knew better than to put away any of Ruby's tools before cleaning them.

"Go on in and ask Ruby to put some of her special salve on your palms. She'll know what you want."

He brought the hose from the side of the house where it was hooked up and turned on the spray. He rinsed off the sickle and the rake, then turned off the hose and went into the store through the side door. He found Ruby and Cass in the kitchen, where Ruby was tending to Cass's blisters.

"Gigi, we have a wheelbarrow filled with grass outside. Where would you like me to dump it?"

"On my compost pile, where else?" Ruby never took her eyes off Cass's hand. "Why'd you let this girl with such soft hands rake so long?"

"I didn't know her hands were that soft." He shook his head as if to shake out the thought. He didn't want his mind to dwell on how soft Cass's hands were. "I mean, I didn't know she'd blister."

Ruby muttered something about someone not having the sense he was born with.

"There you go, Cass." Ruby snapped the lid on the jar of ointment and returned it to the cabinet where she kept it.

"My hands feel better already. What's in that stuff, anyway?"

"Little of this, little of that." Ruby closed the cabinet door and turned to Owen. "You going to take care of that compost today?"

"On my way." He went back out the side door.

"And you be sure to be washing down those tools," Ruby called after him.

"Already done."

He'd just finished dumping out the grass and was about to wash out the wheelbarrow when he heard the door slam.

"You should have saved some of that for me to do," Cass said. "My mother always says a job's not done until the cleanup is over."

"That's a Ruby-ism, too." He finished washing down the wheels and returned the barrow to the shed. He stood in the doorway, mentally debating whether the mower or the weed whacker would best finish the job around the headstones.

"I got you into this. You didn't have to help out."

"Of course I did." Owen laughed. "It's my island."

"How long before I get to call it my island, too?"

"Depends. How long are you sticking around?"

"I could ask you the same question."

"Touché." Maybe the weed whacker. The mower would be too difficult to maneuver around the stones, some of which were embedded in the ground. The weed whacker, definitely. He lifted it from its spot in the lineup of Ruby's tools and put it into the wheelbarrow. He'd load it up with the grass they'd left near the gate and whatever the weed whacker cut down.

"Are you going back?"

"Yeah, I might as well finish up, cut around the grave markers with this." He pointed to the weed whacker. "Then that plot is finished."

"I'll walk back with you. I left my car down at the point. I stopped in to see how the renovations at Lis and Alec's cottage are going."

"Things looked pretty good, last time I was there." Owen headed toward the road pushing the wheelbarrow and Cass followed, a bottle of water in each hand. "The new roof is on, the HVAC guys were just finishing up, and the new kitchen was going in."

"Your sister has a good eye. She was certain that old place could be rehabbed, and she was right." Cass grinned. "Of course, it took a lot of money and some good planning, but the cottage will be fabulous when it's finished."

"Yeah, she was adamant that that was going to be their home. You know that Ruby and Harold lived there after they were married, raised their kids there, right? After they moved to the store, the cottage was vacant for years. Several contractors who looked at it told Lis she'd be better off tearing it down and starting over. It probably would have saved some money, but she wouldn't hear it."

Cass nodded. "I heard the story. When Alec came to me and asked if I could design an addition and some bump-outs, I was skeptical. But once I talked to Lis, I knew I had to come up with something. She wanted the floors her family had walked on, she said. The stairs her grandmother—*your* grandmother—and her sisters had climbed every night to go to bed. Once I heard that, I knew I had to find a way to make it work."

"You did a great job. I've never seen Lis so happy."

"I suspect that has more to do with her rapidly approaching wedding than anything I did."

"I saw your name on the invite list."

"That was Alec's doing, I'm sure. He and I worked together quite closely to get the island project pulled together. Of course, now that's up in the air. Deiter

Construction could, conceivably, be left with twenty-two properties we can't build on." She looked at Owen as if expecting him to volunteer some information she didn't already have, but he was silent.

They'd reached the graveyard, and Cass paused outside the fence while Owen went through the gate.

"It's nice now that you can see the gravestones." She leaned on the fence, and it swayed but held.

"It'll be even nicer once I trim the rest of the grass away." He pulled the string on the weed whacker and it roared to life.

She went through the gate to look over the stones while he worked, and gathered the loose grass with her hands and dumped it into the wheelbarrow.

"It looks great," she said when he'd finished and the weed whacker was silent. "Nice and tidy. But I wish all the names and dates were legible. Still, there's enough here that you can read the history of the family."

"Let me guess. You're thinking in terms of marketing your houses again, how cool it would be if you could give the new buyers a little history of their property." For some reason, the thought irritated Owen.

Cass glanced up at him. "You say it as if it's a bad thing."

"I don't think it's a particularly good thing to be using a family's dead to promote a sale."

"That isn't at all what I'm doing," she snapped.

He could tell by the look on her face that she was offended. Good. He was starting to become offended by the constant marketing of his home. "What would you call it?"

"I call it making the best use of what I have to work with. Look, if I'm selling a property, of course I want to promote its best features. If the property happens to have a graveyard on it, I have to present that in a manner that potential buyers don't think is . . . well, creepy. I mean, how would you feel about living in a house where there are graves right outside your door?"

Her hands were on her hips and she'd removed her sunglasses. The better to glare at him, he supposed.

"I grew up with dead people right outside my door." He snorted. "And no one ever tried to call it anything other than what it was: your dead relatives' final resting place."

"Well, I don't see where the families of all these 'dead relatives' have shown much respect for them. It seems to me that once people move from the island, they don't look back very often, if at all. Do they ever think about what they left behind? Do they even remember the names of the people who were buried on their property?"

Cass went to the far corner of the graveyard, the section she hadn't gone through earlier, and knelt next to a small flat stone. "Rachel Singer. Born August second, 1854—died January twenty-fourth, 1856." She looked up at Owen. "Think anyone ever wonders what happened to her? Why she died so young?"

Cass took three steps to the right and pointed to one of the standing white headstones. "It's another Mary—her middle name is gone, looks like it might have been Ida? Born 1815—died 1820. Looks like it says . . ." Cass drew closer. "'Gone to fever.'" She looked over her shoulder. "She was five years old when she died. And look here." Cass stepped to another grave marker. "Cora Singer, born May eighth, 1790—died November fourteenth, 1820. Looks like she was buried with a baby—see, under her name? Willie Singer, born November fourteenth, 1820—died November fourteenth, 1820. She must have died in childbirth and her baby died with her. It's a sad story, Owen, but it's her story. She lived here and died here." Cass looked around the small plot. "There are a couple dozen stories here. Don't you think someone should remember them? When do you suppose was the last time someone uttered their names?"

Owen stared at her for a long moment. He wasn't sure what he thought. "I don't know. It's not necessarily a bad thing that you want to remember them and you want the people who eventually build a home on this lot to know who came before them. But maybe it's a little crass to use them—to use their names—to make money."

"Did you just call me *crass*? Seriously?" In the blink of an eye, Cass was standing in front of him, her eyes flashing with anger. "You think I spent the better part of my day out here, sweating my butt off, because I thought it would help my father make *money*?" She pushed him, both hands on his chest. "You're even more of a jerk than I thought you were."

She turned on her heel and walked briskly to the road and headed toward the point, where she'd left her car.

Owen stood in the graveyard, feeling stupid and small, and wondering how he could possibly mess things up more than he just had.

Chapter Five

Cass returned to the hotel in time to shower off the grass, sweat, and sunscreen and still make it to the veranda for tea, but even the prospect of spending an hour or so with Grace did little to improve her mood.

"Crass?" she'd muttered as she stepped into the shower. "Yeah, Crass Cass, that's me. Shame on me for wanting to shine the spotlight on generations of people who stood up for what they believed in, paid the price, and went on to settle an island that had been considered uninhabitable. Built homes, raised their families, stayed true to their way of life for a couple of hundred years. Bad Cass."

That Owen failed to understand she was, in fact, honoring Cannonball Island's deceased made her see red. Names that had been forgotten for God only knew how long would be remembered. As she'd walked through the Singer plot, she'd envisioned a little memorial book to be given to each of her buyers. The booklets would contain historical photographs of the island and photos she'd take of the headstones of some of those buried on the buyers' new properties so they'd know the names. She'd seek out photos of previous owners and include them. How better to take the fear from the fact that your new property contained a little graveyard than to put names and stories and faces to those buried there? Cass thought of it as a way of helping the new owners to accept, maybe even feel pride in, that their properties came with the remains of some of the prior occupants. After all, Deiter Construction would be asking premium prices for the limited number of homes they were going to build or renovate.

Besides, it wasn't as if she could remove the graves. That would be illegal and, to her mind, unethical. The islanders who were laid to rest there were there to stay; it was up to her to put the best possible spin on that. She thought she'd found a way to make their presence less objectionable to prospective buyers. Damn Owen for making her feel like an opportunist for doing her job and, at the same time, serving what she saw as the island's best interests.

"Someone looks like she got a bit of sun today," Grace remarked as Cass took a seat at the tea table. Today's group was smaller, though Joanna was present, as always.

"Oh, yes." Cass nodded and smiled at the server, who offered her a choice of teas. "Earl Grey today, thank you."

"At the beach?" Joanna asked.

"No." *Oh, what the hell. Let's test my theory*

right here and now. "Actually, I was on Cannonball Island, cleaning up an old family graveyard."

After a bit of a silence, Grace asked, "Anyone I know, dear?"

Cass suppressed a smile. Was there anyone Grace didn't know in St. Dennis or on Cannonball Island?

"The Singer family. I noticed the grasses were so high around the graves you couldn't even see the stones, so I thought I'd tidy things up a bit."

"I knew the Singer family well," Grace said. "Edward and Paula were the last to raise a family there. They moved to Ohio to be with her folks back in the eighties—she wasn't from these parts—but a few of their boys stayed around for a bit. I think the last of them left the island, oh, my, it must have been ten or fifteen years ago. No idea what happened to any them. I don't recall any of them ever coming back."

"We found one of the sons, still in Ohio, and the company bought the property from the family. And last night, I met one of the descendants at a dinner." Cass almost said, *At Emily Hart's,* but she didn't want to shine the spotlight on Emily's operation, which, as had been pointed out, was probably illegal.

"Oh, yes. Diane Jenkins. She and her husband have been staying here this week. We chatted at breakfast this morning." Grace paused to stir her tea. "She mentioned she was going to look for her grandmother's grave before they left."

"Well, now she'll be able to find it. And others of her ancestors as well."

"That's so nice of you," Joanna said. "But if I

may ask, what would motivate you to do something like that? Especially on such a hot day."

"Because the gravesite was a mess and the people buried there deserved better." As she spoke, Cass remembered why she'd taken those first steps to clean up the Singer plot. Owen Parker's cynicism be damned. "Besides, I think it would be nice for the people who buy the properties to know the family who built their home, the people who lived and died there and are buried there."

"What do you mean, *buried* there?" Joanna raised one eyebrow.

Cass explained the islanders' burial practice and her thoughts on documenting the family plots for the buyers of each of the properties.

"Wait, are you saying you'd have a *graveyard* in your backyard?" Joanna's expression left no doubt what she thought about that.

"More like the front or side yard, dear." Grace declined a refill from their server. "It's actually a charming custom, one that's been practiced for centuries. Remember, for a long time, there were no organized cemeteries in the rural areas. Do go visit the island, and you'll see little white fences here and there. Those fences mark the final resting places of the families who lived in the nearby houses." Grace turned her gaze to Cass. "How good of you to take it upon yourself to clean things up."

"Still, I don't know if I'd want to buy a house that had its own graveyard." Joanna was still frowning. "I don't know if I could sleep at night that close to the dead."

"Dear, you've been sleeping close to the dead from the time you checked in here," Grace said. "My husband's ancestors—and my husband, for that matter—are buried on the far side of the lawn. Actually, I believe you can see the markers from your room. As I said, it's a custom in these parts, one I wish hadn't gone out of favor. I think it's a lovely idea to keep your ancestors close to where they lived." Grace turned to Cass. "I applaud what you're doing. I love the idea of honoring the island's early inhabitants. It brings a sense of continuity and history to the houses you'll be building, a weaving together of the past and the present. I think I'll write about it in my column for the *St. Dennis Gazette*."

"When you put it that way, well, yes, I can see where it might be . . . interesting." Joanna clearly was slowly coming around to the idea. "It would certainly make one feel more a part of the island."

"Exactly." Cass took a sip of tea and looked into her cup to avoid Grace's eyes. Once again, the older woman had saved the day.

"Perhaps you'll let me interview you sometime soon," Grace said to Cass. "It would make a nice feature piece for my newspaper."

"Of course. Whenever you like."

"Now, do you have plans to clean up any of the other plots?" Grace asked.

"I've been thinking about seeing if there's any interest in forming a sort of committee on the island to take care of all of them. I do want to clean up what's there now, but maintenance could be an issue in the future."

"I'm afraid there aren't too many able-bodied residents of the island these days. The population has aged, and I don't know of any young folks who have taken up residence there. I would think you'd be able to recruit my nephew Alec, though, since he'll be an island resident after his marriage to Lisbeth. But I'm sure you'll do the right thing, Cass. I have total confidence in you." Grace stood to signal tea was over for the day, at least for her. "Now, my little break is over. Time for me to get back to work. Thank you all for joining me this afternoon. Do stop back again tomorrow."

Several in the group were slow to rise, finishing either their tea or one of the pastries that had been served. Cass left the table a moment or two after Grace.

"Excuse me, Grace, if you have a minute?" Cass caught up with her at the door between the dining room and the lobby.

Grace turned and smiled. "Of course, Cass. Is something on your mind?"

"I want to thank you for backing my project. I was afraid people would react the way Joanna did at first. I couldn't think of another way to deal with the fact that the houses we're going to be selling have graves on their property."

"Sometimes a little education is all that's needed to overcome our fears and our prejudices, and it appears you have a handle on that." Grace patted Cass's hand. "But I also feel you are sincere in honoring the residents of the island—living and dead—and I respect that. I was serious about writing an article for my paper. I'll look at the schedule and see when a feature would be most appropriate."

"I appreciate that, Grace. I know your paper is widely read on the Eastern Shore, so your article will draw attention to what we want to do on the island."

"Cannonball Island isn't like other places. Its history is unique, and without an effort to preserve it, I'm afraid much will be lost, and that would be a terrible shame. I'd like to see all your homes sell so I can be assured the story not only will be remembered but will continue to be written."

"You know, if the people who have been staying at the inn decide to buy on the island, you'll be losing business," Cass teased. "You might regret making such a good case on our behalf."

Grace laughed. "The last thing I worry about is the inn losing business. We have waiting lists for every weekend from March through December. You should plan to be here for the Christmas holidays— we have wonderful events. There are a number of bed-and-breakfasts in St. Dennis, but we're the only true inn, and the only one right on the water. We have families who've been staying with us for years. I'm not at all concerned about losing their patronage, but I am concerned about losing our local heritage. You can always call on me if you have any questions or need any information you think I might be able to share." Grace took a few steps into the lobby, then turned back to Cass. "You might want to talk to Lisbeth. I understand she's been sitting with Ruby, recording the old stories for a book she was thinking about putting together. Your work could enhance hers, and hers, yours."

"Thanks, Grace. I'll talk to Lis and see what she has in mind."

"You do that, dear." Grace waved and went off in the direction of her office on the other side of the inn.

Cass's plan had been to go back to the island and take some photos at the Singer plot, but she was still annoyed with Owen and didn't want to risk running into him again today. Instead, she returned to her room to take a much-needed nap. The earlier raking had awakened muscles she hadn't known she'd had.

Tomorrow, she thought as she punched her pillow and curled up in the middle of the bed, she'd go to that big-box store out on the highway and buy her own sickle and weed-whacker grass-trimmer thingy.

Who needs Owen Parker? Not this girl.

EARLY THE NEXT morning, Cass set out for the highway, her list of things to buy in hand. She'd need the equipment, certainly, but a goodly supply of the largest trash bags she could find would certainly come in handy when it came time to—ugh—rake the cut grass and take it somewhere, though she wasn't sure where that would be. Would Ruby Carter want the clippings?

Maybe we should plan a community garden, Cass mused as she tried on a pair of garden gloves, which should cut down on the wear and tear on the palms of her hands. No garden this year, but maybe in the future something could be done. She asked for assistance to find the implements she'd come for and spent a full half hour with the salesman, who felt compelled to explain every feature of everything he showed her. Finally she selected a battery-operated weed whacker—the salesman called it a trimmer, but it was the same thing—and something that resembled Owen's sickle, though lighter in weight.

"I can do this," she murmured confidently as she drove over the bridge onto the island and along the bayside road. "I will clean up every one of those plots by myself. It may take a while, but I know I—"

She slammed on her brakes as she rounded the point and the river came into view. There, fifty feet from shore, was a boat. She turned off the engine and got out of the car and stood for a moment, one hand shielding her eyes. For a moment she watched several men gather on the deck before she took off for the beach, her tennis shoes filling with sand as she neared the water. As she drew closer, she could easily identify Jared Chandler, but the others she didn't recognize. She walked out as far as she could on the unfinished dock and glared.

The rat. She'd left a message for Jared with the desk, telling him about her involvement with Deiter Construction and asking him to call her when he got back. Owen probably knew in advance Jared would be here this morning, and neither of them had let her know. *Thanks, guys.*

"Hey!" she shouted, and all five men on board turned at the sound of her voice.

"Hey, Cass!" Jared waved a greeting.

"Something going on I should know about?"

"I just got back." Jared walked to the far back of the boat. "I was going to catch up with you as soon as I had something to tell you." Before she could respond, he said, "I take it you've heard about the ship that's down there."

"I heard that, but not a whole lot else, except that it's going to cost Deiter Construction a delay and a lot of money."

"I'm sorry about that, but it can't be helped until we know exactly what we're dealing with here. Right now, we're going to take some depth measurements, and we'll try to get a read on the visibility down there. I wish I knew more, had more to tell you, but that's all I've got right now."

She remained on the dock for a few minutes and watched two of the men pull on wet suits. Armed with some equipment—Cass wasn't a diver, so she wasn't sure what they were carrying—they entered the water from a platform on the very back of the boat. She stood for a few more minutes, then realized she was wasting time. She couldn't see what the men were doing below the surface of the water or know how long they'd be down there. Best for her to go about her business. She could stand here for the rest of the day and still not learn anything.

Meanwhile, she had work to do. She went back to her car and unfolded the map she'd made for herself the night before. She'd drawn the island, marked the properties Deiter Construction had purchased, and drew an X on the ones having graveyards. She'd drive by each and see which one needed the most work, and she'd start there. She studied the map, numbered the properties, then headed for the first on her list.

At the old Heller homestead, Cass drove onto the overgrown driveway. She stepped out of her car into a sea of grass that came above her knees and tickled her legs up to the cuff of her shorts. She decided there should probably be a path to the graveyard, so that was the logical place to start. She put on her new gloves and got the sickle from the back of her car.

It was cooler than the previous day, overcast and gray. Sun was forecast for the afternoon, but as yet was still hiding behind the low clouds. The breeze off the bay brought whiffs of the salt marsh at the far side of the property, bringing the scent of decaying plant and animal life as summer slowly faded into autumn.

Might be a good idea to show this property early in the season, she mused, *lest the smell off the flats turn people off. People unaccustomed to natural elements might object.*

Cass tried to remember how Owen had used the sickle, but she wasn't sure. She gave it a good swing, but she'd misjudged the length of the handle and, it being unwieldy, caused the blade to careen a little to one side. She'd somehow managed to lop off the top third of a few strands of grass, but that was all. She swung the sickle again, a little closer to the ground this time, but her form still wasn't right. Perhaps if she handled it more like a golf club and less like a rake?

She took another swing, but swung too hard, and the weight of the sickle almost took her with it.

This looked so much easier when Owen was doing it.

"Okay, you are going to cooperate with me whether you like it or not." Cass planted her feet solidly and tried the golf swing again, this time not quite as hard. The sickle barely missed her ankles.

"You keep that up and you'll be shorter by a foot." She hadn't heard him walk up, but she didn't need to turn around to know who was behind her. "Get it? Shorter by a foot?"

"I get it, Owen. Not funny."

"Do you know how unfunny that actually is? Do you realize how close that thing came to your ankles?" He wrestled the sickle from her hands. "You want to clean up the whole damned island, you should have called me. I told you I'd help."

"Was that before or after you called me crass?" She let go of the handle. She knew when she was overmatched. "Why would I think you'd want to work with someone who's so opposite to your moral compass?"

"About that." He planted the sharp end of the sickle on the ground. "I'm sorry. I didn't think before I spoke. It was a stupid thing to say. I understand that it's possible to have two goals at the same time. Which is what I think you were trying to tell me, but it went over my head at the time."

"Who explained it to you?"

"Fine. I deserve that. Go ahead. Pile it on. But I wanted you to know I am honestly sorry, and that I understand."

"So what, exactly, is it you think you understand?"

She was not going to make this easy for him.

She'd thought he of all people, having grown up on the island, would recognize how special it was, how steps should be taken to preserve as much of it as possible. That he'd thought her interest was only financial gain had hurt her. That he had the power to wound her bothered her almost as much as his unfair assessment of her efforts.

"I understand that as an employee you are obligated to do the best job possible for your father and his company, but at the same time, I think you really do want what's best for the island. I apologize for not realizing that right away. I should have known better." Owen paused. "I do know better. And I am very, very sorry."

For a moment Cass was taken aback. A heartfelt apology was the last thing she'd expected. At least, he sounded sincere.

"You're smarter than you look."

"I guess that's a blessing," he deadpanned. "Do you accept my apology?"

"I do. Thanks for manning up."

"So how 'bout I finish up here for you?"

It would have been so easy to take him up on the offer. Her back would have thanked her. Her hands would have been eternally grateful.

"I appreciate it, Owen, I really do, but I want to finish what I started. What you can do is teach me how to use that thing." She gestured at the sickle, which he was still holding.

"You sure?"

"Positive."

"All right. Come here."

He instructed her and watched as she followed through with his directions. When she realized she'd cleared a path to the gate, she turned to him and beamed.

"Nothing to it once you get the hang of it," she said, pleased with the results. "Thank you for taking the time to show me."

"You're welcome, but the offer stands. I'd be happy to work on the others. Anytime."

"Nice of you, Owen, but really, it's something I want to do myself. My tennis partner signed out of the inn this morning, so I'm going to be missing that morning workout. Now I'll spend that morning time working over here on the island. If I don't have a reason to leave my desk, I'd stay there all day. Not good for the head, the heart, or the hips." Cass smiled. "And besides, taking care of something here on the island makes me feel more a part of it. Makes me feel as if I'm more than just someone who wants to buy a home here."

"I get it. Okay, you're on your own. But you know you can call me if you need me."

Cass paused, wondering if he knew Jared had returned.

"I suspect you'll be pretty busy, now that Jared's back. I saw him out near the mouth of the river earlier. He had a couple of divers with him." She paused. "You wouldn't have been one of them, would you?"

"No. He sent me a text a while ago to let me know he had me on the schedule to dive tomorrow. I told him I think they were diving in the wrong place."

"Where do you think the ship is?" She mentally

crossed her fingers. *Please, somewhere away from our dock.*

"Ruby says the story she heard was that the ship went down on shoals that used to be out in the bay, in line with the mouth of the river, and it was pushed by the currents and the tides into the river itself. I'd like to look where she suspects it might be. I never argue with her." He appeared to think that over. "Well, rarely. She's always right."

"So you're saying more in the river than in the bay?"

"If Ruby's right, then yeah. More in the river."

Damn. "Sounds like you'll have lots to keep you busy. Think maybe you could keep me in the loop? You know, about what you find and where."

"Sure."

"Thanks. Now, maybe you can show me how to work the weed whacker." She rested the sickle against the fence and walked to her car. "I watched how you started yours yesterday, but this one isn't like yours."

"Let's take a look." Owen followed her to the car and looked over her purchase. "Fancy. You went for top-of-the-line, I see. Long-lasting lithium battery. Probably cost double what the gas-powered units sell for, but the battery is easier to maintain and you won't have to add gasoline to make it run. Good choice."

"Thanks. The salesman—he called it a trimmer—did show me where the on switch is, but I looked at so many of these things this morning, I can't remember what he told me."

"Trimmer, weed whacker—two names for basically the same piece of equipment." Owen leaned over her shoulder and reached around her. He was close enough that she could feel his breath on her cheek. She tried to ignore the tickle that went up her spine.

"It's right here on the handle." He pointed to it.

She activated the switch and the trimmer turned on. She turned it off right away. "Got it."

"So you're all ready to go." He stepped back, but he was still close.

"Again, thank you." She took the weed whacker into the enclosed yard and made it clear she was ready to work.

He nodded and started to walk away, then turned back. "Cass, about crabbing . . . ?"

"What about it?"

"How 'bout you let me teach you? If you're going to be an islander, you have to know how to catch crabs. This could be your way of thanking me for teaching you how to use that thing." He stood with his hands on his hips, his long legs tan under the shorts that were cut off at the knee, his shoulders broad and muscled and dark from hours spent in the sun.

She almost had to force herself to look away from all that male gloriousness.

"All right."

"Morning's the best time for crabbing, but it looks like mornings are going to be out for a while, with you weed-whacking and me diving, so let's shoot for tomorrow afternoon."

"What time in the afternoon?" She'd be really

interested in hearing about what he found on his dive. On the other hand, she wasn't sure placing herself in the path of temptation was such a good idea, and the more she was around Owen, the more she was tempted.

"Does four work?"

"I have tea with Grace at four."

"You have what?"

"I have tea with Grace Sinclair. She hosts afternoon tea at the inn, and I go every day. I look forward to it."

"How long does it take to drink a cup of tea?" Owen frowned.

Cass smiled. "It's more than just a cup of tea. It's conversation and spending time with Grace and some of the other guests. It's fun and relaxing. Actually, it's about the only fun, relaxing thing I do these days."

"I can be fun. We could spend time together crabbing and conversing. Of course, we'd have to whisper so the crabs don't hear us."

"It's the whole thing—the ambience, the little group who shows up every day." She paused, then put it in terms she thought he'd understand. "The inn's chef makes scones and éclairs and incredible pastries."

"No way I can compete with Grace's chef. I've had his pastries. Okay, how 'bout five thirty?"

"Five thirty should be fine."

"How 'bout we meet on the pier out at the point?" Owen knew Cass was well familiar with the point, that section of the island that stuck out farthest into the bay, because her father had done his damnedest to talk the current owner into selling it. That owner being Ruby, the answer was always an unequivocal no.

"Perfect. I'll see you there." She turned back to the job at hand and went to work.

If he said anything else, it was lost in the whine of the weed whacker. When Cass glanced over her shoulder, he was gone.

THERE WAS STILL plenty of daylight left when Owen parked his Jeep at the edge of the clearing and began to unload his crabbing gear: two buckets—one for bait, one to contain the crabs after they'd been caught—and a long-armed net. On his way out to the pier, he passed the old house—the cottage— where Ruby and Harold had lived when they were first married and where they'd raised their children before they moved above the store, the place that had become the object of Lis's obsession.

Owen still marveled that the place had been salvageable. He'd walked through it a week ago and he'd been amazed by the transformation.

"Silk purse, sow's ear," he'd murmured when he saw the nearly finished structure.

He'd obviously lacked imagination because he'd told Lis she was crazy to take on such a project. He thought maybe her being an artist might have had something to do with the way she could see what the space could become.

Funny, he had the "sight," but apparently his sister was the one who had vision.

The old fishing pier grew out from the very end of the point and jutted into the bay for twenty-five feet. Islanders once gathered there late in the afternoon, their fishing poles or crab nets in the water, and exchange gossip while they waited for their dinner to take the bait. Owen remembered walking to the pier with Gigi, carrying her bucket of bait, and how she'd greet everyone she passed by name. He'd been five or six at the time, which would have made her close to seventy. She'd taught him to crab and to fish off this pier, he recalled as he neared the very end.

It occurred to him that since he'd returned, he hadn't seen anyone on the pier except Lis. Almost all the old-timers were gone, died or moved away, and few had come to the island to take their places. It saddened him to think of all the old ways that had been lost over the years because no one was around who remembered.

My fault as much as anyone's. I left, too.

He felt Cass's presence without realizing, and he turned to look over his shoulder.

Cass had a long, even stride and her legs effortlessly ate up the distance between the road and the bay. She wore khaki shorts and a navy tank top, a Ravens baseball-style cap, and dark flip-flops. Her dark shades were shaped like cat's eyes, and the bag she wore over her shoulder swung slightly as she walked. She waved and smiled as she drew near, and he had to swallow the lump in his throat before he called out a greeting.

She really was hot.

"So glad the breeze shifted," she was saying as she walked along the rickety pier. "I wouldn't be out here if those damned flies were around."

"Those greenheads are vicious. I never miss them when I'm away."

"They don't have flies in Costa Rica?" She dropped the bag she was carrying.

"There are flies, and then there are *flies*," he said solemnly. "They breed 'em big and mean on the Eastern Shore."

"Well, then, they should stop. And what's with this pier? It's wobbly in a couple of places and it's missing some boards."

"It's old, and I guess no one's given any thought to repairing it. It just doesn't seem to be used as much as it used to."

"That's probably a blessing. Someone could very easily fall through this thing, and then Ruby'd be in for a good lawsuit." Cass bounced up and down a little as if testing the pier's stability. "So let's do this. Where do we start?"

"Okay. There are two schools of thought when it comes to catching crabs. Well, three, actually, but we'll leave out the way the watermen trap on a large scale." Owen sat and patted the space next to him for Cass.

She lowered herself cautiously. "I don't want to get any splinters."

After she settled herself, he handed her a string. "We're going to tie bait around the end of the string and then lower it slowly into the water as far as it can go." He reached into one of two buckets he'd brought with him and drew out something that looked fleshy and gross.

"What in the name of all that's holy is that?" She moved back as if her entire body had gone into cringe mode.

"It's a chicken neck. There are some—me being one of them—who believe there is no better bait for catching crabs." He tied the string tightly to the bait and offered the string to Cass.

"That's disgusting, but okay. I'm game."

"To a crab, it's a gourmet meal." He dropped the baited end of the string into the water and looped the other end around her left index finger. "Now, lower it bit by bit—don't go so fast. You don't want the crabs to think, *Incoming bait*. You want them to just sort of find it on their own."

Cass rolled her eyes. "Like crabs think."

"Who knows how advanced their intelligence might be? No way of measuring it, far as I know." He watched her lower the bait until it disappeared.

"So now what?"

"Well, now you want to bring it back up just enough so that you can almost see it. There, yes, that's perfect."

"What happens now?"

"Now you sit quietly until you feel a little tug on the string. Sometimes it's subtle, but pay attention and you'll know when a crab is nibbling on the bait."

"Then what?"

"Then you'll tell me you think you have a bite, and you'll very slowly, like inch by slow inch, raise the string. You don't want the crab to feel it's being lifted. When you can see the crab, I'll come at it from underneath with the net and scoop it up."

"That sounds easy enough."

"We'll see how easy you think it is when you've lost the first dozen crabs on your line."

"Are you having a line, too?"

"I already do." He pointed to his left hand where a string looped over his finger.

"How can you pick up mine with the net if you're trying to catch some yourself?"

He held up the net with his right hand. "Baited string on the left, net on the right. Not my first day on the dock."

They sat side by side in silence for several minutes until Cass whispered excitedly, "Owen, I think I've got something."

"Okay, stop swinging your feet," he whispered back as he reached for the net. "Now pull it up as slowly as possible. That's good. Really slow, now . . ."

He dipped the net into the water, and the crab fled.

"Damn." Cass frowned. "You scared it away. That net went into the water like . . . like . . ."

"*I* scared it away?" He snorted. "Maybe if you hadn't tugged so hard those last few inches . . ."

"Phfft." She waved away his protest. "Next time, I'll do the net thing myself."

"You're not ready." Owen shook his head.

"You're at a weird angle to my string. That crab could see the net coming."

"Oh, one bite and she thinks she's an expert."

"I'm going to net my own crabs. If they're on my line, they're mine. I get to net them."

"Okay. Let's see what you can do, big talker." He placed the net between them.

Owen watched as she let the chicken neck drift back into the water. Moments later she tapped him on the arm.

"I felt another tug." She lifted the net with her right hand and lowered it slowly into the water several feet from the string.

Owen practically had to sit on his hands to keep himself from grabbing the net because as she raised the string, he could see the crab—a large blue claw—clinging to the bait.

"Oh, boy," she whispered, her face lit with excitement.

"Slowly, now."

"Shhhh." The crab was less than two feet from the surface, the net slightly below it. Cass eased the net until it was under the bait, then snapped the net over the crab and pulled it and the bait to the surface.

"I got one!" she shouted with both surprise and delight. "I caught a crab! And, Owen, look how big she is!"

Owen stood and grabbed the net from her hands. "He. Look how big *he* is."

"How can you tell the difference?"

Owen held the net over the larger of the two buckets he'd brought with him and turned it so they were looking at the back side of the crab.

"See that long, narrow shape there on its abdomen? If this were a female, that would be wider and more round. They say the male's looks like the Washington Monument, the female's like the dome of the Capitol. And actually, we don't say *abdomen*, we say *apron*."

"Got it. That was fun." She sat down again and dropped her line into the water, then glanced at Owen. "No nibbles yet?"

"Sometimes it takes a few minutes for the crabs to find the bait. No worries," he said confidently. "I expect a nibble anytime now."

The only nibble was on Cass's line. She happily netted her second crab, which Owen helped disentangle from the net and drop into the bucket. The crab landed facedown.

"It's a female." Cass pointed to the crab's abdomen. "There's the Capitol dome, right there."

"You're a quick study." Owen resumed his place on the dock and once again wound the string around his finger.

Cass did the same. "Thanks. This is fun."

Within three minutes, her line twitched again. Another crab to add to the bucket. "Another female."

"A sook. A female is called a sook. Males are jimmies."

"Thanks."

It seemed to Owen she had an even harder time hiding her pleasure when the next tug came on her line. Another sook, another plunk as it dropped into the bucket.

"We should be keeping score." Cass grinned and leaned over the bucket. "That would be Cass, four, Owen . . . how many did you catch, Owen?"

He made a face and she laughed out loud.

"Someone is feeling pretty damned smug right about now, isn't she?"

"Yes, someone is." She dropped her line back into the bay, a broad smile on her face.

"Wait, I think I have one." Owen peered over the side of the dock, then grabbed the net. Moments later, he lifted the net with the bait and the crab.

"Cass, four, Owen, one. You're catching up."

He laughed good-naturedly and let the crab fall into the bucket.

By the end of an hour, the score was Cass, nine, Owen, six.

"Beginner's luck," he told her after they decided to call it a day.

"Maybe. Could be technique." She held up the string with the now-chewed-up bait still attached. "What do we do with this?"

"Just untie the chicken neck and let it drift on down into the water. Might as well let the others have a feast since we'll be back again sometime to catch them, too."

"We will?"

"Sure. It's still one of the best places around for crabs, as evidenced by the fact that a total novice just made quite a haul." He reached a hand down to help Cass stand. "You can't tell me you don't want to do this again?"

She smiled as she brushed off the back of her

shorts. "I would do it again. Where did you say you got those chicken necks?"

Owen shook his head. "Secret source. You want crab bait, you have to go through me." He held up the bucket of crabs. "I think we have enough here for a couple of crab cakes. You in?"

"I wouldn't know what to do with them."

"I'll clean the crabs and make them into the best crab cakes you ever had. You bring the beer. But it has to be really, really cold beer, because the crabs are going to be spicy enough to make your tongue tingle."

"And where would this be happening? The cleaning? The cooking? The beer drinking?" She paused. "Didn't you have some wine from the dinner at Mrs. Hart's?"

He looked at her as if she'd blasphemed. "Cass. One does not drink wine with crabs in any form."

"Why not?"

"Because it would be a sacrilege."

"Who declared that?"

"It's tradition. You're so set on upholding traditions, this is one you need to keep. You can drink wine with fish, which you will note we have not caught." He picked up the bucket with the bait in it. "Crabs. Beer. End of story."

"Okay." Cass sighed. "When and where?"

"Tomorrow night. The general store. Be there or . . ."

"Yeah, yeah, I know. Or be square."

Chapter Six

Owen zipped up the top of his wet suit and walked to the end of Jared's boat, which Gordon Chandler, Jared's father, had named the *Cordelia Elizabeth*, after his lady love, the mystery writer Delia Enright. The diving platform was in place and Owen's equipment all ready to go. His half mask hung around his neck, and around his waist he wore a belt that held a flashlight, a knife, and an underwater camera with which to record his finds.

"I'd feel better if you waited for Mario." Jared came out of the cabin and crossed the deck. "You know that diving alone is basically a dumb thing to do."

"The water's not all that deep here. I'm thinking maybe thirty-five feet at the most. I've been in water a lot deeper and rougher than this on my own. Diving in a river as calm as this one is a piece of cake." Owen leaned over to put on his fins. "Besides, I don't plan on being down there all that long. Just long enough to check out the scene. Twenty minutes, tops."

"You know, you could wait for me to suit up."

"Not necessary." Owen strapped on his air tank.

"If anything looks off, come right back up."

"Don't worry, pal. The last thing I'm going to do is risk this pretty face." Owen descended the steps to the platform and went to the edge, easing into the water before securing the mask on his face and placing the regulator into his mouth. Just as Owen flipped forward, he was aware that Jared had begun to say something, but it was lost as Owen propelled downward.

Owen knew the water in the river would be dark, but even he was surprised at just how low visibility was. He turned on his flashlight and aimed toward the bottom, eager to see what lay below. Alone in the silent dark, he swam at an angle to his destination, stopping every ten feet or so to equalize the pressure. Soon the light picked up shapes and shadows on the river bottom, and he descended more rapidly, his heart beating just a little faster at the sight unfolding before him.

The outline of the ship appeared like a phantom, the hull mostly buried in silt and sand, but there was no mistaking what it was. Because he'd only brought one flashlight, he was unable to take in the entire vessel without moving the beam of light from end to end. Next trip down, he'd bring lights with broader beams and other divers to hold them.

Owen drifted slowly along the broken hull. The current was not swift today, so he easily observed the condition of the wood and the placement of the ship. He shot picture after picture until he had photographed the wreck from every angle. Later, they'd map the entire area and uncover what was left of its cargo, if anything, and what might lie beneath the layers of sand.

He swam over and around the wreck several times, memorizing its shape and the areas where the cargo had most likely been. He noted what he saw as well as what he didn't see. When he was satisfied, he headed toward the surface.

He rose as slowly as he'd descended and found Jared leaning over the side of the boat to watch him emerge from the water.

"What did you find?" Jared asked even before Owen had pulled himself onto the diving platform.

"Pretty much what we thought we'd find." Owen pulled off his mask and stepped onto the ship's deck. "Whether it's the merchant ship Ruby talked about, or another, we won't know until we can get some better light and some equipment down there, get the airlift going to suck up the sand. See what's left in the hold, if anything." He lowered his air tank carefully to the deck. "I couldn't tell if it rested on another vessel, though. We'll have to wait to determine that."

"The magnetometer located something else in the bay," Jared told him. "Farther out. It may be that 1812 warship the state had contacted me about before this became a priority because of the construction that had already begun on the dock."

"It wouldn't surprise me to find there's more than one vessel down there. The one in the bay poses no obstacle to Brian Deiter's construction operation, but the one in the river is going to require some changes to their plans to build a dock. I think he's going to have to build elsewhere, so he might as well start looking now rather than wait for the state to make a determination on this site. It's going to take a while." Owen stripped off the belt, then the top of the wet suit. "Doesn't surprise me at all, though, that there's something right where Ruby said there would be."

"She's pretty spooky sometimes," Jared agreed. "Did I ever tell you about the time I stopped by to see if you were around and she invited me to dinner?"

"No. When was that?" Owen rolled down the neoprene diving shorts that he'd donned over a bathing suit.

"A few years ago. Right before you married Cyndi." Jared paused. "What ever happened to her, anyway?"

"She moved to Boston after the divorce."

"Why Boston?"

"A job, I guess. She didn't exactly fill me in on her plans. I was in Alaska at the time."

"I never understood how you could leave a woman like her home alone all the time. I mean, I like my freedom as much as the next guy, but still . . ." Jared rubbed his chin.

"What does that have to do with anything?" Owen sat on a bench that ran along the side of the boat. He opened a cooler and searched amid the contents for a beer. He found one, popped the top, and took a sip. "You were going to tell me about stopping by the store and talking to Ruby."

"Oh, right. So she invites me to dinner and

we're eating at that table in the front of the store, that round one over on the right near the window? And out of the blue, she says, 'Jared, you be heading south before long.' Well, yeah, I was headed back to South Carolina where my dad had opened up his new headquarters, so I said, 'Yes, ma'am, I am.' And then she says, 'You take care, be stormy weather by and by. Mind your instincts.' "

"So?"

"So before I could even join my dad, he calls me and tells me he wants me to fly down to the Gulf and take over a job from another salvor who had turned out to be a sham. Didn't bother to get permits from Florida, didn't have the proper equipment on board, that kind of crap. The guy who'd found the site knew of Chandler and Associates' reputation, so when he needed a replacement for the dud, he called my dad in a panic."

"I repeat, so?"

"So I get down there and something seems off. I didn't like the look of the boat, and the equipment was suspect. The crew was sloppy, the divers were sloppy—nothing was up to our standards. I didn't want the job and told my dad. The guy running the op offered me everything but his firstborn. I admit I was tempted—but something told me to back off. Which I did. Of course, they were able to find another salvor to take over. Four days into the job, a hurricane blew up and the boat went down with everyone on board." Jared blew out a long breath. "How do you figure Ruby knew?"

Owen shrugged. "She has the sight."

"What does that mean?"

"It just means she knows stuff sometimes."

"She always knows everything that's going to happen?"

"No, not always. It depends."

"On what?"

Owen answered honestly, "I have no idea how it works. Why some things are clear to her and others aren't even on her radar."

Ruby'd explained it to him once by saying it was no different from the way some in the family had blue eyes and some had green. It was just the way the genetic cookie had crumbled. But Owen was reluctant to get into it even with a longtime friend.

"You ever think about having her pick lottery numbers? Ever take her to the track?" Jared opened the cooler and took out a bottle of water.

"Not on her radar. And, no, I don't know why."

"Aren't you curious about how it works? Ever ask yourself why some things and not others?"

"Every day."

Such as why he was always on the money when judging the character of new acquaintances, but couldn't usually foresee future events the way Ruby sometimes could. Why he could get an instant read on some people but not others. But the truth was, he'd tried so hard for so long to silence the voice, to *not kno*w, that most of the time he wasn't sure if it was instinct or his third eye that hinted at things.

"But back to the dive. I think you're going to need at least three more divers plus yourself, the best lighting we can set up down there, and we need to map it out. I did see some of the ship's frame, but not the amount of structure I'd expected. This is freshwater here, so the disintegration of the wood isn't what it would be if it were in salt water. Ruby thought the ship might have been set on fire, which would explain why there isn't more to the frame. We'll be able to tell more once we get the silt and sediment out of the way and see if there's any charred wood."

"We have a new dredge engine and pump, new hose—everything's brand-new. We can map the site with side-scan sonar, then use the dredge engine and pump to clear away the sand, and we'll see what it all looks like with the naked eye, see what we can recover. I love all the new technology, but there's nothing like seeing a wreck with your own eyes." Jared tapped his fingers on the water bottle. "I'll be going down myself. If it's a merchant ship from the 1700s, I definitely want to take my time with her. Plus, the state is going to insist on it." He nodded. "So let's get started mapping the site, then we'll see what we can do about securing enough lighting for us to explore the wreck."

"You think about mapping using the grid system?"

"Takes longer."

"True, but there's nothing like going over a site square by square, especially when you have no idea what you might find. You miss less that way." Owen took another swig of beer. "Up to you. It's your job."

"Yeah, but you have almost as much experience as I have. You ever think about doing this full-time? I'd hire you full-time myself if I could talk you into it."

"But then I'd be pretty much tied down, and I'm still not ready to spend all my time doing the same thing."

"You've worked for me in the past."

"I've worked as a consultant for others, too."

"If—when—you think you're ready, you'll call me first, right? I get the first shot at hiring you?"

Owen nodded. "Of course. Just don't hold your breath."

He glanced skyward as clouds began to gather. A low rumble of thunder could be heard in the distance. "Doesn't look like we'll be diving much more this morning."

"We can wait if we have to. No need for you to hang around. If it clears up enough, maybe I'll start getting the area mapped and we'll see what we can see."

"Want a hand with that?"

"Nah, I'm good. Mario's here, and Tony. We can cover it."

"You know where to find me when you need me."

"OOOH! CRABS!" LIS poked her head into the kitchen at Ruby's store.

Owen had just finished steaming the crabs he and Cass had caught the previous day and placed them on a platter. All but one had survived in a bucket filled with seaweed and bay water. Earlier he'd tossed the deceased crustacean onto the beach, where it was immediately attacked by several hungry gulls that had a tug-of-war for feeding rights.

Lis reached for a crab, and her brother smacked her hand.

"What? You can't share?" Lis frowned.

"I'm sharing, but not with you."

"You think you and Gigi are going to eat all those?" Lis peered over his shoulder. "There's some pretty hefty claws on that plate, Bro."

"I'm doing crab cakes for dinner tonight and there are just enough." He frowned, looking over the crabs, red from having been steamed and still piping hot, stacked on the platter. "I hope I have enough."

"You'll have plenty for two people." Lis took a bottle of water from her bag and removed the top.

"Three people."

"Who's the third?" Lis took a long drink from the bottle.

"Cass," he said casually, in his best no-big-deal voice.

"Cass Logan?"

"You know another Cass?" Owen opened a cupboard and sorted through Ruby's spices looking for the Old Bay.

"Huh." Lis leaned back against the counter, a satisfied smile on her face. "I knew it."

"Knew what?" he asked without turning around.

"Knew you had the hots for her." Lis drank the remaining water in the bottle.

"I don't have the hots . . ." He glanced over her shoulder, ready to protest, but instead, he paused. "I don't know what it is I have for her."

"Cryptic." Lis boosted herself onto the counter.

"I admit I'm attracted to her—I mean, come on, what guy wouldn't be?—but there's something else. I like her. I admire her work ethic and her wanting to do right by the island. To keep its history from being destroyed. She sees things here that the rest of us either have forgotten or never saw at all. And besides being pretty, she's really smart."

"Wow. That might even qualify as deep, coming from you."

"Yeah, well, no one's more surprised than I am."

"So you went out and caught some crabs and you're going to woo her with your crab cakes. That borders on diabolical."

"*We* caught some crabs. I took her crabbing out on the point yesterday."

"Really? You took the city girl crabbing? I wouldn't have guessed you were *that* clever." Lis nodded slowly. "This is more serious than I thought. Did you dazzle her with your net-handling skills? Lure her with a pile of chicken necks?"

"How do you know there were chicken necks?"

"You never use anything else. So how'd she do? Did you make her tie off her own bait? Was she grossed out?"

Owen laughed. "I tied the bait, and while she did appear to cringe a little when she first saw the bait bucket, to her credit she was a good sport about it." He found the container he was looking for and set it on the counter. "And actually, she caught more crabs than I did."

"And how did your manly ego react to being bested by an amateur?"

"Beginner's luck," he scoffed as he began to clean the crabs, removing the claws first.

"Want some help?"

"No, because you'll eat more than you pick."

"I'm a world-class crab picker. Gigi taught me when I was knee-high, and I'm still damned good. I was always better than you."

"You wish."

For a moment, the only sound in the kitchen was the cracking of a crab's shell.

"I saw Jenn Castro a couple of days ago," Lis said to break the silence. "Alec and I went to Ballard to look at some tables a guy makes out of reclaimed wood."

"Who's Jenn Castro?" He tossed the crab meat into one bowl, the pieces of shell into another.

"You remember her. She's married to Cyndi's cousin Andrew."

"So what about her?"

"So she said she heard Cyndi was going to be visiting her parents sometime soon, she wasn't exactly sure when."

"So?"

"So I just thought I'd mention it, that's all."

"Well, if it's a warning you're giving me, I appreciate it, but I have no interest in what Cyndi does or doesn't do or where she goes. That ship sailed a couple of years ago, Sis."

"I know, I know, but there was something in the way Jenn said it. . . ." Lis shook her head. "Maybe it was my imagination, but it almost sounded as if it was more than a simple heads-up."

"What more could there be? Cyndi's parents moved to Ballard a couple of years ago, so we probably won't even run into each other." Another empty shell into the bowl, another crab to clean and pick.

"I don't know. She just gave me a weird feeling, that's all."

"I have about as much interest in my ex-wife as she has in me. I haven't heard a word from her in years, and that's just skippy as far as I'm concerned. We were a bad idea that never should have happened. Fortunately, we were both able to walk away before things became too complicated."

"Shortest marriage ever. Never even made it into the family Bible. Gigi was appalled."

"No, she wasn't. Gigi thought I shouldn't have married Cyndi in the first place. She tried to talk me out of it more than once."

"Teach you to ignore Ruby's advice."

"No fooling."

"How come you didn't see it yourself?"

"Maybe I did. Maybe I ignored it."

"That was dumb. If I had the sight, I wouldn't ignore it."

"No, you'd buy a bunch of lottery tickets every week and end up with your own reality show."

Lis laughed. "I asked Ruby once why she didn't use it to pick the Kentucky Derby winner, and she all but took my head off. 'No good come of abusing a gift, any gift. Sure way to be losing it.' You could probably do it, right? Pick lottery winners? Call the outcome of horse races? Clean up in Vegas?"

"Gambling's not my thing. Besides, if I don't use it, I don't have to deal with it."

"Why don't you want to deal with it?"

Owen shrugged. "There're things I just don't want to know. I don't want to know what happens in the future—what if I don't like what I see? I don't want to know what other people are thinking. I just . . . I don't want to know."

"You'd read Cass if you could."

"Maybe make an exception in her case," he conceded with a slow smile. He wasn't about to let Lis know he'd tried and failed. Again. He held up the bowl of crab meat. "Think I'm going to need more?"

"How many crab cakes were you planning on making?" She looked into the bowl and raised an eyebrow.

"At least two each."

"That would be six total."

"Who says girls can't do math."

"You don't have enough crab meat." She hopped down off the counter. "Now, if I were a good sister, I'd offer to bring over the crabs we caught this morning so you could add to your mix." She smiled sweetly. "But then, of course, we'd expect to be invited to dinner."

"How many crabs did you catch?" he asked cautiously.

"About three times as many as you did."

"No way."

"Way. We took out a rowboat Alec rebuilt and just drifted along. Early morning, the sun just rising, the gentle lap of those little low-tide waves against the side of the boat, a thermos of coffee, and the love of my life manning the net." She sighed. "It was so romantic."

"You've got it bad, girl."

"No kidding. Which is why I'm marrying him." She flashed her engagement ring. "Thanks again for agreeing to walk me down the aisle and give me away."

"Can't give you away fast enough." His eyes twinkled when he looked at his sister. "Besides, who else is there? Gigi's too old, and—"

"Too old for what, boy?" Ruby came through the door from the front of the store, her hands on her hips.

"Too old to walk Lis down the aisle."

For a moment, Ruby looked as if she was about to protest or scold, but instead she said, "Depends on how long the aisle be."

"It can be as long as we want it to be." Lis put an arm around Ruby. "If you wanted to walk down the aisle with Owen and me, the walk will be whatever you say."

"That be something to think about, Lis. Might be I'd want to. Course, I don't know what your mama would think. She might be wanting that duty for herself."

Lis snorted. "She hasn't even said if she's coming back for the wedding. She's very much involved with her new family. One of her stepchildren is about to make her a step-grandmother again, and that's all she talks about on the phone. She sends me texts every week with pictures of the grandkids."

"Don't be holding that against her, Lisbeth," Ruby admonished. "Other than you and Owen, nothing good came out of your mama's marrying your daddy. Second husband weren't much better. This time, looks like she found someone that makes her happy. Leave her to it. She'll do as she needs, by and by."

"I guess," Lis said. "Still, I wish—"

"She'll do as she needs, Lisbeth," Ruby repeated. "No need to fuss."

"All right. So you give some thought to walking with Owen and me, and we'll scale the distance accordingly." Lis smiled and kissed Ruby's cheek.

"You're still set on doing all at the point?" Ruby asked.

"Of course. Why wouldn't we? We want the ceremony right there on the pier overlooking the bay."

"Best be just the two of you, then," Ruby said. "That pier be going into the bay afore long."

"Alec is fixing it, shoring it up and replacing the broken boards."

"He better get a move on, then, since as of yesterday, it was still needing repair," Owen said. "He doesn't have much time left. Tell him I'll give him a hand if he needs one."

"I'll tell him. Anyway, after the ceremony, we'll have the reception on the grassy area between the pier and the cottage. It'll be perfect. Lucy has a big wedding at the inn, but she's helping out with the planning and she'll be over as soon as her event ends. She already reserved a tent and tables and chairs and a dance floor, and we lined up Sophie

Enright to cater. She's already working on the menu, and I know it will be phenomenal. Grace talked Steffie into making an ice cream flavor just for us." Lis broke into a grin. "Is that the best? Oh, and we're having a special beer made as well. Steffie's husband, Wade, and Clay Madison promised to come up with something."

"I have to admit I'm partial to Steffie's ice cream myself," Ruby said. "Known Steffie since she was little Steffie Wyler helping her cousin Horace plant flowers at that house over there on Olive Street. He left her that place in his will. Always said she'd have her own ice cream shop someday. Now she has that shop . . ."

"One Scoop or Two," Lis supplied the name.

Ruby nodded. "Does right well for herself."

"I haven't been to Scoop since I've been back, but I've sampled my share of MadMac beer, and I have to say, it's damned good," Owen said. "So you're going totally local for the wedding. I like it."

"Everything except my dress. Well, it's sort of local, I guess, since Vanessa at Bling ordered it in special for me from a designer I saw online. She said she was thinking about expanding into the bridal market. The antiques place next to hers has been closed now for six months and there's no sign of it being reopened."

"You don't mean Nita's place?" Owen stopped chopping the onion he was working on and looked up. "She's an institution in St. Dennis."

"No. Nita's a few doors away. I don't even

know who owns the store next to Vanessa. But she said it might be available sometime soon and she'd like to move into the space. Which is a great idea. Weddings are huge right now, and St. Dennis is the perfect spot. The inn is one of the most popular wedding venues on the Eastern Shore. All the town lacks is a bridal boutique."

"Yeah, I noticed that." Owen turned to Lis. "I just said to Jared this morning, 'Know what St. Dennis needs? It needs a good wedding—' "

Lis sent her empty water bottle in his direction, and he caught it in one hand. Owen tossed it back to her.

"So if I pick and clean our crabs and bring them to you, can we come for dinner? Or are you afraid that might cramp your style?" Lis hesitated. "Not that you have any discernible style. Besides which, if you were planning on a move, you wouldn't be making dinner for Cass *and* your great-grandmother."

Ruby stood by silently, though clearly amused.

"Oh, come on. Don't make me beg, Owen. We've already established that you rule when it comes to crab cakes."

"A fact I cannot deny. Okay, if you can get your crabs over here before I begin to work my magic, you guys can join us. But you have to bring a salad and dessert."

"No sweat there. Wait till I tell Alec." Lis raised a fist in victory, grabbed her bag, and headed for the door.

"You knew you were going to give in to that

girl, Owen Parker. Why'd you give her such a hard time?" Ruby asked.

"She's my little sister. I have to remind her of that fact once in a while."

"Be nice to have a little group for dinner for a change. We can eat outside while the weather is still warm. Maybe use that old table that my mother favored."

"I don't remember an old table except the round one in the store. Is that the one you mean?"

"No. I mean the long one up on the third floor. Chairs be there, too."

"Which means I need to get them."

"Course you do. Not gonna be me, traipsing up those steps."

Owen covered the bowl of crab meat and put it in the refrigerator. He climbed the stairs that led from the store to the second floor, then to the third, where the attic held furniture and personal belongings from untold generations of family members. The lighting was poor but he had no trouble locating the table. It stood smack in the middle of the attic floor and was piled high with boxes of who knew what. It took Owen five minutes to remove and stack the boxes, then another five to dust the tabletop and the legs. Even so, it needed a good cleaning. He went back downstairs, where he found Ruby in the store at the counter.

"Ruby, that table is really dirty."

"You be dirty, too, you spent forty or so years just standing around in the attic." She raised her eyes from the register to stare him down. "I suspect you know where I keep the cleaning things. Also suspect you know how to use 'em."

"Even so, there's no way I can bring that table down here by myself."

"Lucky for you, Alec be along before you set dinner out. He be a willing helper."

Owen sighed and went into the kitchen in search of cleaning supplies.

"You're a tough taskmaster, Gigi."

"Gotta earn your keep somehow."

LIS AND ALEC wandered into the store at six thirty. With Alec's help, Owen had the table set up in the garden exactly where Ruby directed.

"Last of the summer things blooming," Ruby pointed out. "Afore long, won't be any color out here 'cept green and maybe some morning glories. Maybe a few dahlias hang on awhile, a few black-eyed Susans, some of the roses. Mostly all else be dying back soon." Ruby stood on the back porch and stared at her flower beds. "Shame to see all that color fade away."

Lis came up behind her. "Happens every year, Gigi. And you have said the same thing every year for as long as I can remember. They'll all be back again next year, just as pretty."

"If I be around to see it. Never can tell."

"And you say that every year, too."

"Never can tell, Lisbeth."

"Gigi, I'm betting you outlive us all." Owen had brought a chair out from the house and placed it next to where Ruby stood.

"Wouldn't surprise me"—Ruby sat down—"the way you run around here and there, diving down under the water one day, flying up to the sky the next." She tapped Owen on the arm. "I'm talking to you, boy."

"I heard you, Gigi." The sports car pulling into the driveway diverted his attention. He tried not to stare as Cass unfolded herself from the driver's seat and smoothed the front of her sundress before looking toward the store.

"We're all out here," Owen called to her, and she raised a hand to let him know she'd heard.

She opened the trunk and removed something before slamming the lid. As she drew closer to the store, Owen saw she carried a six-pack of beer in each hand.

"You got the beer." Owen walked across the yard to meet her.

"That was the deal, right? I bring the beer, you cook the crabs." She looked to the garden when the porch door slammed. "Oh, are we eating outside? I love that. I'm so glad you thought of it."

"Actually, it was Ruby's idea."

"Whoever. I love it."

He reached to take the beer from her but she declined. "I've got them. I'm not sure how cold they are at this point, though."

"Let me put them in the store cooler. Alec brought some beer as well, and his should be nice and cold by now."

"You didn't mention that Lis and Alec would be here." Obviously pleased, she flashed a happy smile, and Owen's stomach did a little flip. She handed over the six-packs. "Some of my favorite people all in the same place. And what a pretty place it is."

Cass walked past him to the backyard, where she greeted Lis and Ruby. Alec came out of the store carrying a chair under each arm, and he, too, got a warm hello from Cass.

Wondering if he was one of her favorite people—though doubting it—Owen went inside and tucked the beer into the cooler after moving around some of the soda cans. He stopped at the back door to gaze out the window. Cass was conversing lively with Lis, and Ruby was smiling as if approving of everything Cass was saying. He gave himself just a minute or two to look at her because he just flat out liked the way she looked. It was as simple as that. He liked the way her short blond hair curled around her ears, liked the way her dress, something light blue that looked like a long T-shirt, just grazed the top of her knees and skimmed over the rest of her, liked the way . . .

Owen sighed. There wasn't anything he could see that he didn't like. He forced himself to look away from the window and retreat into the kitchen, trying to decide if the presence of the others was a good thing or a bad thing. Probably good. If he and Cass were alone, he wasn't sure he'd be able to think of much to say—so out of character for him, but she had that effect on him sometimes. At least the others would keep the conversation moving.

He hadn't been lying when he told his sister he wasn't sure what he felt for Cass. Attraction, of course—he'd admitted that along with a list of other things he liked about her. So what, he asked himself, was so different about her? He'd been attracted to more women than he could remember.

But he didn't remember having been aware of those other things—how smart a woman was, or what she cared about, as long as she cared enough about him. Past relationships—if he could call them that—usually had more to do with how comfortable he was, how hard he had to work to have things the way he wanted them, and he usually hadn't had to work hard at all. And in the past, he reminded himself, women had generally found him pretty much irresistible. He couldn't remember anyone having expectations of him that he hadn't met. Which probably meant that the bar hadn't been set high.

Maybe he was losing his touch. Or his hair. He frowned and ran a hand through it. Nope. That wasn't it.

And most of the women he'd known in the past hadn't spent all that much time talking. Not that Cass was a chatterbox. The conversations they'd had had been *about* something. The island, its history, and its people. The renovations to the houses Deiter had purchased, the designs she'd drawn up for the new ones. He'd even helped her in that, assisted her and Alec in tracking down some of the residents who'd just picked up and left, so they could purchase the properties.

He took the crab cakes from the fridge and turned on the oven, trying to recall if he'd ever spent that much time in conversation with a woman other than his sister or Ruby. He was embarrassed he couldn't think of a one. Even Cyndi and he hadn't spent all that much time talking. Well, she'd talked and he'd pretended to listen.

Had he really been that much of an insensitive ass all this time?

The back door opened and closed, and he heard footsteps coming toward the kitchen.

"Owen?" Cass paused in the doorway. "Ruby said you're doing all the cooking tonight. Is there something I can help you with?"

"Everything's under control, but thanks."

Cass came into the kitchen and peered at the tray. "You made all those crab cakes from those few crabs we caught?"

"Ahh, no. I made about five from what we caught. Lis and Alec caught a bunch this morning and decided to toss theirs in with ours." Owen smiled and turned back to the stove. "If my sister can find a way out of cooking, she'll take it."

"What else are you making?" Cass leaned on the island.

"Baked potato fries. Lis made a salad and she brought dessert."

"Sounds fabulous. Thanks for inviting me."

"You're welcome."

"Can I at least peel the potatoes?"

"No need. I just scrub them and cut them into wedges. A little olive oil, a little salt, a little pepper."

Cass moved behind him, so close her dress brushed against the back of his knees. "Where's your scrubby thing for the potatoes?"

"Really, Cass, you don't have to—"

"I want to. I like to be busy. I can sit around for only so long. Not that the company out there isn't stellar. I just feel like . . ."

"Like what?" He turned around.

"Like being busy. Useful. I'm an okay cook. I'll never win any awards, but I'm okay. I'm pretty sure I can scrub up a couple of potatoes without screwing it up."

"Only one way to find out." He pointed to the vegetable scrubber on the counter next to the sink and the pile of potatoes he'd left there. "Have at it."

"That's some garden Ruby has out there." Cass turned on the water and got to work. "Her flowers are beautiful, and I can't believe she grows all those vegetables by herself."

"She's always had a garden, always planted everything from seed. She shares her flower seeds and can point to every garden on the island—some in St. Dennis, too—where her flowers have taken root. I know Grace planted a bunch of Gigi's seeds at the inn some years ago. I guess the flowers or their progeny are still growing. Gigi's big on perennials."

"I'll try to remember to ask Grace. But how does a one-hundred-year-old woman tend a garden that size?"

"For starters, we're not talking about your average hundred-year-old lady. This is Ruby Carter," he said, his pride apparent. "She's the toughest of the tough, and the wisest of the wise."

"That describes her to a T. But still, there's all that bending, planting, and weeding. Gardening is hard work. Okay, I've finished scrubbing. Where will I find a knife to cut the potatoes with?"

"Top drawer next to the dishwasher, and the cutting board is right there on the counter. Just cut them in half lengthwise, then half again. This summer I did most of the planting and weeding. Other years, some of the neighbors' grandkids came over and helped out in the mornings. Their grandmothers wouldn't let them take money from Ruby, so she paid them in sodas and chewing gum."

"So how'd your dive go this morning?" Cass said casually.

"It was okay. A little cold. But it was an easy dive."

"Find anything?" She kept her eyes on the potatoes, but Owen knew her interest went beyond making casual conversation.

"I did. There's definitely a ship down there. What it is, when it's from, who it belonged to, all remains to be seen. Jared's going to map it before we disturb anything. Once we can get to the cargo and the cabin, we'll know what we're looking at."

"What does that mean in terms of our dock?" She still hadn't taken her eyes from her task.

"It means you probably should start looking for another location."

"Oh, Dad's going to love this news."

"I'm sorry, but if I were you, I wouldn't wait until the state gave me official notice. I'd start looking now and find another place to build the dock."

"Gee, what a swell idea. Why didn't I think of that?"

"I wasn't trying to be a smart-ass, Cass. What's the alternative?"

"We've already spent so much money on that dock. We've dredged and brought in those huge pilings, and they were not cheap."

"You're just lucky you didn't dredge anywhere near the ship. You'd have a mess on your hands if you'd dug that up."

"I guess I should be thankful for that. But still, if we have to take it down and start somewhere else . . ."

"I get it. But I repeat: What's the alternative?"

She blew out a long breath. "I guess there isn't one."

"There has to be at least one place where the water is deep enough that with a minimum of dredging you'll be able to bring your boats to dock."

"You think?"

Owen nodded. "Let me check out the bay side. They used to bring large fishing boats into the cove, so we know there's some depth. I don't know how much of that has changed over the years due to shifting sands and such. But it's worth looking into. Any specific reason you started building on the river side?"

"My dad thought it was more picturesque. He figured when we were done using it to bring in building materials, we could offer docking rights to some of our customers who had boats. He thought it would be a nice perk."

"Maybe it still could be, just probably not in that spot. The bay side isn't as picturesque as the river, but it's better than no dock at all. We'll probably need to get an engineer involved at some point, but I'll leave that up to you. You'll have to get a permit if it turns out you have to dredge, but we won't worry about that unless we have to. In the meantime, Jared has some equipment on board that can measure depth, so I'll ask him to bring his boat over to the bay side when he gets the chance."

"That would be great. Thank you. I'd hate to have to call my dad and tell him the dock has to come down, and by the way, we can't build anywhere else."

"Well, you know what Ruby always says." He smiled at Cass over his shoulder. "'You got a problem, you find a solution. You don't be wasting time worrying about it.'"

"That definitely sounds like Ruby." Cass finished cutting the potatoes. "What now?"

"Dump them into that blue bowl there to your left on the counter. . . . Yes, that one. Then add some olive oil—that's in the cabinet over the bowl—and salt and pepper." He watched her as she followed his instructions.

"That's it?"

"You could toss in some red pepper flakes if you're feeling like a little spice. Then spread them on the baking sheet on the island."

When the potatoes were ready, Owen opened the oven and slid them in.

"That was easy. What else can I do to help?"

"You could go into the store and grab two beers from the cooler."

"I'm on my way." Cass disappeared into the store. She came back carrying two bottles. "I took two from the back. I'm guessing Alec brought those because they're colder than the ones I picked up."

Owen tossed her an opener and she popped the lids off both bottles and handed one to Owen.

"Glass?"

She shook her head no. "It would feel . . . I don't know, maybe a bit pretentious to be eating crabs we pulled out of the bay ourselves and drinking our beer out of a glass. The bottle seems to fit the ambience."

He nodded. She got it.

"So how did you learn to cook?" she asked.

"Our mom worked at night sometimes—she waited tables at the inn on occasion—and my father wouldn't cook." Owen gave her a rueful smile. "Women's work, you know? So when my mother worked late, he ate at one of the local bars, and I cooked for me and Lis or we didn't eat. Gigi showed me how to do some things, others I learned by reading the old family cookbook."

"Recipes that have been passed down, you mean?"

"Yeah. It's more like a folder than a book. It's around here somewhere."

Cass fell silent.

After a moment, Owen asked, "Do I see wheels turning?"

She laughed. "Sorry. I was just thinking how cool it would be to gather some old recipes and make a Cannonball Island cookbook. We could give it to people who buy the houses, and we could—" Cass stopped. "I know. I get carried away. Sometimes I get very enthusiastic about something and my imagination just takes off. This whole project has taken on a life of its own."

"It's a very worthy project, Cass. I admire the way you're handling things here on the island. And a cookbook would be a great addition to everything else you're doing, if you could fit it in between cleaning graveyards, renovating some of the old houses, and tearing down others to build new. How are your designs coming along, by the way?"

"They're done. I keep tinkering with them, but for the most part, they're finished. I'm thinking of marketing some of the renovated homes as perfect little one-person retreats. You know, target singles who are looking for a place to get away." She watched him as if waiting for a response.

"I saw something on TV last week—something Ruby was watching about little houses. They seem to be popular right now."

"Tiny houses are definitely on trend. But ours would be special because they'd have so much history."

Owen glanced at her face. She'd taken on a bit of a dreamy expression, as if imagining what those tiny houses might look like. He took a swig of beer to keep himself from leaning over the granite and kissing that dreamy face.

"History seems to be your thing."

"My first love. If my father hadn't convinced me I'd be more of an asset to Deiter Construction as an architect, I'd probably be teaching history at the high school or college level. My parents both thought teaching wasn't lucrative enough, and my dad wanted me to join his company in some capacity. I'm one of three architects the firm employs, but when a project comes along that I'm interested in, I always get dibs. The other two guys understand that's how it is."

"The perk of being the boss's daughter."

"It's one of the only perks, believe me. He works me as hard as he works the guys, expects more from me because I'm his kid."

"Do you regret becoming an architect?"

"Not really. I actually love designing houses. I like imagining people living in the spaces I design. And a project like this one suits me to a T."

"Because of the history involved?"

She nodded.

"The bay area is crazy with history. From the earliest settlers to the Revolution to the War of 1812, the Civil War, and the connections to the Underground Railroad." He opened the oven, turned over the potatoes, closed the oven, then took a frying pan from an overhead rack. "Have you been on any of the history tours?"

"What history tours?" Her eyes widened with interest. "Someone gives history tours?"

"Well, no, you have to plot them out yourself." He flashed a grin. "Or know someone who knows where to go." He turned on the burner under the pan and added butter.

"Someone like, oh, I don't know. Got anyone in mind?"

"Colonial tour. Revolutionary War tour. Eighteen twelve tour. Civil War tour—I'm your man."

"Are you volunteering your services as tour guide?"

"Anytime. Your choice of tour."

She smiled and leaned her elbow on the island and rested her chin in her palm. "Hmmm. Something to think about, for sure."

He went to the porch door and opened the screen. "Lis, come get plates and stuff to set the table."

"I can help her." Cass turned, and for a moment she was that close, so close to his chest they were almost touching. Owen looked down and almost wished he hadn't. Their eyes locked, and the temptation to kiss her was so strong. All he had to do was lean in just another few inches.

If I'd waited one more minute to call Lis in, I'd be kissing her right now.

Lis and Alec came through the back door, laughing at something one of them had said, and the sound of their laughter broke the spell. Owen took one step back, then a second, his eyes still on Cass's face. He didn't recognize her expression. Relief or disappointment? He wasn't sure.

Lis continued to chatter as she lifted plates from the cupboard, while Alec went into the store for a six-pack of beer.

Lis glanced into the frying pan. "Those crab cakes are monstrous."

"They'll need about ten minutes." Owen moved to the stove and began adding the crab cakes to the pan where the butter was beginning to sizzle.

"I'll take some of the plates," Cass offered.

"I've got them, but you can bring the salad." Lis opened the refrigerator door and pointed to the white bowl. Cass grabbed it and followed Lis out the door.

Owen had just finished adding the crab cakes to the pan when he heard the door again. He knew without turning around it would be Cass, even though she didn't make a sound, and he knew within seconds she'd be right behind him. Instinct? Or was the sight finally pulling through for him?

Cass leaned around him, one hand resting on his shoulder, and every cell in his body went on alert. "They smell amazing."

"They will be amazing."

"Think the potatoes are done?"

He couldn't take his eyes off her mouth. Owen half turned and slid an arm around her. Without hesitating this time, he kissed her ever so lightly on the lips. When he realized she was kissing him back, he cupped her face in his hands and kissed her again. The jolt went from the top of his head to his toes and was so strong, he was sure she must have felt it, too.

Slightly flustered, she pulled away, avoiding his eyes. "I'm not sure that's a good idea."

"Best idea I've had in a long time. Glad I acted on it." He leaned close to her ear. "And so are you."

Diary~

I've been having such fun lately. Toward the end of the summer, I got it into my head that I needed a little break in the afternoon, so I headed down to the terrace—what my daughter, Lucy, calls the veranda when she's doing her wedding-planning thing—where I had a leisurely cup of tea. I enjoyed that short bit of time so much, I found myself gravitating to the same table every day around the same time. I'd often see the same guests out there, so one day I invited a few of them to join me. Well, before I knew it, we had a little group coming together at the same place, same time, every day, and I decided to make it a regular thing. I invited any of our guests who wished to join us to come to the terrace at four every afternoon. I asked our pastry chef to make some tea sandwiches and fancy little cakes and some scones and voilà! Afternoon tea at the Inn at Sinclair's Point was official! I think I shall continue the practice through the coming months, though another venue will have to be found. The winter wind blowing across the bay would put the kibosh on outside dining of any sort, to say the least!

I look forward to this little break in my routine—at my age, such moments of relaxation are no longer luxuries, but necessities. I've gotten to know our guests better—the door, so to speak, is always open to one and all—and I daresay they've all gotten to know our little town better through our discussions. One day we talked about the Enright mansion and how it came to be the community art center, about Curtis Enright and his lovely wife, Rose, and the parties they used to have there. Of course, I had to tell them that there are many who claim Rose—gone now these twenty years—has never really left, how even now there are those who claim to smell gardenias, her favorite scent, here and there around the old house. I myself have had the experience on many, many occasions, but then again, I knew Rose well, so one would expect her to stop by upon seeing an old friend.

Our guests were further fascinated by the history of Cannonball Island, which led into a discussion of the new homes that would soon be available over there. That is, they will be once the whole business of who or what is resting on the bottom of the river is settled. Of course, Ruby and I know it's that merchant ship that the folks at Annapolis turned back. In time, it will be discovered the fire began belowdecks while several crew members, having decided that the small cargo of rum wouldn't be delivered after all, conspired to consume as much of it as they could. The ship was at anchor, hiding in the river with too many idle hands on board. All it took for the fire to blaze out of control was one unguarded candle and five inebriated sailors. However, the real story of that fateful night will not be revealed when the ship is explored: that of the slaves and indentured men who, still chained together, escaped to Cannonball Island. Several folks around these parts are descendants, though they may not know it. It's not my place to tell~

Grace~

Chapter Seven

What, Cass asked herself, was she going to do about Owen Parker?

Owen Parker, who might just be the biggest player on the planet. The same Owen who'd helped her to clean up an abandoned graveyard, taught her how to use power tools, took her crabbing, and who turned out to be a fabulous cook. Oh, and shared his wonderful family with her. Owen Parker, who might hold the title Hottest Guy I Ever Met.

Owen Parker, who had kissed her blind until she barely remembered where the ignition was in her car and where she was supposed to be going.

She hadn't planned on that happening. The dinner, yes. Enjoying his family, yes. Kissing him in the moonlight? Not on her list of things to do.

She'd accepted the dinner invitation hoping to learn a little more about the situation with the dock so she could fill her father in. She hadn't been happy to hear what Owen had to say, but at least he'd been honest and had offered to help her solve the problem. She suspected the possibility was real that there'd be no place on the island where they could inexpensively build another dock, but as Owen had quoted Ruby, "You got a problem, you find a solution. You don't be wasting time worrying about it."

Cass was going to try to live up to that advice. She'd look for a solution before she wasted any more time worrying about it. She just hoped she could talk her father into doing the same.

Everything about the evening had been perfect. The food was delicious. The setting magical—Ruby's garden was full of life and color and fragrance, and a few leftover fireflies made an appearance. Fairy lights, Lis had called them. The company couldn't have been improved upon. The first time they'd met, Cass had recognized she was in the presence of someone very special in Ruby. Alec had been Cass's ally in getting her father to appreciate the potential of Cannonball Island as she envisioned it, and Alec had become a true friend. She'd been honored when he asked her to work with him to renovate the cottage that meant so much to Lis. Cass had been more than happy to be part of making that special dream come true for Alec to give his beloved.

They'd had such a fun time, she'd hated to see the evening end. Even cleanup had been fun. Ruby had retreated to her sitting room with a book she'd been reading.

"I'm almost to the end," she'd told them before she'd shuffled off to her living quarters. "I be certain who the slasher is, but I need to finish the book to know for sure."

Slasher? Cass had mouthed the word to Owen.

He'd laughed out loud. "Ruby loves dark thrillers. The darker, the bloodier, the better."

"I never would have guessed." Cass walked into the kitchen shaking her head.

"How 'bout that one she read a few weeks ago?" Lis had placed the empty salad bowl on the counter. "About some guy who wrapped his pretty victims in cellophane and watched them suffocate."

"No way." Cass's eyebrows had risen nearly to her hairline.

"Way," Lis assured her.

"Wow. I'd have figured her more for a good cozy mystery." Cass started to rinse dishes in the sink. Owen tried to back her away to take her place but she shooed him off. "I'll rinse. You load the dishwasher."

"Fair enough."

"She does read a few cozies from time to time, but give her a good serial killer and she's all in," Lis had said.

Owen turned on his iPhone and searched for his music downloads.

"Is there music to clean up by?" Cass had asked.

He responded by placing the phone on the counter and turning up the volume. "That do it for you?" Owen began to rap along to the lyrics to "My Shot" from *Hamilton*.

Cass had tried to keep a straight face, but by the time he'd finished, she'd lost it. "No way did I see that coming."

"Me either. When he was younger, he wanted to

do the whole boy-band thing," Lis said when she finished laughing. "He doesn't rap any better than he sings."

"Maybe you could rap the toast at the wedding next week," Alec suggested.

"You mock me because you're jealous of my mad skills."

"I mock you because that was so out of character," Alec said. "And not very good, frankly."

"A man has to be multifaceted," Owen said with a straight face.

"Just make sure you practice that toast a few times before the wedding." Lis dried off the bowl she wanted to take home.

"I'll be ready with a knockout toast," Owen assured her. "You'll be in tears by the time I'm finished."

"Great. Something to look forward to. Note to self: waterproof mascara." Lis kissed him on the cheek, then hugged Cass. "Are you sure you don't want help with those dishes?"

"We're good," Owen told her.

"I'll give your dad a call about the dock, Cass," Alec said.

"Thanks, but I think that's a conversation I'll need to have."

"Let me know if you change your mind," Alec said as he and Lis left.

"I don't think I will, but nice of you to offer."

"Do you want to wait to call your dad until after we've had a chance to look around for a possible alternate site?" Owen asked after Lis and Alec were gone.

"I think I should call in the morning, before anyone else contacts him." Cass handed Owen the last plate. "But you will think about where else we could build, right?"

"I promise."

Cass looked at the clock that hung over the doorway. "It's later than I thought. I should be going. I have a date with the Allens in the morning."

"Who?"

"The Allens. They're buried in the front yard of the house next to the chapel."

"The new chapel, the old chapel, or the old *old* chapel?"

"They all look old to me. I can't tell the difference."

"We'll have to include that in your island tutorial."

Cass picked up her bag, and Owen followed her to the back door, his arm resting casually over her shoulder. They walked outside and stood on the top porch step.

"Look up," Owen said.

The night sky was ink black, the ambient light on the island being almost nonexistent. The stars twinkled and several constellations were in full view.

Owen stood as if mesmerized. "Do you know why they call Polaris the North Star?"

"Because it always points north?"

"Pretty much. The earth's axis is pointed almost exactly at that star. It stays in pretty much the same place all year round, while other stars move around the sky. Early explorers used it to navigate."

"So I guess it works as good as a compass."

"It's better than a compass. A compass can only show you the direction of the strongest magnetic force for a certain time and a specific place. The North Star is pretty constant."

"Well, I know it's in the handle of the Big Dipper."

"You mean the Little Dipper." He pointed overhead. "The Big Dipper is there. See the handle? It's in the opposite direction from the handle of the Little Dipper. The handles always appear to be in opposing directions."

"Did you ever navigate using just the North Star?"

"Sure. When I was a kid, that's all we ever used, my grampa and me. He thought compasses were a crutch." Owen laughed. "He thought anything that didn't rely on the use of your own senses was a crutch. The man never went past eighth grade, but he knew more about stuff than anyone I ever knew."

"Was this your mom's father?"

Owen shook his head. "My dad's father."

"You never talk about your parents."

Owen shrugged. "Not much to say. My mom's on her third husband and my father's dead."

"Oooh, harsh."

"My father wasn't a particularly nice guy. As a matter of fact, he wasn't nice at all. He carried a grudge over something that happened back in 1814 and he never let us forget it."

"Eighteen fourteen. That's when . . ."

"Yeah. When the residents of St. Dennis who

were loyal to the British were driven out of town and onto this island. They had to leave behind their homes and anything they couldn't carry with them. My dad's family owned property in St. Dennis that was taken from them and he never got over it. The house is still standing, and it was a source of irritation to him throughout his life. He let that loss—which wasn't even his loss—define his life. He tried to make it define Lis's and mine, too."

"In what way?"

"Anything to do with St. Dennis was forbidden. Which was tough on Lis and me because we had to go to school there. But we weren't to make friends with any of the kids, and we could only hang out with fellow islanders."

"How'd that work out?"

Owen snorted. "How do you think? I never paid any attention to his ranting and raving, and after a time, I was bigger than him, so he didn't force the issue with me. It was tougher on Lis, though, because she couldn't bring herself to defy him the way I did. It just wasn't in her nature back then."

"She seems pretty tough now."

"She earned her toughness. She went away to school and she stayed away for a long time. She just came back at the beginning of the summer."

"And that fast, she and Alec met and fell in love?"

"Alec has always had a thing for her. Always. And apparently, she'd noticed him a lot more than she let on." Owen took her hand as he stepped off the porch, and she followed. "Some people are just meant to be together, you know?"

It had been on the tip of her tongue to ask him who his "meant to be" was, but she thought better of it. She didn't really want to know. Instead, she said, "Well, then, I'm glad they found each other."

Reaching her car, she put a hand out to open the driver's-side door. But somehow she'd gotten turned around, and before she knew it, she was in Owen's arms and his lips were in search of hers. She lifted her head, wrapped her arms around his neck, and kissed him. The crackle of electricity that had marked their earlier kiss became a thunderbolt, but rather than pull away, she moved toward the source of the heat.

She'd never realized how much emotion could be packed into one kiss. When she pulled away, she was almost breathless but did her best to hide it. The last thing she wanted was for Owen to know what effect he had on her.

"So I've decided you need to learn a little more about the Eastern Shore," he said as she tried to clear her head.

"What?"

"I think it's almost criminal for someone who lived in Maryland for so long to have so little understanding of the place the Eastern Shore held in the nation's history. You expect to live here, you have to know what *here* is all about. I'll pick you up at twelve thirty tomorrow."

"Wait, what? What are you talking about?"

"I'm talking about a guided tour." He smiled and opened the car door for her and held it open as she slid behind the wheel.

"I'm going to be working in the Allen graveyard tomorrow. I told you that."

"So start your day a little earlier. Wear sneakers and bring a sweater."

He closed the door without waiting for her response, and Cass had driven home in a fog. It had taken forever for her to fall asleep because she'd relived a hundred times the way his lips had felt on hers, and she'd told herself a hundred times she should back away while she still could. She awoke the next morning with the memory of that kiss still fresh in her mind. She told it to get lost as she rose early and set off for an overgrown graveyard on Cannonball Island.

THE ALLEN PLOT was relatively small compared to the others she'd worked on, so after her early start, by nine thirty she was finished and had the entire rest of the day ahead of her. She had plenty of time to shower off the grass and the dirt. She dressed in navy crop pants and a long-sleeved white T and was right on time to meet Owen in the lobby.

"You look great," he said when he arrived at the inn just when the clock in the lobby chimed at twelve thirty. He took her hand as they walked through the double doors. "You smell good, too." He leaned toward her and sniffed. "Nice. Familiar, but I can't place it."

Cass laughed. "It's coconut-scented shampoo."

"That explains my sudden urge for macaroons."

They arrived at the car and Owen opened the

passenger's door. He held it while Cass climbed in. "How are the Allens doing?"

"A lot better now that their final resting places have been cleaned up. How was your dive this morning?"

"It was great." His eyes lit up. "Jared and a few of his guys had mapped out the wreck site on a grid, so we each took a section. I found a large piece of heavy chain. Ruby said she'd heard the ship had carried slaves and indentured men, so I guess she was right."

"Did you ask Jared about bringing his boat around to the bay side to check the water depths?"

"I'm sorry. I forgot." He grimaced. "That was bad. I should have remembered. We all were so excited about the dive. But no excuse. I'll ask him tomorrow. I promise."

Damn. Cass had held off calling her father because she thought she might have other news for him. She was annoyed that Owen had forgotten, but as long as he followed through tomorrow, it would be okay. Of course, he'd promised yesterday, too. . . .

"So on to the history lesson. Where to today, Professor Parker?"

"I thought we'd start at the beginning." He turned on the car and circled around the parking lot to the driveway. "Well, not the very beginning. For that, we'd go back millions of years, and who has the time for that? Besides, I think James Michener covered all that when he wrote *Chesapeake*. From my schoolboy days, I remember that there was a sort of comet that hit the region, then later there was some glacier activity, and that takes us to the 1600s. John Smith. The local Native American population."

"That's quite a leap, millions of years ago to John Smith and Jamestown."

"Yeah, well, if there were written records left at the time of the glaciers, we'd have something to talk about. For me, *and then there were glaciers* is sufficient to cover that time period."

"Fair enough." Cass rolled down the window and leaned toward it slightly. The air was cooler and crisper than it had been earlier in the week, and just beneath the light breeze she caught a scent of impending autumn. It made her think of walks in the woods with leaves crunching underfoot, cozy sweaters, pumpkins and apple cider, apple pie and pumpkin pie.

"Hey, are you listening?" she heard him say.

"Sorry, I got caught up in a thought," she admitted sheepishly.

"What thought was that?"

"Mostly baked stuff with apples. Like apple pie. Apple crisp. And pumpkin pie. Pumpkin-spice coffee. Actually, pumpkin-spice anything."

"You're psychic, right? Because I make a killer pumpkin pie. Only thing better might be my apple pie."

"Tell me the recipes are in that folder of family recipes."

"Could be. Maybe I'll let you look at my folder someday."

"I'd be honored."

"You should be. It's been carefully guarded through the ages." He made a turn onto the highway and headed north. "Now, back to today's lesson. There were a number of Indian tribes living in the bay area. There are something like a hundred thousand Native American archaeological sites throughout the bay region, a lot of them not even documented yet."

"So are any of those campsites on Cannonball Island?"

"Sure. That would be the area that runs along the river out to the point. Back in early times, the whole area was mostly woodlands. You can still see the signs if you know what to look for."

"And I suppose you know what to look for?"

"Of course. Island boy, born and raised."

"So are we going to see a Native American site today?"

"Not today, but the history is all around you. A lot of the names on the Eastern Shore are Native American. Like the rivers. Choptank. Nanticoke. Wicomico."

"Do you know what any of that means?"

"I know that *Nanticoke* means 'people of the tidewater.' That's about all I remember. My grand-dad knew a lot of the names and what they meant. He collected a lot of pottery shards and things he'd find along the shore and dug up in his garden."

"Isn't it illegal to keep those sorts of things?"

"I guess it is now, but back sixty, seventy years ago . . ." Owen shrugged. "I haven't seen any of it in a long time, so I'm guessing Ruby might have given it all to the library in St. Dennis when they opened their little museum wing. I remember hearing some talk about it."

"So where are we going?" They were on the highway, headed northeast. "What's this tour we're going on?"

"I thought since you're so interested in Cannonball Island and St. Dennis, it would be logical to start with an 1812 tour, since the war played so significant a role in the history of both, but then I thought, nah, it's too extensive. You can't do that all in one day." He looked across the console. "That story began in Baltimore, but since you're from there, you're familiar with the whole Fort McHenry, 'Star-Spangled Banner' thing. And I'm guessing you already know about how St. Dennis was shelled by British warships a couple of times around 1814, but how no house was ever hit, right?"

"No, I don't know that story."

"Here's how it went. The British would sail up and down the bay at night, and they'd aim their cannons on the lights in the windows of the houses onshore. So the people in St. Dennis took to hanging lanterns in the trees and kept their homes dark when ships were sighted approaching the town."

"So the cannons were aimed at the trees instead of the houses? Clever."

"Only one house was ever hit, and the cannonball is still in the wall. Of course, a lot of trees went down, but it was a small price to pay. I'm surprised Grace hasn't told you about it. It's one of her favorite stories."

"It's a good one. So, since we're not going to Baltimore, and we just left St. Dennis, where are we going?"

"We're going to Chestertown, a very old and very beautiful town on the Chester River. Colonial times, the Revolution, the War of 1812, the Civil War—Chestertown's seen it all."

"What are we going to see there?"

"A little bit of everything, and then a surprise."

"What kind of surprise?" Her eyes narrowed.

"One you'll probably remember for a long, long time." His smile and his eyes held mischief.

"Should I be scared?"

"Not if you brought your sea legs with you."

"I don't like the sound of that."

"You'll love it."

That smile again, those eyes.

He glanced down at the tennis shoes on her feet. "I see you remembered I told you to bring a sweater and to wear sneaks. Smart move."

More than smart, it turned out, because Owen had planned a walking tour of the old city. He'd downloaded and printed out an annotated map from the Internet and handed it to her before they got out of the car.

"You being an architect and a history buff, I thought you'd find this interesting." He turned off the engine. "It's a sort of self-guided architectural tour."

Cass glanced at the map. "This is perfect. And very thoughtful. Thank you."

"Sure." He got out and closed his door, then walked around to her side of the car. "Unless you're chilly, you might not need the sweater now. We can stop back for it later before . . ."

"Before what?"

"Before we embark on the second part of our adventure. Now, where would you like to start?"

"The map has places numbered, so let's just follow that. We can start down near the river."

"Good thought." He glanced at his watch. "We have time."

"Time for what?"

"Time to see a few places, walk a few blocks."

"And then what?"

"Then the surprise."

"I'm not sure I like surprises." *What does he have up his sleeve?*

"I bet you'll like this one." He reached for her hand. "Come on. Let's get on with the architectural tour."

They walked a block before Cass stopped in front of a handsome large brick structure.

"This is number one on the map. It's the old customhouse." She glanced at the map again. "It says here this is one of the oldest such structures still standing in any of the thirteen colonies. Original section built in 1740. It's been privately owned since the latter part of the eighteenth century. Oh, and it says here that Chestertown had its own tea party not far from here." She glanced toward the river. "I guess there might be a marker down there somewhere." She looked up at Owen. "Are you sure you're interested in all this?"

"Oh, sure." He nodded vigorously. "Why else would I have planned this?"

"Just checking. I'd hate for you to be bored." She looked at the map again.

"Me, bored? Heck no."

"Let's move on to number two, then." She tugged on his hand and read as they walked. "Italianate in style, built in 1857 by a man named James Taylor."

"Wasn't he a songwriter, singer, back in the sixties, seventies? 'You've Got a Friend'?"

"Ha ha." She smacked him with the map. "The house is on the next block."

When they arrived, Cass studied the front of the building. "Beautiful, and perfectly proportioned and symmetrical. Check out the brackets on the porches and the eaves. Perfect."

She took a photo with her phone.

"On to number three. That would be . . ." She consulted the map. "The Hynson-Ringgold House. Built in 1743. So different in style from the last one. See the difference in the roofline, and the portico is Greek Revival. Now owned by Washington College." She studied the house from different angles, aware Owen was watching her, though he hadn't bothered to follow when she walked from one side of the house to the other, stopping to take photos now and then.

She rejoined him on the sidewalk at the corner, where he waited patiently. "A US senator lived here once."

"It's a nice house. I bet he enjoyed it."

"More than you're enjoying this little expedition, I bet."

"No, no. I'm good. History guy here, remember?"

She slipped her hand into his. "The next place on the tour is on the corner, one block down."

"Great. Let's go take a look." He sounded perky enough, but Cass sensed that his heart wasn't in it. That his eyes were glazing over gave him away.

What did it say about this guy who spent a beautiful, crisp September day looking at buildings he had absolutely no interest in, simply because he knew she'd love it?

"Now this place is pure Georgian," she said when they arrived at the fourth house on the tour. "And a beautiful example of the style. Built a little before the Revolution."

And so on through numbers five through eleven. As she started toward number twelve, Cass noted Owen once again looking at his watch.

"Are you supposed to be back soon?"

"No, why?" He stuck his hands in his pockets.

"You keep looking at your watch."

"Well, there is something else. I guess we should be headed in that direction pretty soon."

"The big surprise . . . ?"

He nodded. "We should stop at the car so you can pick up your sweater."

"Okay." Curious, she followed him back to the car.

"I would definitely come back to this place," she told him as he handed her the sweater. "I love how so much of the town has been preserved. I could stay here all day."

"Some other time." He grabbed her hand and headed toward the water.

Minutes later they were standing on a crowded dock, at the foot of which was tied what looked like an old-time schooner, all its sails rolled up.

"What . . . ?" Cass's eyes widened.

"Cass, meet *Contessa*." He guided her by the elbow to the end of the dock.

"What . . . ?"

"She's a replica of a 1768 British schooner. Beautiful, isn't she?" Owen's eyes were shining excitedly as he gazed upon the ship.

I must have looked like that, Cass thought, *taking in those fabulous historic houses on our walking tour.*

"Can you believe that volunteers built this baby? The original was a merchant ship that the British used to patrol the coastlines after the tea tax was enacted. So from around 1768 till the early 1770s, she sailed up and down the coast from Boston to the Chesapeake looking for smugglers. After they retired her, she was taken back to England and later sold to a private owner. When it was decided that a sailing ship would be a great educational tool, she was chosen as the prototype."

"She's . . . quite something." Cass stared at the ship as some others on the dock moved forward to board her. "Why did they need a ship?"

"The Contessa Education Foundation sponsors trips for schoolkids, sails them around the bay so they can see its vastness, maybe appreciate it a little more, acquaints them with the history and the ecology of the Chesapeake. Its uniqueness, its culture." Owen had taken her elbow and steered her toward the ship. "They also offer paid cruises to raise money for the foundation."

Wait—did he expect her to go *on board*?

Apparently he did. He led her across a metal-mesh bridge and stepped onto the deck and held out a hand to Cass.

"No, no, I don't think . . ." The words stuck in her throat.

"Come on. She's beautiful. And she doesn't bite, I promise."

"But I don't like . . ." Panic arose as she found herself standing on the deck.

"You don't like boats?" he leaned over to ask.

"Water," she whispered sheepishly. "I don't like to be on the water."

"Seriously?" He took her arm and led her to one side of the deck, away from where the others were boarding. "Are you afraid or what?"

"I just feel uneasy. Like it's not natural. I think we were meant to keep both feet on dry land."

Before he could reply, someone—apparently the man in charge—began talking about booms and gaffs. The next thing she knew, some of the passengers were working alongside the crew amid cries of "Heave ho" and "Drop the line" and "Haul away" as a huge sail rose above the deck.

"Oh, crap, get me off this thing." Wild-eyed, she grabbed the front of Owen's shirt with both hands.

"Um, it's a little late. We're moving."

Cass closed her eyes, rested her head against his chest, and hung on to him with all her strength. "Tell me when it's over."

"Cass, it's a two-hour tour. If I'd known you had a fear of water, I'd never have bought the tickets. I swear, I had no idea you'd be afraid." He sounded almost as distressed as she felt.

"Well, now you do."

"You seemed fine when we were crabbing the other day. You never said anything."

"We were sitting firmly on a dock, not standing on the deck of a moving ship."

"What is it that you're afraid of?"

"Things that are out there that you can't see." Her voice lowered to a whisper. "Things underneath the boat."

"But if they're under the boat, they *stay* under the boat."

"What if we got into an accident with another boat? Or hit rocks?"

"Look around. Do you see any other boats in proximity to us? And I promise there are no rocks in the Chesapeake big enough to rip a hole in this baby."

"So you say."

"Cass, what do you do when you go swimming?"

"I don't remember reports of sharks in any pool I've ever been in."

"You've never been in the ocean?"

She shook her head no.

"The bay?"

"The nearest I've come to the bay was the other day at the pier."

"Just pretend you're back there, sitting on the pier at the point, okay?" He held her to him, one hand gently stroking her back as if to calm her. "Look, you just hold on to me, keep your face buried if that makes you feel better."

"I guess there's no point in asking if they'd turn around and let me off?"

"Not a chance. We're in the middle of the Chester River heading out toward the bay."

"Oh, crap, don't tell me." She buried deeper.

"Hey, you weren't even aware we'd sailed out here, so it must be a pretty calm ride, right? Why not just take a look, Cass? The scenery is beautiful."

"I don't think I can. I'm sorry. I know you planned this surprise for me because you thought I'd enjoy it, and here I am acting like a frightened five-year-old." Tears welled up and she was at a loss to control them. They tumbled down her cheeks and onto her shirt.

"Everyone's afraid of something." He tried to soothe her.

"I'll bet there's nothing you're afraid of."

"That's a bet you'd lose." He changed the subject. "We have to move to the other side of the boat. The wind is changing and they need to move the sails."

One of the crew asked Owen if he'd like to help man the sails. He hesitated momentarily. "Not this time around, but thanks."

"Go ahead," Cass told him. "I'll be okay."

"I've done it before. Let someone else have a chance to see what it's like."

"They let *anyone*, passengers, strangers, sail the ship?"

"Under very close supervision and with instruction. It's not that hard. Really." He patted her on the back. "You're not going to die, Cass."

"People die from fright. I've read about it."

"This is a side of you I've never seen. You're always so together, so in charge."

"True, on dry land."

"I can't tell you how sorry I am. How have you managed to live all these years on the Chesapeake without getting on a boat?"

"I haven't been living here for all that long. I lived in Rhode Island for a while."

"What did you do there?" He leaned against the side rail of the boat and took her with him. She knew he was just trying to keep her talking to take her mind off her being on a vessel that was sailing— sailing! Not even engine powered!—toward the open Chesapeake at a fancy clip.

"I moved there after college. I was in grad school and my husband—" She felt Owen freeze.

"What husband?" he asked softly.

"The one I divorced not long ago. He was in ROTC in college, so he owed the government four years of active service. He joined the army, liked it a whole lot more than he liked living with me, so we got divorced."

"I'll bet there's more to it than that."

"That was the short version. It's a story for another time."

The man who appeared to be the head crewman tapped her on the arm. "Miss, would you like to take the rudder?"

"I don't even know what that means."

He smiled. "It steers the ship."

"You let total amateurs drive this thing?" She let go of Owen's shirt and turned, staring at the man with horror in her eyes.

"You won't actually be steering. You'd just be holding on to the wheel to keep the ship steady. We're pretty much on a slow and even course. There won't be any turns made until we circle around to return back to Chestertown."

"Go ahead, Cass," Owen urged as he tried to straighten out the front of his shirt, which she'd bunched and twisted into a wrinkled mess. "Might be good for you. Keep your mind off . . . you know. The whole boat thing. Besides, you know you like to feel you're in control."

"How would you know that?" How *does* he know?

"That's a story for another time, too." He smiled as he tossed her words back to her.

"Come on, miss. It's right over here. . . ."

"Don't leave me," Cass whispered to Owen as the man gently took her hand.

When they reached the wheel, the crewman said to the man who was holding it that his replacement was here. Then the crewman showed Cass where to place her hands.

"What if it does something wonky? You know, like if the wind took it that way?" She pointed off to the left.

"Unlikely, but I'll be right here if that happens." The crewman patted her shoulder gently in encouragement. "You're doing fine."

Cass was aware that Owen mouthed, *Thank you*, as the crewman stepped away, but she chose not to mention it. She still didn't like it, didn't like being out here on the water where she felt so vulnerable, but Owen had been such a good sport about the walking tour, she felt obligated to force herself to stare straight ahead.

The bay was smooth, the waves small, and she was getting used to the feel of the deck beneath her feet. It was breezier and cooler here than it had been at the crowded area at the far back of the ship, and without her asking him to, Owen placed her sweater around her shoulders.

"Thanks."

"You're welcome." A moment later he asked, "How are you doing?"

Cass took a deep breath. "Not so bad. It's actually pretty smooth, isn't it?"

He nodded and pointed out landmarks along the way. "There's Ballard. Great little town with a terrific dock bar. We'll go some night when they have music, and we'll sit out on the dock and listen and watch the boats pull up."

"Sounds like a fun place." She felt her shoulders relax. "This really isn't so bad."

"Good. You're doing great, Cass. I'm proud of you."

She could have cried again. He was being such a sweetheart, understanding and nonjudgmental. He was making it hard for her to remember that he wasn't the guy for her.

Gulls swooped overhead as they sailed along,

and the sunlight danced across the waves. It was peaceful here; Owen had been right. She liked the way the wind blew through her hair and over her skin. She was beginning to understand how some found the sea appealing. It wasn't for her, but she could see how it might be for others.

When she was replaced at the wheel and she and Owen returned to the very back of the ship, she had relaxed sufficiently to gaze at the shoreline and off into the distance, but the underlying anxiety was still there, only not as fierce as it had been. As the ship turned in a slow, wide arc and headed back to the river, she took a deep breath. Maybe she'd survive this short voyage after all.

"Are you okay?" Owen had kept an arm around her shoulders the entire time.

"A lot better, especially now that we're heading upriver and toward the dock."

"We'll be pulling up to the dock before you know it."

She could have said, *I will be aware of every passing minute*, but she refrained. When the dock came in sight, she wanted to whoop, but she refrained from that, too.

"You did really, really well for your first time out on a boat," Owen said once they'd departed the ship and were walking back to the car. "Next time, I'll take you out myself. Alec has a—"

"I don't think so, but thanks. I think I've been there, done that, and don't need to go back."

He fell silent as they reached the car. He unlocked it and opened the passenger-side door for her. She smiled her thanks, and while it looked as if he was about to say something, he merely smiled back and closed her door. On the drive back to St. Dennis, he slipped a CD into the player, and they talked about their favorite music and concerts they'd been to.

"So, John Lennon or John Mellencamp?"

"Lennon," she replied without hesitation.

"Lennon or McCartney?"

"Oooh, tough one." She frowned. "I have to go with McCartney."

"Beatles or Stones?"

"Another tough one. The Stones are still at it, though, so maybe them. They've outlasted pretty much everyone."

"Stevie Nicks or Madonna?"

"I can't believe you'd even ask that." She rolled her eyes. "Stevie, of course."

He nodded his agreement. "Mark Knopfler or Eddie Van Halen?"

"That's a trick question. Two totally different guitar styles. I pass," she fired back.

"Fair enough. Now, this might be the toughest of all. The king of rock and roll: Elvis or Chuck Berry?"

"Wow." She thought it over. "My mom is a fan of early rock and she's a big Berry fan, so I'm going with him."

"I agree. Grace Slick or Janis Joplin?"

She looked at him blankly. "I don't know who Grace Slick is."

"End of game. You lose."

"How can I lose if no one else was playing?"

"I'm sorry, but all questions must be submitted in writing," he said solemnly.

Cass laughed.

He drove less than a mile, listening to the radio and tapping out the beat of a song on the steering wheel. Finally, he said, "So tell me about your husband. Where's he now?"

"Ex-husband, and he's probably in the Middle East somewhere. I lost track of him before the divorce was final." Cass pretended to be staring out the window when she was actually trying to avoid eye contact. The end of her marriage had come with painful realizations, and she didn't like to look back on that time.

This whole day had been a mash-up of good day/bad day.

"So what was it that did you in? Him being away from home a lot?"

She sighed. Apparently she'd have to talk about this at some point, so she might as well get it over with.

"He liked—no, *loved* being in the army. He would come home on leave and wouldn't know what to do with himself. He couldn't wait to get back to his unit. I wasn't prepared for that." She turned and looked at Owen. "He was my college sweetheart. We had our whole lives mapped out. He'd do four years while I got my architecture degree, then we'd set up house somewhere and have a bunch of kids. It became apparent after a few years that *that* wasn't going to happen. He wasn't a bad guy. Even he wasn't prepared for how much he loved military life. I was miserable and resentful, and he was feeling guilty and trapped. One of us had to be the grown-up and pull the plug. That was me. He never would have done it, no matter how unhappy he was, because he knew he'd let me down. But as long as I stayed, he could convince himself that, deep down, I was okay with it."

"Was he shocked? When you told him you wanted a divorce?"

"Shocked?" Cass smiled ruefully. "Relieved. Grateful. Happy as a pig in . . . well, you get the idea."

"I'm sorry. It sounds as if you started out with the right idea, but it went off the rails somehow."

"I couldn't have said it better myself." She watched the scenery on Route 50 fly by. "How 'bout you? Any wives—ex or otherwise—in your background?"

"One ex."

"You were married?"

"One time, yes."

Cass tried to hide her surprise. She would have bet just about anything that he'd never been married. The question had been one of those toss-out things, something you say in conversation, sort of like asking if the other person ever broke their leg after you've talked about the time you broke yours. She hadn't been prepared to hear him say he'd been married.

"Who was she?"

"Someone I went to school with from first grade. We'd always been friends, but we started dating in high school, on and off, then later, for years, on and off. I don't remember how many times. Looking back now, I think it was always a matter of me coming home after one of my jaunts and she'd break off with whoever she was dating, and we'd date for as long as I was here if I wasn't seeing someone else. Then one day she gave me an ultimatum. She was tired of me bouncing back to her, then leaving for one adventure or another—sometimes that adventure may have involved another woman—then bouncing back, leaving again. You get the picture."

"Marry me or lose my number?"

"How'd you know?"

"Not hard to figure out that one."

"So, yeah, we got married. Bad idea right from the start, and we both knew it. I still don't know why I did it. Maybe I was tired, or maybe she caught me in an off moment, or maybe I wanted to see what it would be like to stay in one place all the time. Maybe I'd come to depend on her as a constant in my life, because in spite of everything, we really did like each other. I don't know. Needless to say, it didn't last very long. Well, the marriage lasted a few years, but only because I was in Alaska and they couldn't serve me with the divorce papers. I wasn't dodging her, I just moved around a lot, which I was in the habit of doing. When I finally came back, we decided to try again, but that lasted about two weeks before we both agreed it had been a dumb idea from the very beginning."

"Did you love her?"

Owen hesitated for a moment. "Not the way I should have. If I had, I wouldn't have gone to Alaska in the first place."

"Why did you?"

"Adventure. Something and someplace new. The thrill of the unknown. Take your pick."

"So how long has it been final?"

"It'll be two years in November."

"Does she still live in St. Dennis?"

"No, and as far as I know, her parents moved a few towns over."

"You never contacted her?"

"No. Why would I?"

"I don't know. Just to see how she is . . . how her life is going."

"Well, in keeping with the nautical theme of the day, let's just say that ship has sailed. It wouldn't do either of us any good to revisit that time. It's done. Move on."

"Turn the page," Cass murmured.

"Exactly." He nodded. "You want to see your ex again?"

"No."

"Why not?"

She shot him a dark look. "I don't want to see him because I don't want to remember how bad he made me feel."

"That's pretty much what I said. Just different words." Owen reached over and took her hand. "How did we get onto this topic that has clearly bummed out both of us?"

"I don't remember, but it is a downer."

"I know the perfect cure for chasing away bad thoughts."

"No, please. Not another boat ride."

"That was a ship, not a boat, but no."

"Is this going to be another one of your surprises? Because if it is . . ."

He laughed and the mood in the car lifted. "You'll love this one. I promise."

"That's what you said about the *Contessa*."

"Trust me. This will be good."

It wasn't just good, it was great. Once back in St. Dennis, he turned onto Kelly's Point Road and drove to the end. They got out of the car and he steered her to the left side of the narrow boardwalk and the old crabber's shack that had been converted into an ice cream shop.

"Oh, One Scoop or Two. Everyone talks about this place, and I meant to come down here and never did."

"Shhhh." He lowered his voice to a whisper. "That's like a sin around here. If you want to live here, you have to make a weekly stop—at the very least—to see what Steffie has concocted."

The sign outside the shop promised ice cream using local ingredients and made by hand.

"She comes up with the wildest flavors." Owen opened the door and held it for Cass. "Let's see what she has on the chalkboard today."

"Chocolate thunder, peach blossom, wildflower honey, black raspberry divine, pumpkin spice . . ." The woman behind the counter rattled off the flavors without looking at the board. She was tall, slender, and had a long blond ponytail and an easy smile. "Of course, we have the standards: vanilla bean, double chocolate fudge, strawberry supreme. I think we also might have some chocolate raspberry and maybe a little bit of peanut-butter pie left. I can check in the back if you want."

"Ah, that's okay, Stef. I think I'm good." Owen turned to Cass. "You want to hear more?"

"No, no. She had me at pumpkin spice."

"An excellent choice. I just made it this morning, and it's fabulous, if I do say so myself." Wielding a scoop, Stef opened the case. "Cone or dish?"

"Cone, thanks."

"Sugar or waffle?"

"Sugar."

"Stef, this is my friend Cass Logan." Owen turned to Cass. "Stef makes all her own ice cream every day."

"I'm impressed," Cass said. "That's quite a selection."

"Thank you. I try to be modest about it, but . . . why?" Steffie smiled broadly. "It's all I ever wanted to do. Oh, that and marry the coolest, handsomest, hottest guy in St. Dennis. With apologies, Owen, but you're Cannonball Island, so you weren't a contender."

Owen laughed and studied the chalkboard.

"So did you?" Cass couldn't help but ask. "Marry the cool, handsome, hot guy?"

Steffie held up her ring finger and wiggled it. "Two babies later and we're living happily ever after."

"Good for you." Cass felt her stomach flutter with something that could have been envy, if she'd wanted to put a name to it.

"Steffie's husband, Wade, is half of MadMac Brews," Owen explained.

"That he is." Stef handed over Cass's cone. "You're up, Owen. What's it gonna be?"

"Gotta be one scoop of chocolate thunder, one scoop of peanut-butter pie."

"You're on." Stef completed the order and walked to the cash register, where she gave Owen the cone and the total. "How's my friend Ruby these days? I haven't seen her in a couple of weeks."

"She's doing great." Owen handed Stef a ten. "I'd take her something but I'm not going right home."

"You can bring her back later." Stef gave him back his change.

Owen and Cass sat at the table nearest the counter and chatted with Stef, who was more than happy to tell Cass how she made up the names for the various flavors of ice cream she served.

"I can attest to the absolute deliciousness of the pumpkin spice." Cass left her seat for the counter and another few napkins.

"You have a drip." Stef pointed to the front of Cass's shirt. "Come on in the back and I'll see if we can get it out before it sets."

"Oh, thanks, but you don't have to do that."

"I'd hate to see that pretty top ruined by the stain from the spices I used in that recipe."

Cass looked down at the spot on her shirt.

"It'll only take a minute." Steffie waved her to the back of the store.

"I'll be right back," Cass told Owen.

"I'll be right here, working on my double-decker." Owen leaned back in the chair.

"Do you think it will leave a permanent mark?" Cass frowned as Stef wetted a cloth at the sink in the back room.

"I hope not." Stef handed Cass the cloth.

"This must be your workroom." Cass looked around at the many shelves and cabinets that lined every inch of wall space as she dabbed at the mark.

"It is. I tried doing it at home, but with young kiddies"—Stef shook her head—"it just wasn't going to work. So now my husband and I take turns in the morning staying home with them while the other works, and either my mother or his sister watches them in the afternoons."

"Convenient to have family around."

The bell over the shop door rang and Cass heard footsteps cross the wooden floor. "I think you have a customer."

Stef looked out through the doorway. "Hi, Ken. I'll be right with you."

"I think I got it all." Cass studied the front of her shirt.

"You did." Stef nodded.

"Thanks. I appreciate it."

"You're welcome." Stef walked back to the front of the shop and Cass followed.

Owen was sitting in the chair where Cass'd left

him, looking up at the bearded man who stood five feet from the table. There'd obviously been some conversation, but from the expression on Owen's face, it hadn't been particularly friendly.

"What can I get for you today, Kenny?" Steffie called.

The customer turned from Owen and went to the counter.

Cass returned to the table. "Thanks to Stef, I have a stain-free shirt."

"Looks good. Are you finished?" Owen asked somewhat abruptly.

"Yes."

"Come on. I can eat ice cream and walk at the same time." He got up and waved to Stef.

The man at the counter turned, and the two men exchanged a look Cass couldn't decipher. Neither spoke a word. Cass had wanted to say a parting word to Stef, but Owen led her by the elbow to the door and they went outside.

Cass tried to keep up with Owen's long stride. "Is something wrong?"

"No, why?"

They reached the car. "Who was that guy?"

"Just someone I knew from school." Owen unlocked the car and waited till she got in before slamming the door.

Obviously there was more to it than Owen admitted. His mood and his body language had changed in the time it had taken Cass to blot away a stain from her shirt.

Whoever he was and whatever he'd said had

caused a cloud to cast a dark shadow over what had been a sunny day and had yanked Owen from that happy place he and Cass had shared.

She could feel the distance spreading between them, and she was at a loss to stop it. She wanted that sweet, thoughtful guy she'd spent the day with to come back, but she sensed that whatever had happened in Scoop was standing between them.

The only thing she knew for certain was that Owen had retreated into himself, and there was no way of knowing when—or if—he'd be back.

Chapter Eight

Owen found Ruby at the counter with a customer when he entered the store. He waved as he went into her living quarters and poured a glass of cold water in the kitchen. He took a long drink, splashed the remainder of the water into the sink, and waited for Ruby's customer to leave. When he heard the front door close, he went out to the store. He needed to talk to his great-grandmother and didn't want an audience.

"Gigi, you have a minute?"

"Always have a minute for you. Maybe more, if you need them." She gestured to the round table along the wall. "Want to sit a spell?"

He nodded and waited until she'd made her way across the room, her feet shuffling in her white tennis shoes. After she'd seated herself in her chair, he took the other and rested his forearms on the tabletop. Neither spoke for a few minutes, but Owen could feel her eyes on him, and he had the feeling they were searching. It wasn't the only time he'd thought she had such an ability. He'd seen her do it to others. He didn't know how she did it, but when he was younger, he imagined she had some sort of invisible ray that could secretly probe your mind. At times, just suspecting she was capable of reading his thoughts had kept him on the straight and narrow. He'd secretly thought of it as Gigi's own form of search and destroy. As a boy, he believed the Gigi Ray was indeed awesome.

He no longer thought of her as possessing the Ray, but he knew she had abilities most people didn't have. He'd long accepted it, even as he'd never accepted or appreciated similar tendencies in himself. But earlier in Scoop, when Ken Lockhart had walked in, the hair on the back of Owen's neck had stood straight up, and he'd sensed . . . something.

"You seen my sister yet?" Ken had asked, his eyes narrow and dark.

"Nice to see you again, too, Ken. It's been a while."

"I asked if you've seen my sister."

Owen's Spidey sense began to tingle. "Not in a couple of years." Owen tried to recall the last time he'd seen his ex-wife. "Maybe two years. Why?"

"Might be time you caught up with her again."

"She knows where to find me."

"That's a fact."

"What are you trying to say, Ken?"

"Just that you need to mind your own."

With that, Ken had turned his attention to the flavor board. But the look he'd shot across the room as Owen and Cass were leaving had spoken volumes. Unfortunately, Owen was at a loss to understand what the message might have been. All he knew was that the hair on the back of his neck was still standing straight up.

"Gigi, I got this feeling," Owen said after relating his exchange with Ken. "I can't even put it into words."

"If you'd spent less time trying to push away what you knew all these years, you might not be needing words."

"What does *that* mean?"

"What I been telling you all along, but you be determined to deny the gift what was in you by nature. Maybe if you'd been watching, listening, not turning a blind eye and a deaf ear pretending you didn't see or hear, you'd have seen what you needed to see, heard what wasn't said."

Owen sighed. "You mean the sight, or whatever you want to call it."

"I call it a gift, boy, and it's not about just seeing or hearing. Sensing, knowing. Understanding what you sense, believing what you know without being told. You been refusing to see, and I been telling you time'd come when you want that sense and it be gone, sure enough. That's where you be right now." She folded her arms across her chest and stared him down. "I don't mind being the one who told you so."

"Okay, yes." He nodded. "I wish I could figure out what it was I sensed."

"Tell me."

"It was like there was something there I should have known, but didn't. Something *hidden*." He paused, almost embarrassed by what he was going to say, so he lowered his voice. "Like something was reaching out to me. Something . . . Gigi, I felt a pull, but I don't know where it was coming from. I know it wasn't a pull toward Ken. And it wasn't about Cyndi. I'd have known if there was still something there, but there isn't and there hasn't been." He thought that over for a few seconds. "That's not exactly true. In spite of everything, I still think of her as a friend. I'll never think less of her because of what happened. She's not a bad person."

Ruby stared at him but said nothing.

"Do you know?" he asked.

"Tell me again what he said."

"That I should catch up with her, and that I should mind my own."

Ruby nodded. "He be right, son. Time to mind your own."

"Mind my own what? My own business? I always do that."

Ruby stared at him as if waiting for him to say more.

"You're not going to tell me what that means, though, are you?"

"Not my place."

"What was pulling at me?" Owen whispered.

She appeared not to have heard, though he knew she had. "Ada be on her way about now. That woman sure can talk." Ruby glanced at the door seconds before her neighbor Ada Banks entered.

"You'll find what you find, and you'll do what you'll do. You'll do right in spite of everything that's been done to you."

"Oh, hey, thanks. That makes it all so clear," he grumbled.

"Hadn't been such a stubborn cuss all these years, you wouldn't need me to see for you what you should be seeing for yourself."

He watched Ruby greet her neighbor and smiled in spite of himself. He'd thought talking to Ruby would help clarify the mixed feelings he had and maybe even explain the odd vibe that had floated from Ken. It had been more than just a reaction to Ken's coolness and cryptic message. There'd been something visceral, something that spoke directly to something inside him, but damn if he knew what it was all about.

He'd put it aside for now. Maybe one day soon he'd find out where in Ballard Cyndi's parents had moved, and he'd stop over and see what was going on. Owen had a more immediate concern. Once he'd been bombarded by whatever he sensed from Ken, he had one thought in mind: talk to Ruby. In his haste to get back to Cannonball Island, he'd all but pushed Cass out of the car. After the day they'd spent together, he'd owed her better than that.

"I'll be back," he called to Ruby as he left the store and headed for the inn. Because walking to the inn would give him more time to think, he set off on foot to St. Dennis.

It had been years since he'd walked into town, though when he was a kid, his two feet had been his primary means of getting around. But once he'd gotten his license and discovered the joys of driving, walking became passé. This time around, he needed to be alone with his thoughts and to sort through them. But once he arrived at the inn, he stood outside, wondering what to do now that he was actually here. He took his phone from his pocket and sent a text:

Got a minute?

CASS GRABBED A towel from the nearby rack and wrapped it around her before reaching for a second one to dry her hair. She was still confused by the way the day with Owen had ended. The drive back to the inn had been all but silent except for the radio. She was relieved when they arrived at the inn and he'd stopped near the back door.

"I guess you missed afternoon tea." He'd pointed at the clock on the dashboard.

"That's okay. I'll see Grace at dinner. She invited me to join her and her daughter, Lucy, and her daughters-in-law. I think she realizes I don't have any friends here—well, other than you, Ruby, Lis, and Alec—so I think she wanted me to meet some others. Nice of her, don't you think?"

Owen'd nodded, but his mind was clearly elsewhere.

She sighed. *Why try to fight it? Just say goodbye.* "So thanks so much, Owen. I had the best time. It was a really great day."

"Except for being forced onto the *Contessa*."

"Even that was pretty cool, after a while." She'd

hastened to add, "Not that I'm in any hurry to go back out on the water, but it was okay. And you were right. I didn't die."

"I was pretty sure you'd be okay." He'd obviously been trying to lighten things up, but he missed.

They'd sat in an awkward silence until he said, "You don't want to be late for your dinner." His fingers tapping on the gearshift had made it pretty clear he was ready to leave.

"Right. Thanks again." She'd forced a smile and let herself out of the car. Before she closed the door, she said, "Owen, you'll remember to talk to Jared?"

Owen had nodded somewhat absently and waved before he pulled away.

She'd gone through the double doors without looking back. *I don't understand men. In particular, I don't understand that man, who all of a sudden seems to be running hot and cold.*

Once back in her room, she'd gone straight to the French doors and opened them. She'd leaned on the railing that surrounded the balcony and tried to mentally rewind back through the day up until the time things had gone off the rails. The drive to Chestertown had been amicable, and the walking tour he'd planned had clearly pleased and surprised her. There'd been no mistaking the satisfaction Owen had taken in her joy as she all but danced from one historic property to the next. He'd listened to her describe what she saw with a smile on his face, his hands in his pockets. He might have been bored to death, but he had made an effort to hide it.

Yes, he'd forgotten to talk to Jared, but as long as he took care of that tomorrow, she was okay with it.

Then there'd been the *Contessa*. He thought he'd planned yet another surprise treat for her, and when that hadn't gone as he'd planned, he'd done his best to help her through the two-hour cruise even as he'd tried to hide his disappointment. The drive back to St. Dennis had been pleasant enough, fun conversation and reflection on their past marriages, their expectations and their failures. They'd stopped for ice cream on a whim, and he'd still been chatty and relaxed.

Then the guy with the beard had come into Scoop, and everything changed. She'd felt it as surely as she'd felt the bay breeze on her face while she stood on the deck of the *Contessa*.

One way or another, she was going to find out who the bearded guy was and what he'd said that had brought the curtain down on what had, up to that point, been a near-perfect day.

With one eye on the clock, Cass dried her hair, dressed quickly, and put on the minimum of makeup and made it downstairs to the cozy dining room just as the others were being seated.

"Ah, there she is," Grace greeted her arrival, and made introductions all around.

Cass made mental notes and hoped to keep everyone straight even while her mind was elsewhere. Lucy, Grace's only daughter, was the inn's wedding and event planner and was married to Clay, who partnered with Steffie's husband in the brewery.

Jamie wrote self-help books and was married to Grace's son Dan, who ran the inn. Cass realized she'd read one of Jamie's books about the importance of honesty in relationships and thought wryly it might be time for a reread.

Before her marriage to Grace's youngest, Ford, Carly owned several art galleries and currently was in charge of the town's art center. Ford, Grace told Cass, had taken over the *St. Dennis Gazette*, their family's newspaper. All three women were vivacious and friendly and chatty, and under other circumstances Cass would have delighted in their upbeat company. As it was, she could barely keep up with the conversations that swirled around her. She slipped out before dessert, citing a headache that was very real.

Cass was halfway to the stairs when her phone pinged to indicate an incoming text.

She read, then reread, the text.

Got a minute?

She paused at the bottom of the stairwell, debating how to respond. Her first inclination was to ignore the text altogether. She could always claim not to have seen it until a later time, such as the next day. Or she could text back a simple no. But wondering why he was asking would drive her crazy speculating, and she wouldn't get a minute's sleep.

What's up? she typed, and waited.

A moment later came his response: We should talk.

Duh. Ya think? she wanted to reply, but before she could begin to type, her phone pinged again.

Are you busy right now?

Why? she typed back.

She was waiting for him to get back to her when the lobby doors opened. She glanced up at the sound and was startled to see Owen striding toward her.

"I was just texting back to ask you for your room number." He slipped his phone into his pants pocket.

"Where were you?"

"Outside. Look, can we go someplace quiet, where we can talk?"

Cass looked around, but most of the sofas in the lobby were occupied. They couldn't go into the bar; they'd have to pass through the dining room, and she'd already left Grace and her family to go to her room with a headache. Cass could think of only one place in the inn where they'd have privacy with no chance of running into Grace.

"I guess we could go to my room." She pointed to the stairwell. "Second floor."

"Okay." He fell into step with her as they climbed the stairs and followed her down the hall.

Cass felt a little awkward unlocking the door and pushing it open. They hadn't exchanged a word since they left the lobby. But if what he had to say had anything to do with their just keeping things friendly, she wanted to hear that now, tonight. It hadn't felt that way all day, but if he'd had second thoughts, better to know now. She'd take it, and fine, they could just be friends. She braced herself for it.

But when she closed the door behind them, he reached out for her with both arms.

"Come here. Please." He'd tugged until she was

close enough for him to wrap his arms around her. His lips brushed against hers lightly, and whatever annoyance she'd felt faded. "I'm sorry," he whispered.

"You should be. You have some 'splaining to do." She decided to go straight to the moment when things had shifted between them. "That guy in Scoop—"

"—is my former brother-in-law. Cyndi's brother."

"What did he say that made you freeze up like that?" She pulled away, that confused feeling returning.

"He asked me if I'd seen Cyndi, and when I said I hadn't, he told me I should."

"So that was enough to cause you to shut down? And don't deny that you shut down, Owen." Cass took a deep breath. She saw no reason not to speak her mind. "One minute things were great, and the next minute . . . well, the next minute, they weren't."

"It wasn't so much what he said, as the way it felt."

"Look, if you still have feelings for your ex-wife, it's fine. You don't have to pretend you don't. I'll understand. But you need to say it."

"I don't have that kind of feeling for her. I told you. I don't hate her; I'll always think of her as an old friend. But I'm not carrying a secret torch for her."

"Then what was it about seeing him that made you act like you couldn't get rid of me fast enough?" There. That was what she hadn't been able to put into words even to herself. But that was how she'd felt.

"It had nothing to do with you."

"It sure didn't feel like it. Actually, it felt like it had everything to do with me."

"I really wish I could explain to you what happened, but I can't because I don't understand myself. I got this very strong feeling that . . ." Owen paused as if trying to find the words. "That there was something I didn't know that he was trying to tell me, something I should have known, something he was angry about, but he wouldn't say what it was."

"That doesn't sound like a random hunch. Are you sure there isn't something you're not telling me about your relationship with her? Are you sure she isn't still in love with you?"

"No way is she in love with me. Trust me on that. She and I knew when it was over, it was over. No, it wasn't about her."

"What else could it be? Did you owe him money or had you insulted him in some way in the past?"

"No. Not that I'm aware of, anyway. And I never borrowed a thing from him. He was never around. No, it was more like he knew something, something I should know but it's hidden and he's pissed off about it."

"That's pretty specific." Cass laughed. "What are you, a mind reader?"

"No. I can't read minds," he said softly.

"If you and his sister have been divorced for two years, what could he possibly be angry about now?"

"That's what doesn't make sense. I was never good friends with him—frankly, I never really liked him all that much, and now that I think back on it, neither did Cyndi. So his attitude—his whole demeanor—is baffling. I'm afraid I let it get to me and I overreacted. I am so sorry you were caught there, at that moment."

"I get it. But I wish you'd said something sooner, like when you dropped me off."

"I wish I had, too. I should have, but I was still sort of startled by the whole thing, and I was trying to think it through, trying to understand. It's bothering me because it felt so personal, but maybe I just read too much into it."

"We all get hunches from time to time. And there is another explanation."

He raised an inquiring eyebrow.

"Maybe he's just an asshole."

Owen covered his face with one hand for a moment, then laughed. "Well, unless he's changed a lot, yeah. That fits."

"So there you go. Mystery solved."

"Cass, I had a great time with you today. Like, one of the best times I've had with anyone in a very long time. I'd like to do it again, soon."

"I guess you just can't get enough of those old buildings and all that architectural talk."

"Yeah, I could spend all day looking at rooflines and porch brackets. About as much as you'd like to spend a few more hours on the deck of a ship headed out to sea."

Cass pretended to grimace. "How 'bout next time we try to find something mutually agreeable?"

"Next time I'll let you in on the planning."

"Not that I didn't appreciate the thought that went into today. And I really loved Chestertown."

"We'll go back sometime just for dinner." He pulled her a little closer. "There's a restaurant right on the river. We can sit and watch the *Contessa* go by."

"As long as other people are on it, I'm all in." Then, because she couldn't help herself, she said, "Speaking of ships . . ."

"I know. Jared. I'll talk to him tomorrow, and if he can get a read on the bay side, I'll let you know."

"Sounds like a plan."

"Speaking of plans—how 'bout being my date for my sister's wedding?"

"I'd love to. But you know I was invited—because of my work with Alec—so I'm going to be there anyway."

"So now you can be there with me." Owen seemed to think about that for a moment. "Well, you can meet me there. I'm walking Lis down the aisle. Ruby and I are, together. But after the ceremony we can be together. Sit together. Dance together. It's going to be a fun wedding."

"Alec has been telling me about some of their plans. A little unorthodox in some respects, but it does sound like fun." Cass smiled. "So, yeah, we can be together. Dance together. And stuff."

"'Stuff' always intrigues me." Owen smiled back. "So it's a date. Not that I won't see you before then."

"I'll be around."

"Are you coming over to the island in the morning?"

Cass nodded. "Next up is the Davies place. If I finish early enough, I'll start on the Blakes'."

"I know both places. If I'm finished diving early enough, I'll stop over to check your progress." He drew her back to him and kissed the side of her face, then lightly touched her lips with his. "So I'll look for you tomorrow somewhere between the Davieses' and the Blakes'."

"I'll be the one in the dirty tank top and the grass-stained shorts swinging a sickle."

"Should be easy enough to find." He paused to give her one last kiss before leaving.

Cass closed the door behind him and leaned back against the wall. Even though she still didn't understand what had really transpired between Owen and his onetime brother-in-law, it gave her an odd sort of peace to know that Owen didn't seem to know, either, but that he'd taken the time to seek her out and explain things to her. It made her feel as if she mattered. The feeling she'd had earlier in the day began to seep back in, the feeling that all was right in her world, and she welcomed it.

She went to her closet and scanned the clothes she'd brought with her, but nothing said *Eastern Shore wedding in early autumn*. She'd be forced to go shopping, and she knew just where she'd be heading as soon as she cleaned up from her cemetery duties in the morning.

CASS WAS HALFWAY through the Davies graves when she heard an incoming text and knew it was from Owen before she even looked at it.

Making a second dive. Will probably not finish till later this afternoon. Sorry I won't be able to help this morning. TTYL

All of which was okay with Cass. She'd been stretching out the work anticipating Owen's arrival, so now she could finish up, run back to the inn to shower and change, and she'd be in the center of town by noon. And by center of town, she meant Bling, the upscale boutique with the gorgeously dressed windows that brimmed with all its tempting dresses and bags and shoes.

She sent Owen a reply—OK. Talk to Jared?—and made it to Bling by eleven thirty.

Cass took a deep breath as she walked into the shop. She knew she'd find just the perfect thing for the wedding, and maybe a few other little some-things. She hadn't been shopping in forever, and she was due. She knew she'd come to the right place the minute Vanessa, the shop owner, smiled and said, "I have just the thing for you."

She led Cass toward the back of the store where the fancier dresses were kept and pulled out three items from the rack. A deep blue lace with long sleeves and a sweetheart neckline, a blush-pink lace with short sleeves and a boatneck, and a light blue silk with three-quarter sleeves and a deeply rounded scoop neck.

"The dark blue lace is classic, the pink is beautiful with your skin, but the light blue is a little sexier. That scoop shows just enough of the girls to make it interesting." Vanessa held up first one, then another.

"I think I'll try on those last two. The light blue and the pink."

"You can't go wrong, either way." Vanessa led her to a dressing room. "You give a shout if you need help. I'll be up front. It's a light day, so . . ."

As she spoke, the front door opened and another customer came in.

"I spoke too soon. But call me or just walk up front so I can see how they look."

Cass went into the dressing room and closed the door. She tried on first the pink lace, but thought it might be just a tad summery for early fall. Besides, the silk dress had been speaking to her since Vanessa held it up. Cass slipped it over her head and adjusted the front. Vanessa had been right. There was just enough cleavage to be interesting, but not so much as to be inappropriate for a wedding. She stepped out of the dressing room and peeked into the front of the store.

Vanessa was at the counter wrapping up a sale to a tall, pretty blond woman who was chatting up a storm. In her arms she held a child who was clinging sleepily to her neck. ". . . and as soon as I saw this bag, I knew it was mine. I love animal prints, don't you?" The blonde held up the bag to admire it again. "Perfect."

"I'll get a box for you." Vanessa turned toward the back of the store and saw Cass. "Oh, that's fabulous on you. Walk out here so I can see. Do you have some really high, strappy shoes?"

"I do, but they're in Baltimore." Cass checked herself in a mirror. She did love the way the silk glided over her hips. "I might be able to drive up there between now and next weekend."

"Tell me you're going to the big wedding." Vanessa took a box from a shelf along the wall and returned to the front counter to pack the bag for her customer.

Cass nodded.

Vanessa nodded. "We'll be there, me and my honey. We don't really know the bride. I've met her, but I don't really know her, but we do know the groom. Oh, and if you want to try on a pair of stunning heels, I just happen to have a pair there on the display."

"The floral ones?" Cass lifted a shoe that looked like a watercolor on silk shantung. "These?"

Vanessa nodded. "Your son is so good," she told her customer as the woman handed over her credit card.

"He's sleepy. He doesn't sleep well anywhere but his own bed, and for the past few days we've been at my parents'," the pretty blonde replied. "I hope he adjusts soon."

"How long will you be staying?" Vanessa rang up the sale and handed the slip to the woman, who leaned over the counter to sign it.

"I'm not sure." The customer passed the slip back to Vanessa.

"Well, it's a nice time of the year on the Eastern Shore." Vanessa slid the box into a shopping bag and handed it over the counter. "Enjoy your bag. Come see me again."

"I will." The blonde picked the bag up by the handles and started to the door, but with no hand free, she paused. Cass hastened to the door and opened it for her.

"Oh, thanks." The woman flashed an engaging smile and left, the child in one arm, her bag in the other.

"That was nice of you," Vanessa said. "I should have realized she'd need help, but I was distracted wondering where I'd put this pretty silver necklace with blue beads and white pearls we got in early in the summer. I hope I didn't sell it. It would be perfect with that dress." Vanessa looked through her jewelry displays. "Oh, here we go." She lifted it from under the counter and placed it on the glass. "Since it was summer merchandise, I can let it go for half price."

Cass made a beeline to the counter and held up the necklace. "I love it."

"Do you want to try the shoes?"

"I do. Seven and a half, please." Cass fastened the necklace and admired it in the mirror. "I do like this."

"It's sweet, right?" Vanessa handed Cass the shoe box.

Cass put on the shoes and stared at her feet. "These are so pretty. It's like having works of art on your feet, so how can I resist? I'll take the whole thing. Dress, necklace, shoes. I haven't been shopping in a long time, so I'm due."

Cass took off the shoes and put them back into the box, which she left on the counter, then went back to the dressing room and changed out of the dress.

"Nothing perks you up like a good shopping day." Cass put the dress back onto the hanger before handing it to Vanessa.

"I know, right?" Vanessa had already bagged the necklace and the shoes, and she now slipped a plastic carrier over the dress. "I feel the same way. I love to get something new for myself. I'm surrounded by all this, but I rarely have time to try anything on. I will find something for the wedding, though. Everyone in St. Dennis and Cannonball Island's been invited. It should be some party." She glanced up at Cass. "I'm guessing you're not going solo."

"Actually, my date is the brother of the bride, Owen Parker."

Vanessa's hand stopped writing.

Cass couldn't help but notice. "Is something wrong?"

"Oh, no. But funny coincidence? That woman who just left? Her last name is Parker, too."

Chapter Nine

Cass signed the slip for her credit card purchases and thanked Vanessa, all the while trying to restrain herself from running out the door. Once outside, she stopped on the sidewalk to scan the cars parked on Charles Street, searching for a glimpse of the blond woman. Cass spotted her across the street in front of the local coffee shop Cuppachino. The woman had opened her car's rear passenger door and was strapping her son into his car seat. She closed the door and walked around to the driver's side and got into the SUV, started the car, and drove off. Cass walked toward the stoplight and waited until the crossing sign flashed on. The SUV was the third car in the line, and it took all Cass's willpower not to stare as she crossed the street.

You're being ridiculous, she told herself as she walked toward the municipal parking lot. As Vanessa said, *Parker is a common name. She could be a cousin or a tourist or who knows what. And besides, Owen never mentioned anything about having had a child. Surely that would have come up in conversation.*

She took a deep breath. It had been a coincidence, that was all. Silly to have reacted the way she had.

I almost stalked that poor woman. Get a grip, Cassie!

She'd barely gotten back to her room when her phone rang. When Owen's name appeared on the screen, she juggled the bags and the room key to answer the call.

"Whatcha doing?"

"I'm just getting back from shopping in town. Just getting ready to hang some pretty things in my closet."

"Let me guess. Bling."

"How did you know?"

"Only shop in town that sells pretty things for ladies, if you believe my sister. Did you have lunch?"

"Nope. But I'm thinking about it."

"Think about having lunch with me."

"I thought you were going to be underwater until later."

"I was. We were suited up, but Jared developed a migraine and he wanted us to wait until he could make the dive. He doesn't get headaches often, but when he does, they can last for hours. I didn't feel like waiting around, so here I am. So how 'bout it?"

"Okay. Do you want to meet me downstairs in the dining room?"

"I have something different in mind. I'll pick you up in ten minutes."

"I'll see you then." Cass hung up and went into the bathroom to check her makeup. She added a little more blush to her cheeks and a little more mascara, a little more lip gloss.

The yellow skirt and white linen shirt she'd worn to Bling still looked fresh, so she grabbed her bag and left the room. She knew she was early, but she didn't feel like waiting it out in her room. A walk around the grounds would be so much better than sitting and watching the clock.

It was another beautiful day, much like the one before, so Cass took a minute to walk around the building to see if there was in fact a family grave-yard there on the grounds, or if Grace had been teasing Joanna at tea the other day. But halfway around the inn Cass found the gathering of graves, surrounded not by a white fence, but boxwood.

Less conspicuous, she thought.

"Comparing graveyards?"

She turned to see Owen striding toward her in khaki cargo shorts and a pale green polo, dark glasses covering his eyes and leather flip-flops on his feet.

"I saw you walk around the building as I was pulling up the driveway." He pointed to the neatly trimmed grass and the grave markers. "A far cry from what you've been dealing with, right?"

Cass nodded. "Of course, the inn has a whole grounds crew, so it makes sense the family plot would be well cared for."

He stood at the opening between the shrubs, his hands on his hips. He looked tan and handsome and sure of himself.

Don't play me, please, a voice inside her whispered. *I really want you to be one of the good guys.*

"That's Grace's husband, right there." Owen pointed to a headstone a few feet away from her. "Daniel."

"Did you know him?"

Owen nodded. "He coached a softball team I was on when I was a kid. One of his kids played, and back then, if you wanted to play, one of your parents had to be involved in the league. Coach, run the snack bar, keep the equipment and bring it to the games—something to contribute. I guess they still do that."

"What did your dad do?" She walked toward him.

"My dad?" Unexpectedly, Owen laughed. "My dad didn't do anything. He wouldn't even allow me to play on a St. Dennis team. My mom helped out at the snack bar twice each week so I could play, even though he'd told us both we weren't to go. That was one of the few times my mom openly defied him."

Owen fell silent for a moment. "I told you how my dad felt about St. Dennis."

"It's sad."

"It was at the time. It doesn't matter anymore." He held out a hand to her and she slipped hers into it. He'd left the car by the inn's front door, and they walked around a hedge of roses that were still in bloom.

"I always come and go through the back door," Cass noted. "I've never been on this side of the inn.

It's pretty. I like the rocking chairs on the front porch." She nodded in the direction of the chairs and the guests occupying them.

"I guess 'cause the lobby's in the back. If I remember correctly, there's a big ballroom right off the front where they have weddings and big parties."

"So if we're not eating here, where are we going?" She got into the Jeep.

"A place called Blossoms out on River Road. Sophie Enright owns it. It used to be a bit of a dive— it'd been empty for as long as I can remember—but she bought it a few years ago and fixed it up. She has a really creative menu and they make everything from scratch."

"It sounds great."

"It is." He turned the Jeep around and drove slowly down the driveway as a number of walkers crowded the drive.

Once on River Road, he pointed out various landmarks and homes of note. "You know who Dallas MacGregor is, right?"

"Oh, please. Like I don't read *People*? She's a huge movie star who lives in St. Dennis and has her own production company in some old warehouse somewhere around here."

"We just passed it."

Cass's head all but swiveled off her neck as she turned around. "That building back there? The long one with the metal roof?"

Owen nodded. "Actually, there are three of them, but you can only see one from the road. I heard on good authority that she's planning a big announcement in another week or so," he teased, wiggling his eyebrows.

"What's good authority and what's the announcement?"

He pulled into a parking lot between a stone building with glass windows on the front and sides, and a plant nursery.

"The authority is her brother, Wade—married to Steffie of Scoop fame. Dallas just finished the script for a new film that will be shot right here in town."

"Oh, wow. We'll get to watch." Cass hopped down from the Jeep after he opened the door for her.

"Maybe even get to be an extra." He took her hand. "She's filmed here before. Gigi said just about everyone in town appeared in one scene or another."

"Gigi was in a movie?"

"She said there wasn't a role for anyone over ninety-five. But I understand Dallas is going to rectify that omission in the next one." He opened the door, upon which BLOSSOMS had been painted in a pretty scroll.

"This is so cool," Cass said as they waited to be seated at one of the square tables, each of which had a vase of fresh, colorful zinnias.

"Check out the wall." He gestured to the opposite side of the room.

"I see lots of photographs."

"Photos of old St. Dennis. I'll show you in a minute."

A waitress led them to a table across from the photo wall. She brought them a bowl of roasted chickpeas and took their drink orders. Specials were listed on a menu that stood in a metal stand on the table.

"What's good here?" Cass asked.

"Everything. The menu changes daily depending on what Sophie can get fresh that day and what she feels like making. So today we have she-crab bisque and grass-fed-bison burgers with garden lettuce and tomatoes." He leaned back. "I think I'll have the burger. I can't resist anything with fresh tomatoes. It says here they're grown right out back."

"The BLT is speaking to me, and I think I'll have to try the bisque."

The waitress returned with their iced teas and took their orders.

"Lis said Sophie grows a lot of what she serves," Owen pointed out, "and the flowers for all the tables as well."

"She must be Superwoman. Run the restaurant, grow the stuff, cook the stuff . . ." Cass shook her head.

"And she's also an attorney. She was working in her brother's office in town, but last I heard, she's pretty much given that up."

"She's definitely Superwoman."

"It helps that her husband has a landscaping business—it's right next door, actually—and he helps out a lot with the gardening. Plus they live upstairs, so neither of them has a commute." Owen pointed to the picture wall. "So. The pictures. By the time Sophie was ready to open this place, she was pretty much out of money after buying the building and making the repairs it needed. This place'd stood vacant for a long time, so she had a lot of expenses. But she had to do something to spiff up the interior, and a plain old paint job wasn't going to do it for her. She wanted to do something that no one else was doing, and she wanted the place to reflect the character of the town. So she asked some of her friends and friends of her brother's and their grandfather's if they'd give her copies of their old photos for the wall. Sophie had the pictures enlarged, and bingo. Décor. Take a good look later, you might recognize some faces."

"Grace is probably the only person I'd know."

"Grace is there, along with her husband and most of her family. When others found out what Sophie was looking for, they went through their attics and scrapbooks and came in with all you see there. There are wedding pictures and graduation pictures going back over a hundred and some years. Gigi said Sophie wanted the wall to be a tribute to old St. Dennis, and it definitely is that."

"Nice. I'm itching to take a look. I hope that couple sitting next to the wall leaves soon." Cass had lowered her voice to a near whisper.

"They look as if they're nearly finished. And the name of the place? Blossoms? She named it after her grandmother Rose Enright, and her grandmother's two friends, whose names were Lilly and Violet. When they were girls, people referred to them as the blossoms."

"That's so sweet. I love that." Cass popped a chickpea into her mouth, chewed it, and then reached for another. "These things are addictive."

"Not my taste, so you feel free to empty that bowl all by yourself."

She laughed and pulled the bowl closer. "So did you figure out what that guy was all about?"

"What guy?"

"Your ex-brother-in-law."

Owen shook his head. "Maybe I just imagined that he was trying to tell me something." He paused. "But I just remembered Lis said she'd run into one of their cousins and she was sort of cryptic, too. I have no idea."

Cass thought about the blond woman and the child from Bling. "Do you think Lis and Alec will have children?"

"I'm pretty sure they want to." Owen tilted his head to one side. "What made you ask that?"

Cass shrugged. "I don't know. Maybe something Lis said the other night that I meant to follow up on."

"I guess I missed that conversation."

She could have told him he hadn't missed it, because the conversation hadn't taken place, but she was fishing and had needed a segue.

"Maybe. Maybe we were talking outside while you were in the kitchen."

"What did she say?"

Cass shrugged. "I don't remember how the topic came up." She sipped her iced tea through a straw. "Did you have children? When you were married?"

"Me?" He seemed taken aback by the question. "Hell, no. If I had a child, you wouldn't have to ask. That child would be with me. Well, part of the time, anyway. Don't you think I'd have mentioned it when we were trading divorce tales?"

"Well, yes, I suppose you would have." She smiled apologetically. "The question just seemed to blurt out. I do that sometimes. I'm sorry if it was too personal."

"It's not too personal. But the answer's no, I have no children from my marriage or any previous relationships."

Of course he would have told her—why wouldn't he have?—but the woman in Bling with her sleepy child had sent Cass's imagination into high gear. She felt herself relax, as if exhaling a breath she hadn't realized she'd been holding.

"I'm assuming you have no children in your past?"

"No. None. And, yes, I would have told you, too."

Their sandwiches were served, and they both dove into their food.

"Everything okay?" the waitress asked as she breezed past on her way from another table to the kitchen.

"Great. Thanks," Cass replied.

Having just taken a bite of his burger, Owen merely nodded.

A moment later he said, "Before you ask, no, I didn't have a chance to talk to Jared. I thought I'd hit him with my request over a bottle of beer when the dive was over, but we never got that far today.

Hopefully he'll feel better later and we can have that conversation."

Cass forced a smile. She had assumed Owen would have said something first thing this morning. She had to remind herself that her priorities might not be the same as Owen's, and that he couldn't control that Jared had a migraine. Still, she was disappointed. She clung to the hope of finding another place around the island to build their dock, and that hope was a lifeline to her.

"I never had a migraine, so it's hard for me to relate," she said. "But I've known people who've suffered with them, and I realize they can be murder. Tomorrow's another day."

"I sure hope so. I'm eager to work this wreck and see what's really down there. Is there a second vessel under the ship? Are there traces of one of the lost islands?" Owen's eyes shone with anticipation.

He was like a kid on a quest, she realized. But was it all about the hunt, or was it about finding the hidden prize? "This is like a treasure hunt to you, isn't it?"

"Sort of. I'm just curious by nature. It doesn't matter what we find so much as the fact that we discover something that hasn't been seen for a couple of hundred years. It's all treasure of one sort or another."

The couple at the table nearest the photo wall rose and walked to the counter.

"Quick, before someone else sits there." Cass nodded in the direction of the wall. "I'm going to take a look."

She was out of her seat before Owen could respond. She stood in front of the wall of photos and scanned the faces, but couldn't pick out anyone she knew.

"That's Grace and Dan Sinclair's wedding picture." Owen came up behind her, and one hand on her hip, he reached around her to point to a bride whose windblown veil covered part of her face. "And that's Alec's parents, Carole and Allen—she was Grace's sister—and their brother, Cliff. He raised Alec after his parents were killed in a car accident. Cliff was a boatbuilder, built most of the skipjacks for the watermen in St. Dennis."

"I didn't know that about Alec. I did know he was Grace's nephew."

"Cliff taught Alec his carpentry skills, left him the boatbuilding business and a house over on Lincoln Road in town. Alec and Lis have been living there."

"I thought they were going to be living in the cottage out on the point."

"They are. Alec's looking for someone to rent the house while he decides what to do with it. He doesn't really want to sell it, mostly for sentimental reasons, but he doesn't want it to sit vacant, either." Owen pointed to another picture. "Here's Dallas MacGregor and Grant Wyler on their wedding day. They had a double wedding with Dallas's brother, Wade, and Steffie, who is Grant's youngest sister."

Owen pointed out other married couples in their wedding finery on their big day.

"This should be called the wedding wall." Cass glanced from one happy couple to another.

"There are plenty of pictures of people doing other things besides saying 'I do.' We have high school graduations going back to the turn of the last century." Owen showed her several. "New babies. Here's Grace showing off her son Ford."

Cass studied the photos. "Steffie in front of Scoop. Opening day maybe?"

"I guess. I wasn't here for it. But that would make sense, because here's Vanessa cutting the ribbon in front of Bling, and Brooke Madison—Brooke Enright now—standing in the open door of her bakery."

"So if you want your picture on the wall, you have to graduate from somewhere, get married, have a baby, or open a business," Cass said thoughtfully.

"Something like that."

"How long do you have to live here to earn a spot?"

"Long enough to make your mark, one way or another."

Cass turned and walked back to their table, a determined smile on her face. She was going to bring new life to Cannonball Island, and if that wasn't making a mark, she didn't know what was— whether or not her picture ever hung on the wall at Blossoms.

"What's that smile for?" Owen sat back down at the table. "You look like you're up to something."

"Just thinking about all the work I have to do." She took a long sip of iced tea. She *was* thinking about all the work she'd set out for herself. "That reminds me. I mentioned to Grace I was thinking about putting together a booklet of stories about the island. She said Lis had written down some stories Ruby told her and was thinking about putting them into a book, and I should get together with Lis. Do you know if your sister's done anything on that project?"

Owen shook his head. "I know she did interview Ruby a number of times and recorded their conversations. I don't know if those conversations ever got into island history beyond what happened in our family. But if you're serious, you should give Lis a call. I don't know of any written history of Cannonball Island beyond a footnote in a book about St. Dennis." He paused. "You are serious, I can see it in your face. You get this look when you decide to do something. Like weed-whacking all those little graveyards or scrubbing up potatoes."

Cass laughed. "Yes, of course I'm serious. Aside from the public relations benefits of having a book to offer our buyers, I think there should be a written history of Cannonball Island. We both know it's unique."

"It is that. I don't know how much Lis has done with the information she's compiled. I know she's been painting up a storm since she came back home. She uses one of the upstairs bedrooms at the store as a studio, so she's in and out a lot. She was there when I left to pick you up, so you might be able to catch her this afternoon."

The waitress returned to the table to ask about dessert and coffee, which Cass and Owen both declined.

"I was all in for the pumpkin mousse, but I saw the look on your face when I asked her to repeat the selections," Owen said after he'd paid the check and they'd gotten back to the car. "You look like a woman with a mission."

"I would like to talk to Lis if she's still at the store. I could call her, but since it's on my mind . . ." Cass clicked her seat belt and he closed the passenger-side door.

"I know. Strike while the iron's hot and all that." He slid behind the wheel and started the Jeep. "That pumpkin mousse really did look good, though."

"What a sport. I'll make it for you sometime."

"Really?"

"Ahhh . . . no. Not likely. Sorry. I'm really not a very good cook. But it's not too late for takeout."

"Why didn't I think of that?" He stopped the car, both hands on the wheel. "Don't even think about driving off and leaving me here." He put the car in park and hopped out.

Cass sat in the front seat writing a list of things she wanted to ask Lis about.

Five minutes later, Owen was back, a bag in his hand and a smile on his face. He got back into the car. "Thanks for the idea. Ruby will be happy. She loves pumpkin mousse."

"All's well that ends well, so you didn't need my probably-not-very-good mousse after all." Cass smiled and dropped her little notebook into her bag. "Besides, aren't you the guy who bragged to me about how he could make all things apple and pumpkin with one hand tied behind his back?"

"I don't recall the tied-up part, but yeah, I'm pretty good. And one of these days, I will turn your head with an apple pie that will be swoon-worthy."

"If you're that good, why don't you make your own pumpkin mousse?"

"Pumpkins aren't in season yet, and anyway, they take too long to bake. There's all that cutting and pulling out the seeds. Time-consuming."

"You mean you make it from scratch?"

"Doesn't everyone?"

She couldn't tell if he was serious or putting her on. She tried but couldn't think of a comeback, so she sat quietly as they made the turn into the parking lot at the inn.

"Thanks for lunch. I enjoyed the food and the company. And I loved Blossoms. What a very cool place." She opened her door without waiting for him to open it for her. She wanted to get into her car and drive directly to the island. With luck, Lis would still be in her studio and wouldn't mind a short break. "I guess I'll see you at the store. I want to catch up with Lis if I can."

"Why don't you drive back with me?"

"I don't want you to feel that you have to chauffeur me around. If Lis isn't there, I'll probably come right back to the inn. You have other things to do."

"I'm sure Ruby has things for me to do. So I'll see you over there. And you're right to want to get to Lis when you can. She's so busy getting ready for the wedding, it's hard to pin her down."

"That's what I was thinking. See you there." Cass smiled and closed the car door. She waved to

Owen as he turned the Jeep around, then crossed the parking lot to her car.

She pulled into the wide driveway at Ruby's store and parked in the same place she'd parked a few nights ago. Ruby was on the front porch, so Cass waved as she got out of the car.

"You be dressed mighty fancy for a girl looking to clean up somebody's graves," Ruby observed as Cass came up the steps to the porch.

"I did all the grave cleaning I'm doing for one day, Miz Carter. I was hoping to find Lis here, but I don't see her car."

"She be up in her studio. Alec dropped her off on his way over to the point. He's been promising to fix up the pier, and it looks like today be the day."

"It does need fixing. We—Owen and I—were crabbing off the end of it, and it was pretty rickety."

"Been like that for a time now. No one been around to fix things. Looks like that be changing." Ruby's eyes were on Cass. "Lots of changes be coming 'fore long."

"Changes can be good."

"Some be, yes. Just gotta be open to what comes next, make the most of it." Ruby turned to go into the store and Cass followed. "You'll find Lis in the room at the top of the steps. Take some water up, she been up there a long time and likely she be warm right 'bout now. Those front windows been closed a long time, never did open right. Take one for yourself, too."

"Thanks, Miz Carter." Cass stopped at the cooler in front of the worn wooden counter and grabbed two bottles of water, held them up for Ruby to see, and went directly to the stairwell, which seemed to grow out of one wall. She took the steps slowly, liking the view of the store from her elevated height: the floors scraped and scarred by two hundred years of islanders' feet, the wooden shelves that held the basics but little more, the old neon Coca-Cola sign over the door that still, defying all odds, remained lit. Something about the place drew her. The few times she'd been inside, she hadn't had this overall view. It was a place out of time, and she wondered what would become of it once Ruby was gone.

Like Owen, Cass didn't want to think about a time Ruby was no longer with them, because the earth might very well tilt off its axis when that day came. She continued up the steps to the second floor.

"Lis?" she called from the top landing.

"In here."

Cass nudged open the door to the front room and found Lis standing in front of an easel where a large piece of thick white paper rested and on which she was tracing something Cass couldn't quite make out. Paintings—framed and unframed—stood along one wall. The wooden floor was bare except for some newspapers under the easel, presumably to keep paint from dripping onto the floor, but were apparently an afterthought. Here and there, smears of paint in various colors smudged the floor so in places it took on the appearance of a rainbow.

"Oh, hey, Cass. How are you?" Lis glanced over her shoulder, then rested her brush onto the palette that sat atop a nearby table, also covered with newspapers. The table didn't appear to have been protected any more than the floor had been. "What are you up to?"

Cass handed Lis one of the water bottles. "If I'm disturbing you, I can stop back. Or you can give me a call when you're free." Cass couldn't take her eyes off the painting on the easel. As she drew closer, she could see the sketch on the paper was a portrait of Owen.

"I'm ready for a break and happy to have someone to chat with for a few minutes." Lis opened the water bottle, took a long sip, and rested one side of the bottle against her chin. "It gets so hot up here sometimes. I need Owen or Alec to get the windows open. They're the old-fashioned kind, with ropes inside to hold them up?"

Cass nodded. She'd seen those same windows in her grandparents' old house outside Baltimore.

"And they stick, so they're a bear to open, and someone has to hold them up while someone else—usually me—has to prop something in there to hold the window open. In the meantime, it gets hot in here."

"Want me to see if I can help?"

"Nah. At this point, it's easier to sweat. I don't plan on working too much longer. I have some things in the car I want to drop off at the cottage."

Cass's eyes were drawn back to the easel.

Lis followed her gaze. "Yeah. My brother. He's really hard to capture. He has so many expressions. It's been a real trial for me, trying to get him right. I thought I'd give it to Gigi. Owen's gone so often and she doesn't say much, but I know she misses him every day he's away."

Cass stepped closer, her eyes on the portrait. "You're really good. I can almost see that little bit of snark in his expression."

Lis laughed. "Nice way to put it. Yeah, he has that, but there's more to him, and it's that *more* I'm having trouble with." She turned her gaze to Cass. "I guess you know what I mean. You seem to be spending a lot of time with him."

"Not so much."

"Oh, please. Just about every time I see you, you're together."

"I don't see you all that often."

"Ha. I don't blame you for denying you're seeing him. I wouldn't admit to it, either."

"I'm not denying anything. I'm just saying that I'm not seeing him. Not really."

"Would you please listen to yourself?" Lis rolled her eyes. "Total denial of a provable fact. The proof being he took you to dinner at Emily Hart's."

"Well, yes, but it was only so I could hear some of Ruby's stories for a booklet I'm thinking of putting together. Which is actually why I wanted to—"

"He took you crabbing."

"He was sort of appalled that I planned on being an islander but had never been crabbing before, but look, the reason—"

"He took you on a tour of Chestertown and took you on the *Contessa*."

"Well, yes, but—"

"And—and this one is the biggie—he brought

you to dinner here." Lis smiled with apparent satisfaction at having made her case. "And he cooked."

"So what? We caught crabs, I didn't know how to cook them, he did." Cass opened her hands, palms up, assuming she'd proven her point. "What's the big deal?"

"In all my memory, Owen has never brought anyone here for dinner. Feel free to check with Ruby if you remain the skeptic."

"That can't be true. He must have at least brought his wife . . . his ex-wife."

"He told you about her? Hmmm. Interesting."

"Why?"

"He never talks about her anymore. Which is just as well. It wasn't a good time in his life."

"He said the divorce wasn't particularly hostile."

"No, but it still wasn't good for Owen. I think he tried to be what he thought he should be, and he failed, and it made him think less of himself."

"Wow. That's heavy." Cass sat on one of two wooden chairs that stood near the double windows that offered a glorious view of the island and the bay off to the right.

"I know. We all worried about him. I think he thought the fact he couldn't be a good husband meant he was going to be too much like our father, after all the years he tried to be the exact opposite. I don't think it occurred to him that he wasn't the right husband because she wasn't the right wife. Anyone who knew them could see that. They weren't just mismatched, they were just plain wrong for each other, but he blamed himself when it didn't work out."

"Heavier even still. He said he thought it hadn't been a good idea from the get-go," Cass said softly. "And he told me your father . . . had issues."

"That's a kind way of putting it." Lis snorted. "But there you go. Another point for my side. I can't believe he told you about our dad."

"It was just a casual conversation, Lis. Don't read anything into it."

"You don't get it. There are two things Owen hates to talk about, his failed marriage and our father. He told you about both."

"I really don't think it means anything. We're just friends. He's been helping me with the gravesites I've been trying to clean up, and he's taught me how to use some of the tools I've needed. That's all."

"You keep telling yourself that, girlfriend." Lis sat in the other chair, and the two women stared at each other for a moment. "So what did you have on your mind today, besides your relationship with my brother?"

Cass decided to ignore the comment about her relationship with Owen and focus on her purpose in being here. "Grace mentioned you were thinking about writing a book of Ruby's stories."

Lis nodded. "I had her tell me some of the family tales, which I recorded, but I haven't had time to do anything with them. I wanted to put them together into a book of some sort when I could get to it." Lis looked around the room. "As you can see, I've been busy. There's something about being here on the island, and here in this place where my great-grandparents lived for so long, that seems to have opened the creative portals. I paint every day, and some days I feel I could go nonstop into the next day and the next. Of course"—she smiled—"Alec would have something to say about that."

"Funny you should say that about feeling creative. I keep coming up with one great idea after another for our building project. Not just designs for the houses, but ideas for marketing and promotions that tie in to the island's history. It's like every time I hear about something that's connected to the island's past, I want to incorporate it into what we offer our buyers."

"Like what?"

"Like writing a little booklet for each homebuyer and telling them about the family that built the original home. Putting together a cookbook with local recipes. Telling the legends that've been passed down through the years." Cass smiled. "Making the little graveyards look pretty so people won't think it's weird to have a few generations of another family buried in their front yard."

"Ah, that's a tough one." Lis laughed. "But I have no doubt that if anyone could make that seem like everyday, no big deal, that would be you."

"That's my goal. And the reason I wanted to talk to you was to see if you wanted to collaborate on a book about the island. You know, the stories you've collected from Ruby over the years. It would be a shame to see them lost."

"I agree. That's why I started recording them. But ours wasn't the only family that moved here during 'the crossing'—that's how Ruby sometimes refers to the time our family and others were kicked out of St. Dennis. I was thinking how cool it would be to talk to some of the others on the island— maybe even some people who have moved away— and get their stories, but I don't have time."

"I have time. I'm not a native islander—right now, I'm not even an islander, but I will be as soon as I have a house. I could collect some stories."

"I could make copies of my recordings for you." Lis picked at a spot of paint on her forearm. "Maybe we could work on something together. I'd thought of using some of my paintings of places on the island along with the stories. You know, like the cottage on the point. I have a painting I did before the renovations started." Lis got up and went to a portfolio on the table. After shuffling through the contents, she held up the work she was looking for.

"Lis, it's magical." Cass's jaw all but dropped. Lis had perfectly captured the essence of the old cottage with its half-hung shutters and sagging porch, the overgrown vegetation that reached to the roof, the window glass that was too dingy to reflect what little sunlight came through the towering pines. The cottage looked abandoned, but waiting, and in that was the magic. "No wonder you have galleries in New York fighting for the right to exhibit your work."

"Where did you hear that?"

"I read it in an article in one of the old *St. Dennis Gazette*s at the inn."

"The painting's not for sale." Lis held it up. "None of the work I did around the island will ever be for sale. It's going to hang in the cottage, and in the store downstairs where Ruby can look at it every day, and someday in Owen's house when he realizes he's meant to be here. At least, Ruby predicts that's going to happen." Lis returned the painting to the portfolio.

"I don't think that's what Owen has in mind."

"Owen can kick and scream and protest all he wants, but Ruby knows what's coming. She won't always say, but she knows. If she says he's sticking around, he's sticking around." Lis grinned.

"I guess we'll have to wait and see. I was under the impression he was only here because Jared asked him to dive with him."

"So he says. Just remember where you heard it first."

"Marking the date and time in my memory. So. What other places around the island did you paint?"

"Take a look." Lis gestured to the portfolio and stepped back.

Cass went to the table and began to look through the paintings, her awe for Lis's talent growing. "These are remarkable. Here's the general store. Ruby's garden. Emily Hart's Victorian porch?"

When Lis nodded, Cass continued going through the portfolio. "One of the old chapels. Oh, another of the chapels." Cass smiled. "Looks like you did all three. I can't tell them apart, but I vaguely recall the stories of ministers who couldn't get along, so they each built their own chapel. Oh, here's the bridge to St. Dennis. And the pier at sunset. Perfect."

Cass paused for a moment. "I understand why you wouldn't want to sell any of them, but what if you made prints to sell to the new homebuyers?"

"I hadn't thought of that. I was just thinking of maybe using them in whatever sort of book I ended up doing. Obviously I haven't given as much thought to this as I could have."

"You've been busy planning a wedding. You're excused."

"Maybe we could sell the prints, display them down at the art center. Maybe even photograph the befores and afters for each new homebuyer. Heck, if I had time, it would be very cool to paint the befores. Some of those ruins have a certain beauty. And we could use the proceeds to fund the restoration of the chapels."

"Great idea. I wasn't sure what could be done about those properties. They're eyesores, quite bluntly."

"They are. I don't know who owns them. I'd say check the deeds, but I'm not sure where you might find them. Cannonball Island isn't known for such formalities as property deeds. I understand that these days, it's made things tough for the state and county tax collectors. I can check the county tax records."

"I think my dad already did that. There were a lot of properties that didn't even show up on the books."

Lis drank the rest of the water in her bottle and tossed it into a nearby trash can. Cass got the feeling that was Lis's way of saying she was ready to go back to work.

"Well, I'll let you get on with what you're doing." Cass took one last look at the incomplete portrait of Owen on the easel.

"Do you think he'll like it? The fact that I painted him?"

"I think he'll be flattered. I think he'll be pleased, whether he admits it or not."

"I hope so. Oh, look at this one." Lis went to the row of framed paintings that stood facing the wall and selected one and held it up.

"Oh, my God, it's Ruby! It's her to a T. Right down to that tiny mole next to her right eye and the wisps of hair that always come free from her bun. Oh, and the eyes. They couldn't be more right if this were a photograph. Has she seen it yet?"

Lis shook her head. "I was thinking of unveiling it at the exhibit next month at the art center. I wasn't planning on taking any of my other works. Just this one." Tears were in Lis's eyes when she turned to Cass. "She's the most beautiful woman I ever knew, and I wasn't sure I could do her justice."

"You have. You definitely have. I think she'll be thrilled."

"I hope so. Owen and Alec both think I should show her before the unveiling, but I think she knows about it." Lis smiled. "You know how she knows things without being told."

"She said changes were coming, so I guess she knows something."

"When did she say that?" Lis returned the painting to its place near the wall.

"Just a while ago, before I came upstairs."

Lis shook her head. "It could mean anything. She could mean because of my wedding."

"That's probably it. Hey, thanks for the time." Cass turned toward the door.

"Sure. My pleasure. I'll get a copy of those recordings for you." Lis walked Cass to the door of the studio. "I'll see you at the wedding, if not sooner. You are coming, right?"

"Yes." Cass hesitated. "Actually, I'm going as Owen's date."

"Really?" A smile spread across Lis's face. "And you didn't think to mention that earlier?"

"It slipped my mind."

"Of course it did."

Cass was in the hall and almost to the steps when, without having planned it in advance, she turned to Lis. "What was she like? Owen's wife?"

"Cyndi was all right. A lot of fun. Easygoing. Liked a good time." Lis shrugged. "She was his girl when it was convenient for him. He was a rat that way. If she was dating someone else when he came back from one of his adventures, she'd drop the other guy to be at his beck and call. That whole routine would have grown old real fast for me, but she didn't seem to mind. At least not when they were younger. But when they got to closing in on thirty, I guess she figured it was fish or cut bait. I never did know what she said to make him fish, but eventually he married her. I think he tried to be happy, tried to make her happy. But he's got those restless feet, you know? Couldn't settle down, though I think he thought he could. They'd been friends for a long time, and I think he felt he was letting her down, but he had a chance to go to Alaska, so he went. He thought he'd be gone about a month, but it lasted almost a year. She started the divorce proceedings after he'd been gone about six weeks because she was smarter than the rest of us had given her credit for. She and Owen didn't fight about it. It was just one of those things neither of them should have done, and they both probably knew it, but they did it anyway."

"That's pretty much in line with what he told me." Cass started down the steps.

Lis walked to the staircase and leaned on the railing. "For what it's worth, I don't think his feet are as restless as they used to be."

"Good to know." Cass started down the steps. "By the way, what did Cyndi look like?"

"Really pretty. Tall. Long legs. Incredible body. Real pretty face. All the guys in town fell all over her." Lis smiled wryly. "For all the obvious reasons."

"What color hair did she have?"

"Oh, she was blond. A tall, leggy blonde."

A tall, leggy blonde. The phrase repeated over and over in Cass's head as she drove back to the inn. That was a pretty accurate description of the woman in Bling. The tall, leggy blond woman whose last name was Parker. How could that be a coincidence?

Still, it wasn't beyond the realm of possibility, was it? Common name. Lots of women are tall and blond. Lots of tall blond women could very well be named Parker. Maybe the woman was married to a cousin.

The child in the woman's arms had looked to be about a year and a half old. Owen said they'd been divorced for about two years.

Do the math, Cassidy.

She knew in her heart that Owen wouldn't have looked her in the eye and lied about something as important as having a child. So it had to be a coincidence or someone married to a relative of the Parkers'. Nothing else made sense.

Whatever the answer was, she'd put it aside for now. It was almost four, and time for tea with Grace at the inn. If nothing else, she could look forward to some pleasant conversation and some tasty treats, and maybe she'd come away with yet another compelling marketing idea to add to her growing list of things to do.

Chapter Ten

Cass spent the next few days focused on work. She'd spoken with her father and they'd agreed to start clearing the sites they'd bought and begin to tear down those small houses that couldn't be salvaged. She made a schedule and emailed her father a list of properties where the demolition could start right away. He called her in response, happy to hear that at least some progress was going to be made.

"Your mom and I are driving down on Friday. We booked a room for the night at that inn where you're staying."

"You got a room at the last minute? You're lucky. They're usually booked solid. Someone must have canceled for the weekend."

"Not the weekend, just Friday night. We're supposed to be going somewhere on Saturday, I forget where. One of those invitations your mother says yes to and tells me about later."

Cass called down to the reservation desk and reserved a room for her parents, then emailed instructions to the job foreman, Ted Sterling. She'd worked with him several times before and he knew she'd be on-site to make sure things were being done to the letter. She had few concerns about the quality of the work when things were in Ted's hands, but she'd had run-ins with him in the past over her authority. He never failed to make her feel she should have been born male if she wanted to have her hands on the construction end of her father's business. While she always made it a point to try to start fresh with him on every new job, sooner or later he'd say something to get under her skin. She was certain he believed she ran back to her father every time, though she never had. She'd be the first one on the job site when he arrived on Wednesday morning.

"Getting a Dumpster over that bridge is going to be dicey," Ted told her when she met him at the property she'd designated lot number one. "They're pretty heavy."

"Maybe we won't need a Dumpster. Maybe we can use pickup trucks. I plan on using a lot of the material from the takedown houses in the new construction, so whatever is salvageable is going to stay right on-site."

"You do know that's going to triple—quadruple—the time to take these places apart if my guys have to go board by board, brick by brick?" He tried to mask his displeasure, but she wasn't deaf to the undertone, a mixture of annoyance and impatience. "Which means it's gonna cost you more than you planned."

"I have planned for it, so we're good. My father's

aware of it as well. It can't be helped." She explained the rationale of being able to use the original wood and bricks as a marketing hook. "So I'll see you and your crew at seven tomorrow morning on lot one."

"We'll be there."

"Good. Bring a couple of pickup trucks and some tarps in case it rains before we get to reuse the material."

Cass was on the job site at six forty-five the next morning, a large cup of the inn's coffee in hand, when the first of the crew arrived. By seven, all hands were accounted for. She explained what she wanted and ignored the rolling eyes and shaking heads of the crew. She stood in the driveway and watched the chimney of the old Morrison house come down, brick by brick, just as she'd requested, but not before she'd photographed the building from every angle.

Ted took her aside, her printed-out list in his hand. "So I'm a little confused on the scheduling here. We're going to take all these places down before we start building anything new?"

"We're going to dismantle until I find out where we can build a dock to bring in the materials to start the new construction."

"You've already started building a dock on the other side of the island."

"Yeah, well, that one's off the table." She explained that the sunken ship was responsible for the work stoppage.

"So you think you can build something over here to bring stuff over from the mainland?" He turned and looked toward the bay as if scouting for a location.

"I do." She willed herself to remain calm. She didn't want her face or her words to reflect the doubt she was beginning to feel, especially since she hadn't had any indication from Owen that Jared would be depth-finding for her.

Ted took off his baseball cap and ran a hand through what little hair he had left. "You know we use different crews for demo and construction, right? And that the guys we use to build the houses aren't going to be the same guys you use to build the dock?"

"Do you honestly think you have to tell me that? Really? Is this my first rodeo?" She made no attempt to hide the sarcasm in her voice. She leveled him with a stony gaze and went to her car to calm down. The situation was stressful enough without having the foreman lecture her on any aspect of the job. She knew he thought she'd be calling her father to complain about him, so she deliberately took a folder from the car, laid it out on the hood, and pretended to be reading while she drank her coffee and tried to appear calm.

She'd been questioned by subcontractors as well as Deiter's own construction people before, and she'd always handled it with as much good humor as she could muster, but she wasn't in the mood on this project. She had a lot riding on it—her reputation, her father's money—and she wasn't about to admit to Ted or anyone else that if she couldn't build the dock and thereby couldn't get what she needed onto the island, she'd have to try to sell the already-cleared lots to someone else to recover at least some of her father's investment. Giving up on Cannonball Island was the last thing she wanted.

Her fingers itched to text Owen and ask him if he'd spoken to Jared yet, but she knew there was no point. If he'd done so, wouldn't he let her know? Besides, he'd called her on Monday night to let her know they'd be diving for the next couple of days if the weather held.

She walked back to the house and went through it with the crew of five, pointing out what she wanted them to save—and therefore carefully remove—and what they could trash. She addressed everyone's concerns and answered their questions. The water-damaged counter in the kitchen could go; the wide boards covering the outside wall would stay. The window glass should be removed carefully, but the rotted frames were beyond salvaging. Cass stepped back to give the guys a wide berth while they worked.

"Sorry about that, before, you know . . ." Ted told her as she walked past.

She nodded that she'd heard and had sort of accepted his sort-of apology as she always did and returned to her car, this time intending to call her father and let him know the work had begun. As she reached through her open driver's-side door for her bag, she heard an engine out in the bay. Habit made her turn to the sound. Jared's boat was forty feet off the beach.

She shielded her eyes with her hands. Several

men stood on deck, but the sun was in her eyes and she couldn't distinguish one from the other. She leaned against her car, her eyes fixed on the boat, waiting to see what would happen.

Ten minutes later, one of the men on deck dove overboard and swam to shore, long arms plowing through the waves until he reached shallow water. He stood and walked ashore, his shorts weighed down by water to just above the scandal line, his bare chest gleaming in the sun, an Adonis rising from the sea.

Oh. My. Heart.

"Hey, Cass. Guess what?"

She had to clear her throat before she answered. "Hey. Owen," she managed to squeak out.

He slogged across the sand, water dripping, his dark hair stuck to his forehead, and he crossed the road, his bare feet leaving prints on the warm macadam. She wanted to look away, but she couldn't. She'd thought he looked good in a polo shirt and jeans, but in less than that by half, he was mesmerizing.

He approached the car. "I've got great news."

"What's that?" She had to force herself to focus on his face. The rest of the view was that good.

"Jared measured the depth at fifteen feet right about where he is now. Which means you can probably get a permit to build your dock because you won't have to dredge." Owen stood with his hands on his hips. "Unless, of course, you think your people are going to be wanting to bring in some really huge crafts. So go ahead and tell your dad things are looking pretty good and he can go ahead and send his engineer down. Jared has a printout so the engineer can see what we saw, but it all looks pretty good."

"Thank you. I'll tell him. Thanks for remembering."

"Sure. I know it was important to you."

"And tell Jared I said thanks."

"Will do."

"I thought you were diving all week."

"The pump on the dredge engine is malfunctioning, so Jared's taking it back to their shop and picking up another."

"Is he waiting for you to swim back out?" She nodded in the direction of the boat.

Owen laughed. "No, he's on the phone with some girl he met at a bar in Annapolis over the weekend." Owen glanced over his shoulder. "Is your father planning on putting in a boat ramp?"

"I don't think so. He's not going to be offering a marina. He just wanted a place where the owners who want to come and go by water could moor up for a few nights. They'll have to winter over somewhere else. He's not going to be offering fuel or anything else."

"Just a place to tie up."

"Exactly. And I think he only planned on maybe having room for six boats at the most. First come, first served."

"I get it. Makes it sound more exclusive. Good plan." Owen looked toward the house. "So what's doing here?"

"The first demo has begun. This is one of the complete teardowns."

"They doing it all by hand?"

Cass nodded. "I'm trying to save as much as possible. This one doesn't have a whole lot that we'll be able to use, but I want anything that can be saved."

"It'll be interesting to see how much you can salvage from each house."

"I have a pretty good idea. I went through every place and made lists. I can tell you how many floorboards should come out of that house and go into the reuse pile."

"I'll just bet you can." He turned and his eyes held hers. "I'll bet you're damned good at everything you do."

"So they tell me."

He was close enough that she could have reached up and smoothed the wet hair back from his face, but here, in front of one of her crews, she'd have died first. Instead, she backed up a step or two. "You're welcome to come see what we're salvaging from this place."

"Thanks, but I think I should go back to the store and shower off the bay. I swear I can almost feel that sea grass reaching up from the depths to slash at my legs as I swam by."

"Do you have visions of crabs chasing behind you, claws outstretched, hoping to lop off a toe or two?"

"I didn't, but I do now. Thanks for that."

"Anytime."

"So Friday night is the rehearsal dinner. Want to tag along?"

"I can't. Sorry. At least, I don't think I can."

He raised an eyebrow.

"My dad and mom are driving over to see what we've done, so I'll be showing them around. I already booked a room at the inn for them."

"I'd invite you to bring them along, but that wouldn't be much fun."

"Probably not."

"If anything changes, text me, okay?"

Cass nodded, and for a moment she thought he was going to kiss her. The moment passed, and he turned and headed for the dune and the path that led to the back of the store. She watched until he disappeared from sight.

Holy crap, she thought. She'd been adamant about remaining impervious to his charm, but it wasn't his charm that was wearing her down. It was the sight of that toned, tanned body emerging from the Chesapeake. How did a girl guard her heart against that?

"THIS IS LOVELY." Linda Deiter took her time looking around the inn's lobby. "Just what I'd expect an old inn on the Chesapeake to look like. It's casually elegant but homey at the same time."

Cass's mother took in every inch of the lobby décor. Dressed in a white linen shirtdress that amazingly hadn't wrinkled on the trip from Baltimore, she looked the part of the wife of a successful builder. Gold bangles were on her wrists, and diamonds on her fingers. From her coiffed hair to the fat natural-pearl earrings to her designer sandals that Cass knew had cost a bundle, Linda Deiter was a showstopper. At sixty-five, her skin was still luminous and her eyes were still bright. Cass prayed the beauty her mother had been born with was hereditary so Cass, too, could shine as naturally when she was her mother's age.

"I've enjoyed staying here. The owners are very friendly and there's always something to do." Cass took her mother's arm and walked with her to the stairwell, pausing to point out various paintings that hung on the walls.

"There's your father." Linda waved and caught her husband's eye.

"Did you check in?" he asked from halfway across the room.

Cass watched fondly as her father wrestled with the sunglasses that had fallen from the top of his nearly bald head. As stylish and put together as Linda was, Brian Deiter was . . . not. He had a talent for always looking just slightly in dishabille even in custom-tailored suits. Today he wore a polo shirt that had pulled out in several places from the waistband of his navy-blue shorts. Both his wife and his daughter had always found it oddly endearing.

Linda nodded. "All you have to do is have our bags sent up."

"*Bags*? Plural? I thought you were only staying for one night."

"We changed our minds. We did have an event for tomorrow night, but it was one of those things your father couldn't have cared less about, and frankly, I didn't really want to go. So we had a good excuse to beg off—we had to come see the progress our daughter's making on a big project. It sounded good, and it's tough to argue when a parent plays the kid card." Linda squeezed Cass's arm. "Besides, I feel as if it's been months since I've seen you. I missed you."

"Aw, that's nice, Mom, but it hasn't been all that long."

"Maybe it just seems it."

They climbed the steps to the second floor, Brian huffing and puffing several steps behind them.

"Why isn't there an elevator in this place?" he complained when they reached the second floor.

"The building's well over a hundred years old, Dad. They didn't have elevators when the place was built." Cass repeated what she'd been told when she'd asked the same question.

"They never heard of retrofitting?"

"There is a service elevator in the back hall somewhere, but I think they didn't want to disturb the historic ambience of the lobby."

"They can keep their ambience," he continued to grumble. "I'll take an elevator over ambience any day of the week."

"You could use the exercise," his wife told him. "You're getting a little paunchy."

Cass watched in amusement as her father tried to pretend he hadn't heard.

Her parents' room was in the wing opposite Cass's, and by the time they arrived, the bellhop was there with their bags and the room had been opened for them.

"I should have hitched a ride up with you," Brian muttered as he tipped the young man.

"So what's your plan, guys?" Cass went to the French doors and opened them, then stood back on the balcony so her parents could admire the view. "What's on your agenda?"

"Well, first thing I'd like to see is this island you and your father have been raving about. I've looked over your preliminary plans, and I love what you're wanting to do there. Such sweet little houses. And who thought of using original materials in the new construction? My girl." Linda made no attempt to hide her pride in her daughter.

"I gotta agree, Cassie. I think we're all gonna be real proud of this project once it's finished."

"Well, before we can finish, we have to start. Did you call the state about the permit for the dock?" Cass stepped back into the room.

"I had Lee call. She's the engineer I'm using here, Lee Stafford, so she'll handle that."

"I love that you can see so much of the Chesapeake from here, Cassie." Linda was still on the balcony. "Brian, come out here and see this view of the bay."

Brian rolled his eyes and did his wife's bidding, and Cass smiled to herself. For all his occasional bluster, Brian was putty in the hands of his pretty wife, and everyone knew it.

"Like I've never seen the bay." He was still muttering. "Yes. Pretty. Lovely view. Let's show your mother the island, then get lunch."

"How about showing your wife some lunch and then we'll look at the island?"

Cass voted with her mother, and they headed downstairs to the dining room, which Cass had highly recommended.

"Tomorrow maybe we can grab breakfast or lunch at this sweet place called Blossoms on the other side of town." Cass described the restaurant for her parents.

"That sounds darling. Let's save that for dinner," Linda suggested.

"I won't be around for dinner. I have a wedding to go to. Alec Jansen's getting married tomorrow, Dad."

"Nice boy, Alec. We couldn't have gotten this project off the ground without him. Him and that woman in the general store. Topaz?"

"Ruby," Cass corrected him.

"Of course. Ruby Carter. Wonderful lady." Brian shifted from one foot to the other while they waited to be seated.

Crab in several forms was on the menu, so they each ordered a different dish to share and chatted easily through lunch. Brian was obviously eager to get out to the island, so no one lingered over their meal. Cass started to offer to drive, then remembered her sports car was best suited to two passengers, so she let Brian drive.

"This place looks almost deserted," Linda exclaimed after they'd driven over the bridge and onto the one paved road on the island. "Oh, wait, there are some cars parked up ahead."

"That's one of our job sites, Mom. Those cars and pickups belong to our work crew. That's the first of our houses to be taken down. Stop, Dad, and let's give Mom a tour."

Brian pulled over to the side of the road and parked.

"Well, the house has a view of the bay and it's nice and close to the beach."

Cass knew her mother had tried to find something positive to say, as she always did. "It's okay, Mom. We knew it was a teardown when we bought it."

"Oh, good. I was hoping it wasn't one of your rehabs." Linda and Cass got out of the car and Brian followed. "Because it looks like something that should be torn down."

In her pricey designer sandals, Linda headed up the sandy driveway to the shell of the house. Workmen were stacking bricks from the chimney and pulling old nails from the floorboards they'd already removed and were tossing the nails into a bucket. Cass wasn't sure what if anything she'd do with those old iron nails, but she thought they might be worth saving for some unforeseen project.

The men stopped momentarily when Brian appeared on the scene, but, at a signal from Ted, returned to their tasks.

"We're going to enlarge the footprint of the house," Cass told her mother when Brian and Ted stepped to the driveway to talk. She took her mother by the elbow and led her carefully to the back of the house. "At one time there was a patio back here. I'd like to restore it and have it extend the full length of the house."

Linda nodded thoughtfully as Cass described where the different rooms would be in the house. "Well, you weren't kidding when you said these places would be small. Two or three bedrooms and two baths." Linda frowned. "That's not much of a beach house, Cassie."

"I think of them as little getaways. They aren't intended to impress. They're supposed to be cozy, comfortable little cottages where you can come and relax without all the trappings that complicate life."

"They'll certainly be cozy."

"I'm going to be keeping one for myself. I have it down to two sites, but I can't decide between them."

"A little place like this would be perfect for one person." Linda nodded. "This would be a nice little weekend place for you."

"I'm thinking of making this my home. I spend so little time in my condo in Baltimore, and I think it's because I don't love living there."

"You think you'd love living here?" Linda frowned.

The sound of pounding feet drifted from the road, growing louder as the runner drew closer. Cass glanced around the corner of the house, a smile on her face. She had a pretty good idea who the runner was.

Owen spotted her and raised a hand in greeting, then diverted from the road onto the overgrown lawn.

"Hey, Cass." He was dressed as he had been the last time she'd seen him running, though this time his shirt was still on.

"Hi, Owen." She took several steps to meet him. Her mother followed her around the corner. "No diving today?"

"Jared's not back yet. I don't think he'll make it back till Monday or Tuesday. He has plans for the weekend." Owen noticed her mother standing at the corner of the half-demolished building. He smiled and waved.

Cass turned to see her mother staring. "Mom, this is Owen Parker. Owen, my mother, Linda Deiter."

"I'd shake your hand, Mrs. Deiter, but I'm afraid I'm a little sweaty right now." He seemed both apologetic and slightly embarrassed.

"It's quite all right." Linda nodded but didn't join them.

"So no change in your plans for tonight?"

Cass shook her head. "I should show my parents around town and have dinner with them. They decided to stay through Sunday, so I should spend at least one of their two nights with them."

"I got it. How 'bout I pick you up before the wedding instead of meeting you there? No reason for us both to drive. It should be a fun time. It certainly will be interesting." Owen smiled wryly. "Our mom decided to come to the wedding after all."

"How long's it been since you've seen her?"

"Too long. I tried to get together with her on my way back here a few months ago, but she was busy.

Anyway, what's a Parker wedding without a little drama?" He glanced behind her and realized her mother was still standing there. "Speaking of moms, I think yours is waiting. I'll see you tomorrow." With a wave toward Linda, Owen turned and jogged off across the lawn.

Cass noticed he stopped to say something to Brian, but she turned her attention back to her mother.

"So I don't want to take you inside because it's dangerous, but I think you get the idea of what I want to do, right?" Cass stood with her hands on her hips.

"Who was that?"

"Owen Parker. I told you."

"But who is he?" Linda seemed to be searching Cass's face.

"He lives on the island. His great-grandmother is Ruby Carter." Cass tried to think of something else to say other than *He's the guy who sets my pulse racing and who turns my knees to mush.*

"What does he do?"

Cass thought it over and found herself opting for the most socially acceptable answer. "He's a professional diver."

"No, I mean what does he do to stay in shape like that?"

"Oh." That had been the last thing Cass expected her mother to say. "Well, he runs a lot."

"Whatever else could be said about this little island of yours, one can't complain about the scenery."

"Mother!"

Linda laughed. "Cassidy, you're blushing. Now might be a good time to tell me what else I might want to know about Owen Parker."

"He's the brother of Alec's bride."

"The wedding that's tomorrow? The one you're going to?"

Cass nodded. "I'm going as Owen's date."

"I see. Now, tell me what you think you can do with all that glass that's piled up over there."

Cass walked around the entire property outlining the new house and elaborating on its design. They met up with Brian out front and agreed that the house, when completed, would be an interesting property.

"And right across from where the new dock's going to be," Brian pointed out.

"Don't get ahead of yourself, Dad. Wait and see what your engineer has to say after she talks to the state."

"I have a good feeling about this, Cassie. I think it's going to be fine. Owen just told me about the natural depth in the bay there. He thinks we'll be fine."

"Tell me again why you didn't want to build the dock over here in the first place," Linda said as they walked to the car. "And how do you know Owen?"

"I thought the river was a more picturesque setting than the bay side," Brian said somewhat sheepishly. "And I met Owen at the meeting we had some months ago in the general store when we got some of the islanders together. He's Ruby Carter's great-grandson."

"So Cass said."

Linda got in the car's front passenger seat and Cass got in the back.

"Ruby and Owen were both very helpful to me when I was trying to buy up some of the unused properties. He and Alec tracked down some former residents so we could negotiate the sales through the Realtor." Brian slid behind the wheel. "So where to now?"

"Just drive slowly around the island so Mom can see the point and we can point out the lots we bought."

The drive took less than twenty minutes. As they approached the point, Cass noticed the tent for Lis and Alec's wedding reception had already been erected, and folding chairs were stacked under the canopy.

"That's where the wedding's going to be tomorrow," Cass pointed out to her mother.

"Under the tent?" Linda asked.

"The ceremony is going to be on the pier at sunset, and then the reception will be under the tent."

"Isn't it going to be dark?"

"They're bringing in tons of lights to hang in the trees all along the point, and that's all I know. Lucy Sinclair—her family owns the inn—is apparently a very well-known event planner. She's doing the entire thing, and except for the fact that there will be lights, she's kept pretty much everything else close to the vest. I'm really intrigued to see what she's going to do. Some of her weddings here in St. Dennis have been written up in magazines, so I'm prepared to be impressed." Cass glanced over her shoulder at the cottage that stood near the edge of the trees.

"So is that like a little community-center type thing there?" her mother asked, apparently having followed Cass's gaze.

"No. It's the future home of the bride and groom." Cass explained the history of the cottage and Lis's love for it. She added proudly, "I helped re-design the interior, added some space to the back of the house, and bumped out the bedrooms. It's lovely inside, maybe one of the most charming places I've ever been in. Lis was right to want to save it."

"You really have become immersed in this place, haven't you?" Linda turned in her seat to face Cass.

"I have. I can't help it. It's the sort of place that draws you in. There's something very special about Cannonball Island, Mom. Dad was a genius to see here what no one else had seen in a hundred years."

The rearview mirror captured her father's smile.

"Take a bow, Dad."

"I'm driving. I'll bow later."

Cass pointed out the general store to her mother, and Brian slowed as they passed by. Cass noticed a light in one of the second-floor rooms, and the thought that it was most likely Owen in the shower after his run brought a quick flush to her cheeks. She could imagine soapy water covering that broad chest and beyond, could almost see him with his head back and his eyes closed as the water streamed down his face and the length of his body.

Would she be a fly on that wall? Oh, yeah.

"Now show us around St. Dennis, Cassie," her

father was saying. "Maybe a bit of that walking tour you went on . . ."

"Take the second right after the bridge," she said after taking one last glance over her shoulder. "And then the first left."

She struggled but finally managed to block out the vision, willing herself to stop speculating what she might see should she be able to see through the second-floor walls of the old store.

Chapter Eleven

Owen's hands were sweating as he dressed for his sister's wedding. There was almost an hour before the ceremony, but he was ready except for the navy blazer Lis had wanted all the guys in the wedding party to wear, including the groom. He'd pulled on the prescribed dark khakis and slid the belt through the loops. Buttoning the light pink shirt would be easier if his hands hadn't been sweating. What was up with that?

His little sister was getting married, that's what was up. And he, Owen, would be walking her down the makeshift aisle on the point, where so much of their family history was rooted, and symbolically turn her over to the man she loved.

It wasn't that he had a problem with Lis marrying Alec. If ever two people were meant for each other, it was those two. It was just that she was *his little sister*. He'd felt protective of her from the time they were children, had walked her to the school bus and back home again every day until high school sports got in the way, but even then, everyone knew not to mess with Lisbeth Parker, because if you did, you'd have to deal with Owen on the flip side. And no one ever messed with Owen.

Thinking about their growing up together in the small house halfway between Ruby's store and the river, Owen recalled reading to Lis at night when their mother worked and their father was too busy watching TV to tend to his daughter. Owen had made dinner on those nights because, to his father, cooking was women's work, and he'd rather not eat at all than cook for his family. He'd teased Owen unmercifully about taking over so many of the household chores until Owen shot up in eighth grade and not only towered over his father, but out-weighed him as well. Jack Parker had been a fool about many things, but he hadn't been fool enough to take on the son who'd seemed to become a man overnight.

Owen had tried to shield his sister from their father's hateful rhetoric when he'd been drinking. It bothered him that Lis would fall asleep with ugly words inside her head, so on those nights, he'd read light or funny books to her so she could fall asleep with a smile. And now tradition called on him to hand over her care—her heart, her well-being—to someone else, though in truth, Lis had taken pretty damned good care of herself since she left the island for college, and Alec was the man who'd always owned her heart.

Just another of life's milestones, Owen thought as he put on the navy blazer, tied on the navy-and-pink-striped tie, and slipped his watch onto his wrist. While he found himself referring more and more to his phone for the time, he never felt dressed up unless he was wearing the watch his mother bought him one long-ago Christmas. He looked at himself in the mirror and decided he'd do. He pushed a few errant strands of dark hair back into place and left his room.

His plan was to pick up Cass at the inn and come back to the store for Ruby. He peeked into Ruby's living quarters, but she was still getting dressed and he didn't want to disturb her, so he left a note printed in two-inch-high letters on a big piece of paper—*Went to pick up Cass. Be right back*—and left it in the middle of the kitchen island where she couldn't miss it.

He drummed his fingers on the steering wheel as he waited for opposing traffic to cross the one-lane bridge. Normally on a Saturday night—on just about any night—there'd be no traffic at all. But the wedding was drawing people from all over the Eastern Shore and as far as New York, where Lis had lived for years and her paintings hung in famous galleries. Owen had to remind himself sometimes that his sister was a well-known and respected artist. She'd made her mark painting city-street scenes, but her reputation had grown since she returned home and began painting what she knew best— Cannonball Island and the natural beauty of the Chesapeake.

What did their mother think of that? Owen wondered. Kathleen had shown up in the middle of the night, her third husband on her arm. Their flight had been delayed, she'd told Owen when she arrived at the store. She'd meant to make reservations somewhere, but the decision to come East had been made at the last minute, and it seemed every room in St. Dennis had been booked. There'd been no choice but for Ruby to offer them one of the second-floor bedrooms. It had been years since Owen had shared a bathroom with anyone, and he enjoyed it even less now than he had when he was growing up.

Kathleen's husband was a nice enough guy, and she seemed happy, so Owen had nothing to complain about. He was pleased for Lis's sake that their mother had decided to come to the wedding, even if it had been at the last minute. He'd been glad to see her, and he thought maybe she'd been happy to put her arms around him as well.

Owen turned into the drive for the inn and again had to wait as a steady stream of cars exited onto Charles Street, most of them heading toward the island. He hadn't realized Lis and Alec had so many friends and had invited them all to the wedding. He parked outside the back door of the inn and hurried inside and up the stairs to Cass's room. He knocked twice on the door and waited. When the door opened a moment later, he blinked in surprise.

"Well, don't you clean up nicely." Cass's mother held open the door for him. "Cassie, your friend is here."

She turned back to Owen. "Cass tells me you're giving the bride away."

"I am, yes."

"It must be a very informal wedding, judging from your attire. Or are you changing before the wedding?"

"Nope, this is it, Mrs. Deiter. Lis's choice from the tie to the socks." He held up one foot and pulled up his pant leg slightly.

"Oh." Cass's mother leaned closer. "Are those . . . ?"

"Yes, ma'am. Flying pigs. Pink on navy to match my sister's color scheme." He could hardly keep a straight face.

"I'm assuming there's some significance to the pigs?"

"So am I, but my sister hasn't chosen to enlighten us. She just said, 'It's my wedding, wear what I tell you to wear.' And so I am."

"I think they're adorable." Cass came out of the bedroom putting in an earring and holding a clutch bag under one arm, and Owen's heart threatened to stop on the spot. She wore a dress of softest blue silk that skimmed her body, and high heels with lots of straps that looked like a garden party on her feet. The dress was sufficiently low in the front to show enough of her assets without being inappropriate. He felt his throat go dry.

"And I think you're a good sport, Owen," Cass was saying. "Don't you agree, Mom?"

Linda Deiter nodded slowly. "I do. And I admit I think the pigs are quite cute, if somewhat unusual for a wedding. In my day, you know, nothing would do but formal wear. A tux was the thing."

"It's a new day, Mom, though a lot of grooms do choose to wear a tux. But just about anything goes now. Including pigs that fly. I think navy blazers and dark khaki pants are perfect for a bayside wedding at this time of the year." Cass turned to Owen and smiled. "You wear it well. I'll just be one more minute."

Cass disappeared into her room. When she returned, she carried a cream-colored wrap over her arm. "In case it gets cool later." She picked up her room key from the desk on her way past and tucked it into her bag. "I'll see you tomorrow, Mom. You and Dad have a great night."

"I'll stop by for you in the morning," Linda said. "We can have breakfast together before your dad and I leave."

"It might be a late night, Mom. I may not want to get up early. How about I call you when I wake up?"

Cass kissed her mother on the cheek as she strolled by, then waited at the door for Linda to leave. Cass locked the door behind them and took Owen's arm as they walked to the stairwell.

"You do wear it well. Flying pigs notwithstanding."

"And you look amazing. Beautiful." Owen looked down into Cass's eyes and almost felt starstruck. She was gorgeous. She was hot. And she was with him. He could have pinched himself. Was this really his life? In the past, plenty of beautiful women had loved to spend time with him, but none of them affected him the way Cass did. He needed to think about that one of these days, but it wouldn't be today.

"Do you like the dress?" Without waiting for a

reply, she said, "This is what I picked up at Bling the other day. And this necklace." She turned her head to show it off. "And these fabulous shoes." They reached the bottom of the steps and she held out one foot. "Aren't they the best?"

"Um, well, yeah. They're pretty." He wasn't sure what his response was supposed to be. He didn't think like a woman, so he said the first thing that came into his mind. "Um, well . . . yeah. They're . . . nice."

Cass laughed and took his hand. "*Nice* will do, thank you."

All the way back to the island, Cass chatted about the day she'd spent with her parents, the things she'd showed them, the places she'd taken them. "I'm still learning a lot about the area, so it was fun to discover things I'd missed. Did you know there's a historic house in St. Dennis with a sign out front that identifies it as Cassidy House?"

He tried to think of a response that didn't reflect his loathing of the place.

"Get it? Cassidy? As in my name?"

"I got it."

He drove over the bridge and, once again, went the wrong way to avoid driving all the way around the island to reach the general store. He parked in front of the store and reached for the door handle.

"I'll be right back. Just picking up Ruby."

He went through the store into the back room and called her, but there was no response. In the kitchen he found the note he'd left for her, and the reply she'd written.

Went with Kathleen and Dave.

Owen locked the door behind him, turned the sign to the CLOSED side, and went back to the car. "I guess Ruby was tired of waiting for me. She went with my mom." He'd left the engine running, so he put the car in reverse and turned back onto the road.

"Owen, are you annoyed with me?"

"No. Why would I be annoyed with you?"

"You shouldn't, but you're acting a little strange. Since I mentioned taking my parents on a tour of St. Dennis."

He drove in silence past the bridge, past the old chapels, until they reached the point. So many cars were already parked along the roadside, he pulled into the driveway at the old Mullan place.

"About Cassidy House. Here's the short version." He turned off the car and pocketed the key. "Once upon a time, some ancestor of mine owned that place. Built it, actually. But when he and his family were driven out of town and onto the island, a man who lived in St. Dennis—someone who worked for that ancestor of mine in his mill—claimed the house because it was now for all practical purposes abandoned, and he moved into it with his family. His name was Cassidy. Now, it never bothered Lis or me, but it drove my father to drink. I mean, literally drove him to become an alcoholic. He couldn't leave the past where it belonged, blamed St. Dennis for everything that was wrong with his life, when he should have been blaming himself. He was a really miserable human being, and it was all because he couldn't let go of something that had never been his to begin with."

"I'm sorry. If I'd known, I wouldn't have mentioned it," Cass said softly. She reached her hand across the console and touched the side of Owen's face. For a moment he thought she was going to kiss him, but she merely let her fingers linger on his skin for a moment.

The gesture instantly soothed him. "There's no way you would have." He took her hand in his and held it. "I'd told you about my dad, but I didn't mention that." He gave her hand a squeeze. "It's not worth talking about."

"No, it isn't. Especially today when it's such a happy time for your family."

"It is. I'm really happy for Lis. She deserves only good things in her life." He got out of the car and walked to the passenger side to open the door for Cass.

"The weather is perfect for an outdoor wedding." She took the hand he offered to help her. She stood for a moment and smoothed her dress. "Did my dress wrinkle in the back?" She turned around.

"Nope. It's perfect." He would willingly have stared at the view for a moment longer, but he knew they were right on the border between almost late and late. He took her hand and they hurried across the road and onto the point.

A string quartet was playing to the right of the pier, a song Owen didn't recognize but that Lis said was the theme from *On Golden Pond*. Almost all the guests had been seated, and several turned around as if watching for the bridal party to appear.

The door to Lis's cottage stood open. Lis had planned on getting dressed there, and the bridal party was to meet inside.

"This looks amazing," Cass exclaimed. "What a perfect place for a wedding. Would you look at this? It's positively transformed."

"Lucy did an incredible job." Owen nodded. "Looks like everyone's been seated except for the—ahem—latecomers. Go ahead with Ford, he'll find you a seat. I need to get inside. I'm sure Lis must think I've gone fishing or something and I've forgotten what day it is. I'll catch up with you later."

He took one last look over his shoulder. Lucy had indeed transformed the point into a sparkly wonderland. Thousands of tiny white fairy lights twinkled in every one of the towering ancient pines from the cottage all the way to the pier where the ceremony would be held. White chairs were set up in a fan pattern, with an aisle strewn with flower petals down the middle. Off to the right a large white tent had been set up for dining and dancing after the ceremony. Lis said a cocktail hour would be held outside the tent, which was carefully closed off from the prying eyes of the arriving guests. She'd wanted everyone to be surprised when the tent flaps were pulled back. Owen had no idea what was inside, but he was sure that between Lis and Lucy, it was going to be great.

He went up the cottage steps and pushed open the door.

"There's my boy." Kathleen Parker Long patted his arm when he entered the great room. "And doesn't he look handsome?" For a moment, he was afraid she was going to pinch his cheek.

"Thanks, Mom." He gave her arm a squeeze and looked around.

Two women in floaty pink dresses held bouquets with pink and purple flowers with just a touch of something orange. Owen spotted Alec and made his way to him. Everyone seemed to be sipping champagne but Owen. He grabbed a glass from a tray on a table and took a sip. He'd rather have a cold beer, but there weren't any.

"Hey. You all ready for this?" He clapped Alec on the back.

"I've been ready. I just want to get on with it. What's taking Lis so long?" Alec glanced down the hall toward the bedroom.

"How about I send someone in to find out." Owen looked around for someone to send. "Carly, would you run back and ask my sister what her timetable is? I think we need to get started real soon."

Carly Summit Sinclair—Lis's matron of honor and wife of Ford, Alec's cousin and best man—nodded, grabbed another glass of champagne, and headed down the hall. She returned in less than a minute and told Owen, "Lis wants to see you."

Oh, God, she's got cold feet, Owen thought. He knocked softly on the door, then opened it, expecting to find Lis pacing nervously. Instead, she stood, cool and calm, looking out the back window at a rosebush she'd planted earlier in the summer.

"They're doing really well there. The roses. Everyone told me they wouldn't grow, that it wasn't a good spot for them, but Gigi said she used to have one planted there and it bloomed from May till November. One year, she had roses at Christmas." Lis turned and smiled at her brother. "Or so she claimed. She told me to have faith and it would bloom. And it has."

Owen stared at Lis. He'd never seen her look so beautiful. He'd always thought of her as a pretty kid, but today she was radiant. Her hair was swept up at the back, intertwined with small pink dahlias he recognized from Ruby's garden. Her dress was lacy and long, off the shoulder, and had long sleeves and she looked like . . .

A bride. Today my little sister is a bride.

"Why, Owen Parker. Are those tears?" Lis walked toward him, scrutinizing his face.

"What? Me? No. Of course not." He swiped at his eyes. "Lis, you look . . . pretty."

"*Pretty*? I spent the entire day getting buffed and made-up and hair and yada yada yada, and my brother tells me I look *pretty*?" She snorted. "That's the best you can do?"

"I guess *beautiful* is more accurate. You really do look beautiful."

"Does it pain you to say that?"

Owen laughed. "No. Well, maybe a little. I'm not used to seeing you all fluffed up like that."

"Fluffed? Well, yes, I guess we can add *fluffed* to the rest of it." She reached into a box for his boutonniere. "Hold still so I can pin this on you."

She took a minute to affix the small pink flower and green fern to his lapel, then stood back. "You look pretty, too, big brother. The ladies will be lining up for your attention tonight." Her eyes narrowed thoughtfully. "But you only have one girl on your mind these days, right?"

"Maybe."

"Uh-huh." Lis kissed his cheek. "I hope it works out for you. Life is very different when you find the one you're meant to be with. It's better. Stop fighting it."

"I'm not fighting anything." He couldn't explain to Lis that while he couldn't read Cass, he could feel her somehow, and what he felt, felt right. He almost didn't understand it himself.

"Good. Don't get in your own way. Cass is special. I may not have the eye, but I can see that much. If you want her, you have to let her know. Thinking about her isn't going to get you anywhere. And don't deny that you think about her. I watched your face at dinner last week. You melt every time you look at her." Lis took his hand. "Lecture over. Let's get this show on the road, as they say. Go tell my handsome almost-husband to go on out to the pier. Ask Ford to escort Mom to her seat. Do you believe she actually showed up?"

"Yes, and she's glad to be here."

"Good. I really wanted her to come."

"Did you tell her that?"

Lis shook her head. "I wanted her to be here because she wanted to be, not because my wanting her here made her feel obligated." Lis sighed. "Why do things always have to be so complicated in our family?"

"They don't have to be. She loves us both, but being around us reminds her of a very unhappy time in her life. We both know how we felt, growing up in that house with Dad, but neither of us knows what she felt or what she had to put up with. She always tried to make it seem for us that things were okay, even when we all knew they weren't. She's finally found someone who makes her feel good about herself, and who cares enough about her to come with her to your wedding. The fact that she's here should tell you all you really need to know, Lis. Let's just leave it at that."

"You're right. Of course you're right. So, yes, I'm going to focus on the fact that she cared enough to come." Lis paused. "Do you think I should have asked her to walk me down the aisle, too?"

"You already have me and Ruby walking with you. Unless you want to look like you're leading a parade, I think I'd leave things as they are."

"Good point. Now get moving so I can get married."

"You say that as if I were the one holding things up."

"Out. Now."

"Wait. Shouldn't I be walking Mom to her seat?"

"If you weren't walking with me, I'd say yes. But now I want to get the whole party moving. So go."

Owen tagged Ford to walk Kathleen to her seat along with her new husband, after which Ford would join Alec at the pier, where the officiant—Dan

Sinclair, Ford's brother—waited to perform the ceremony. Lucy sent Alec on his way, with instructions to get everyone in line. She sent a text to the violinists who were waiting near the pier that they should begin to play "Canon in F" for the processional.

Lis's two attendants—a former roommate of Lis's from New York named Olivia, and Carly—went out the door first. Owen found Ruby seated in the living room, waiting for her cue. She wore a long-sleeved dress of purple lace and a cream-colored wide-brimmed hat covered with pink and purple flowers. On her feet she wore—yes, the ever-present clean-as-a-whistle white tennis shoes.

"You're a stunner, Gigi." Owen helped her to her feet.

"It be such a happy day. My granddaughter be back home and my great-grandbaby be marrying her fellow. All right here in this same spot where my Harold brought me to begin our life together. It all be right, son."

He nodded. "I couldn't agree more. Lucy went to get Lis . . . oh, there she is. What do you think of your girl now, Gigi?"

Lis seemed to float through the hallway.

"Pretty as a cornflower." Ruby nodded, and her eyes, much like Owen's, brimmed but did not spill over. She took Lis's hands in hers and simply held them. Finally Ruby said, "It be time, Lisbeth."

Owen opened the door and helped Lis and Ruby on the steps. With Lis in the middle, the three prepared to walk the short aisle to the strains of Clarke's "Trumpet Voluntary." Owen wondered how much of that walk Lis would later remember. While leaving a lot of oohs and aahs in her wake, she looked straight ahead. When she and Alec locked eyes, she smiled, and Alec looked as if he were about to burst with the joy of the moment. Owen left his sister with Alec and Dan on the pier, the sun setting behind them, to take their vows.

Owen gave Ruby the aisle seat so she could see the proceedings better, which put him between his mother and his great-grandmother. Ruby surprised him by reaching for his hand and holding it throughout the entire ceremony. A few minutes later, his mother did the same. He felt as if he were pinned down on each side. He tried to focus his attention on the ceremony, but he found himself drifting in and out.

A sailboat halfway across the bay came into view, and he watched for a few minutes as it passed by. There was no wind, and little breeze, so he imagined the owners were using the engine to keep the boat moving. He wondered where it was moored.

Ruby squeezed his hand and brought him back to the ceremony.

"I, Lisbeth Jane Parker . . ."

His sister had been named after a great-aunt and another long-ago ancestor, and Owen toyed with the idea they could be watching, spirits from another dimension, gathered invisibly on the point as one of their own entered into marriage.

Another squeeze from Ruby, as if she knew his mind was elsewhere.

Of course she did.

It wasn't that he didn't care that this was his sister's wedding. It was just that he was a guy, and there were distractions. Such as knowing Cass was sitting back there looking like the best dream he'd ever had in that silky dress that seemed to flow like water through his hands when he'd touched the small of her back.

Ruby turned and glared at him, and he gave her his most innocent look before turning back to the wedding.

"I, Alec Matthew Jansen . . ."

It was strange thinking about his little sister being someone's wife. Not a bad strange. She looked so happy, her face was glowing.

His mind wandered back to the skipjack that used to sit on cinder blocks behind the store. Once upon a time it had belonged to his great-uncle Eben, who'd taken it out on the bay every day of the week except Sundays from the day he bought it. Owen had been shocked when he arrived home over the summer and looked out the window to find the boat gone. Ruby had given it to Alec as payment for all the work he'd done in the store, building her new living quarters. It turned out that Alec's uncle—the one who'd raised him—had built that boat. Owen was glad Ruby was happy with her new rooms and that she didn't have to climb those steep steps anymore, but he still missed the sight of that boat standing above the dune like a sentinel. Of course, with Lis marrying Alec, the boat was now back in the family, more or less.

"I now pronounce you husband and wife," Dan was saying, and everyone applauded. Which meant that both Ruby and Kathleen let go of his hands, which had fallen asleep while in their clutches.

The happy couple turned to the crowd, and Lis raised her bouquet in a gesture of joy. They danced their way back down the aisle to U2's "Beautiful Day" coming through the speakers that had been hung on the trunks of two of the trees.

"Think you could stay tuned in to your only sister's wedding," Ruby grumbled.

"I'm sorry. But it's not really my fault." He leaned close to her ear and whispered, "It's true what they say about guys and short attention spans, Gigi."

"Don't be seeing you drift away when you be watching football last Sunday night."

"That's different. I had money on that game."

"I don't want to hear about it." Ruby grabbed his arm and all but shoved him into the aisle. At one hundred years, she could still give him a push when she felt like it.

He found a seat for Ruby near the doorway to the tent, then went in search of Cass. He found her chatting with Grace and Jamie, Dan's wife.

"Lovely wedding, Owen," Grace said when she saw him approaching. "Your sister makes a beautiful bride."

"She does."

"And you're looking quite dapper yourself," Grace told him. "I don't often see you dressed up. As a matter of fact, I don't think I've seen you in a suit but maybe once or twice in your life."

"It's not my first choice, but today's a special occasion." His hand rested casually on Cass's waist.

"Lis's dress was gorgeous," Cass said.

"Totally to die for," Jamie agreed. "Vanessa special-ordered it for her. Don't you love that off-the-shoulder look?"

Owen took the opportunity to hunt down a waiter who carried flutes of champagne and another with some scrumptious-looking hors d'oeuvres and led them back to Grace and her group.

"These are yummy," Cass said as she nibbled a shrimp, her lips closing over it slowly.

Owen had no problem keeping his focus on her face. It was an effort for him to look away when the time came to go into the tent, where they found flowers wrapped around the tent poles and Chinese lanterns in shades of pink, purple, and orange hanging from the roof. Farm-style tables ran along both sides of the tent and were joined with one lateral table, where the bride and groom sat with their wedding party, with a dance floor in the middle and the band at the opposite end of the tent. Owen found places at one of the long tables and helped Ruby to her seat. Lis had decided against assigned seating, so Kathleen and Dave and Cousin Chrissie rounded out that end of the table.

The bandleader invited the bride and groom onto the dance floor for their first dance. They'd chosen an old tune, "I Only Have Eyes for You," as their song. The twentysomething lead singer did justice to the song, which had been around, Kathleen explained, since before the Second World War.

"I don't know the song," Cass said. "It's lovely, but I don't know if I've heard it before."

"Alec asked for it because it was a favorite of his parents. He said one night he was sneaking out of bed to get a book he'd left downstairs, and he caught them dancing in the living room after they thought he'd gone to bed. This song was playing, and he said he crept back up the stairs because he knew instinctively, even as a five-year-old, that he was intruding on something very special. He never forgot the song. I guess maybe they played it a lot."

Next the bandleader announced the bride would dance with her brother in place of her father, and together Owen and Lis danced to "Forever Young" and sang along with every verse. Alec danced with Grace—obviously a surrogate for his mother, Grace's late sister, Carole—and Grace uncharacteristically wept through the entire two minutes and twenty-eight seconds it took for the band to play a decent rendition of the Beatles' "In My Life."

Dinner had been prepared by Sophie Enright's crew and featured both Lis's and Alec's favorites—halibut and cheeseburger sliders, respectively. They'd been interrupted numerous times for toasts to the wedding couple. Owen's followed that of the best man, but overcome with unexpected emotion, he'd skipped the rap he'd rehearsed. He concluded with wishing his new brother-in-law tons of luck and lots of patience, because Alec would no doubt need a bundle of both.

By the time dinner had concluded and the cake had been cut and served, the band was in full swing and the dance floor was busy.

"My turn to dance with you." Owen rose and held

out a hand to Cass. He'd danced with his mother, his sister, and even Grace. Now he only wanted Cass.

They made their way to the dance floor, and he put his arms around her. "I've been wanting to do this all night." He nuzzled the side of her face. "You feel really good. We should make a habit of slow dancing."

"Is that what you call this?" Cass laughed and wrapped her arms around his neck. "It's sort of fast for a slow dance, don't you think? And what step is that you're doing?"

"I'm trying to keep in tune with the music." He grinned good-naturedly. He knew dancing wasn't his forte.

"Maybe it's not supposed to be a slow song." She wrinkled her nose and tilted her head to listen. "What is this song, anyway?"

He appeared to be horrified. "It's Blake Shelton. 'Sure Be Cool If You Did.'"

"Well, I don't, so I guess I'm not cool."

"No." Owen laughed and pulled her a little closer. "That's the name of the song. 'Sure Be Cool If You Did.'"

"Ah, I get it."

"But if you don't know Blake, you can't be very cool."

"I don't listen to much country."

"I never did either, but that's all Jared listens to. Morning, noon, night. You work with him for a while, you get to know country music."

"So was this on Lis's or Alec's playlist."

"Alec's. Definitely. He plays this stuff in his shop

while he's working on boats. Says it puts him in the frame of mind to work with wood." Owen shrugged. "I don't judge."

All Owen could think about from that point on was getting Cass alone. The evening seemed to go on forever. As Lis's brother, he couldn't very well leave before she did, even though he wanted to. He danced with Cass every chance he got, just to feel her body close to his. By the time they could finally leave, he was dizzy with wanting her.

Kathleen and Dave were driving Ruby back to the store, so Owen took Cass by the hand and they walked down the road, back to where he'd left the Jeep. He was trying to decide where they should go when Cass said, "Let's go back to my room."

"Okay," he said as calmly as he could, as if he hadn't been hoping she'd offer, as if he hadn't all but willed her to utter those words.

He took his time driving to the inn, as if they had all the time in the world and his heart weren't pounding out of his chest. They strolled across the parking lot and then through the lobby holding hands, climbed the steps leisurely to the second floor. By the time they reached her door, he was about to explode. She unlocked the door and stepped inside, and the minute it closed behind them, he had her flat up against the wall.

He kissed her as if he couldn't get enough of her lips, her mouth, her scent. His hands slid over her body, feeling the silk of the dress, then pushed it up to feel the silk of her skin. She was soft in all the right places, and she made all those places accessible to him, arching against him and pressing into him as if she could not get close enough. In one motion, she unzipped her dress and let it drop onto the floor, then pushed his jacket off his shoulders and unbuttoned his shirt. The heat had risen between them to the point he was sure they'd both spontaneously combust.

He lifted her off her feet and carried her to the bedroom, kicking the door open with one foot. She took him with her onto the bed and helped him remove what was left of his clothing, and he removed the rest of hers. With a groan that came from deep within, he ran his hands over her body from her shoulder to her thigh, stroking, lingering, stroking again. His lips trailed hot kisses down her throat and found her breast, and she moaned, wrapping her legs around him and making him know in no uncertain terms what she wanted, whispering in his ear, "Yes."

Later, he'd vaguely recall having told her how beautiful she was, how much he'd wanted her from the first time he saw her, how good it felt to touch her, how good it felt when she touched him. He was lost in a fog of sensation, of desire fulfilled, and when she opened to him and he entered her and felt the silken smoothness of her wrap around him, he thought that after this night he could die a happy man. He was so happy when he awoke the next morning to find he hadn't died that he pulled her to him and loved her all over again.

Chapter Twelve

$\sim$

"Cass? Cassie?" The knock at the door was insistent. "Cassie, are you awake?"

Cass sat up in bed. "Oh, my God. It's my mother."

"So don't open the door." Owen rolled over and took half the covers with him.

"She knows I'm in here." Cass tugged back her share of the covers.

"If we're real quiet, she'll think you're asleep. Which she should expect you might be at"—Owen sat up and looked at his watch on the nightstand—"nine in the morning after a late night."

"I know, but it's *my mother*, and I'm sitting here buck naked in my bed with an equally naked man."

"Not that there's anything wrong with that," he muttered.

Cass stifled a giggle.

"You're over thirty. You're single. You aren't breaking any law," he whispered.

"I know. I know. But she's still my mother. What if she won't go away?"

"She'll go away. Give her a minute."

It took more than a minute, but Linda finally did give up and left.

"Are you hungry?" Owen asked. "I'm starving."

"Me, too. Want to call for room service? Then again, no. What if my mother comes back and sees the cart being delivered. She'll know I'm in here."

"Let's get dressed and go into town. We can grab breakfast somewhere."

"Okay. Good idea. I want to take a quick shower first."

She wrapped the sheet around herself and went into the bathroom.

Fifteen minutes later, she emerged wrapped in a towel, her hair wet from the shower. "One of the advantages of short hair is that it takes no time to wash and to dry. The bathroom is yours."

"Did you leave any towels?"

"On the counter."

While Owen showered, Cass dressed in jeans and a pink long-sleeved tunic. She tied a scarf around her neck and put on wide silver hoop earrings. Her mind wouldn't leave her alone, insisting on taking her back over every minute of the night before. She hadn't planned on bringing Owen back to the inn, or taking him to her bed, but once she realized that was where they'd been heading all evening, it seemed the most natural thing in the world.

Don't be a fool, the voice inside whispered. *Player . . .*

Not this time, she told herself. Owen'd been

honest with her about everything, hadn't been anything but wonderful in every way. How could she
not believe that he wasn't playing with her? What
man did all he'd done—the crabbing lesson, making her dinner, planning the day in Chestertown,
even putting himself on grave-cleanup duty just
to be with her—what man did all that to have a
woman for only one night? There were times to
trust, she told herself as she dressed and put on
makeup, and this was one of those times. Something special was between them, she'd felt it before,
and last night it had overcome them both. It wasn't
just sex, though that had been great to the point of
being phenomenal, but the attraction between them
was undoubtedly real and went well beyond the
physical.

So take it at face value and see where it leads.
That was her goal.

She heard Owen come out of the shower, and a
few minutes later he emerged wearing just his khakis.

"I seem to have lost my shirt." His eyes scanned
the room. "Ah, there it is."

He picked it up off the floor where she'd tossed
it and shook it out.

"Looks a little wrinkled." He held it up. "How
do I keep from looking as if I'm still in my clothes
from the wedding? Think anyone would notice?"

"Roll up the sleeves and lose the jacket and tie."
She watched him button the shirt. "Too many buttons. You look like you're ready to put the tie on.
Here." She undid a few more buttons and smoothed
out the collar. "That looks a little more casual."

"Thanks. I'd go back to the store, but I'd run into my mother and she'd be wondering why I'm still wearing my wedding duds."

"Ha. So you don't want to face your mother, either. And you're how old? Thirty-eight?"

"She'd get the wrong idea."

"What idea is that?"

"I'm not sure, but it would be wrong, either way."

He finished getting dressed. He looked her over, his eyes skimming from her head to her feet and back again. "You look just as beautiful now as you did last night. How do you always manage to look so perfect?"

"Seriously? Perfect? You must have forgotten about the days you've seen me sweating, dirty, and covered with grass clippings."

"You wore them well."

Cass searched his face and realized he'd meant every word. She went to him and kissed him. "That was sweet. Thank you."

"It's the truth. It doesn't matter what you wear. You can't help being beautiful, just as I can't help being stunned by just how beautiful you are."

"You keep talking like that, Owen Parker, and I'm going to . . ."

"What?" He held her to him, his eyes searching hers. "You're going to what?"

"I'm going to start to think this was more than a one-night . . . you know." Cass looked away. Despite her earlier pep talk, her basic insecurity betrayed her and put words she hadn't wanted to say into her mouth, expressing thoughts she didn't want to have.

"I hope you're kidding." No humor was in his voice or in his eyes. "Of course it wasn't a one-night— Is that what you thought?"

She threw out the truth: "It's what I was afraid of."

"Babe, last night—today—this is not a one-night anything. It's just the beginning of us." His arms tightened around her. "Look me in the eye and tell me you're on board."

"I'm totally on board," she whispered.

"Good. Now, let's go get breakfast before we both pass out."

He folded his tie and tucked it into a pocket of the jacket, which he laid over his arm. They got to the door, and he was just about to open it when she grabbed his hand.

"Wait. Owen. What if my mother is out there?"

"You mean lurking in the hallway, waiting for you to emerge after your long sleep? Afraid she'll pop out from a laundry cart?"

"Stranger things have happened."

"Not in my experience, but okay. What do you want to do?"

"We'll go out separately."

He laughed. "This is ridiculous."

"I just don't want to have a conversation about this and what it means with my mother this morning."

"Okay. I know where the freight elevator is. I'll leave first, and one minute later, you come down the steps and go right to the parking lot. Do you remember where we left the car?"

Cass nodded, then the absurdity of the situation struck her, and she giggled.

"I know." Owen shook his head. "This is silly. I feel like a fifteen-year-old."

"Me, too." She opened the door and poked her head out to look both ways. "Go." She shoved him out the door.

A minute later, she found the room key where she'd dropped it the night before and left the room. Once outside the inn, she went straight to the parking lot and found Owen waiting in his old brown Jeep. He laughed when he saw her.

"What's so funny?" She got into the car and snapped on the seat belt.

"Just the whole thing. Your mother being here this weekend, my mother being at Ruby's this weekend. It's silly, because how old do you have to be before you let your parents know you're sleeping with someone?"

"I think it would be different if it weren't new."

"You mean if this hadn't been the first time we were together?"

Cass nodded, and he seemed to give that some thought as he drove from the parking lot to Charles Street. Once in town, he looked for a parking spot on the street, but had to drive down to the municipal lot to find a place.

"I forgot how busy it gets around this time on Sunday morning. Lots of people apparently like to go out to breakfast on Sunday. Let's hope we can find a place that isn't filled up."

Owen took her hand and they walked up to Charles Street. They tried three restaurants but all had a wait of at least thirty minutes.

"Let's go into Cuppachino," he said after trying Lola's, where the Sunday brunch was legendary but where the wait was a full hour. "At least we can get coffee and a muffin."

"Anything at this point."

They stood in line at the counter and waited to give their orders, then looked for a table. Finally Cass located one on the far side of the room next to the wall.

"Not much of a view, but there's caffeine in the coffee, and sugar in the muffin, so it's all good as far as I'm concerned." Cass took a long sip of coffee and sighed. "This is so good."

"Best coffee on the Eastern Shore."

"So they claim."

"Can't argue with it. It's damn good."

"I told my mother I'd give her a call when I woke up. I guess I should do that now so she doesn't think I'm in a coma or something." She speed-dialed her mother's cell and waited for the call to be picked up. She and Linda spoke for a few moments, then Cass hung up and told Owen, "They're just getting ready to leave. I crossed my fingers and told her I knocked on her door earlier but no one answered. She said they were probably having breakfast in the dining room. But why didn't I meet Owen there instead of going out? I told her I'd call later today and tell her all about the wedding."

He leaned toward her to ask, "So we have the entire day to ourselves. What would you like to do?"

Movement from the left seemed to catch his eye, and he straightened up, an unreadable expression on his face.

"What?"

He didn't respond.

She turned in the direction in which he was staring and saw the tall blond woman from Bling seated on the opposite side of the room with a group of three or four people.

"That's her, isn't it?" Cass said softly. "That's your ex-wife."

He nodded. "Yup. That's her, all right."

"She's very pretty."

Owen nodded. "She always was a pretty girl." He looked at Cass for a long moment. "Don't even think about it."

"Think about what?"

"Don't think about comparing yourself to her. She'd come up short and then you'd feel sorry for her."

"She was in Bling the other day. When I bought my dress." She wondered if she should tell him that she'd known the woman's last name was Parker. Or that she had a child in her arms.

"Really? Huh. What a coincidence." He glanced back at his ex-wife. "I guess I could go over and say hello, but I'm not sure I want to deal with her family. They weren't very complimentary to me after the divorce."

"Well, she's theirs, and we always stick up for our own, right?"

"We do." He turned his attention back to Cass. "I'll wait and catch up with her another time."

Cass was still wondering if she should mention the child with the dark curly hair when Cyndi and her group stood and headed toward the door. Owen's ex was the last in line, and she turned to look over her shoulder and saw Cass across the room. She stared for a moment, then the recollection of having seen Cass the previous week must have kicked in, because she appeared to be about to smile.

Cass knew the exact second when Cyndi saw who else was at the table. Her expression froze and she seemed to blanch. She turned abruptly and left the shop. Cass continued to stare at the door where the woman had been standing.

". . . and maybe go to Rock Hall for crabs this afternoon. What do you say?"

"What? Oh. Crabs. Sure."

"Okay, where'd you go? 'Cause you obviously weren't here."

Cass felt flustered and unsure of what to say. "I looked up and she—your ex—was looking at me, and for a moment it was like she recognized me but wasn't sure where she'd seen me. Then I thought maybe she remembered me from the shop because I thought she started to smile, but she saw you here and sort of went white."

"I have that effect on a lot of my old girlfriends."

"She's not just an old girlfriend, Owen."

"Okay, I know. I just was trying to not give it any more importance than it deserves. She saw you with me and for some reason that . . . what, spooked her? I can't imagine why, unless it was just one of those things where you see someone you didn't expect to see." Owen shrugged. "I heard she was going to be visiting her parents in Ballard. I'll drive over one day this week and just say hello."

"I think she'd probably appreciate that."

"We know her brother would. He sure made a point of telling me in Scoop last week."

Cass took a drink from her cup, holding it in both hands. She put it down on the table, her hands still wrapped around it. "There's something else. When she was in Bling, she had a little boy with her."

"Probably one of her nephews. Last I heard, her sister had two and was pregnant again. And two of her brothers are married, so it isn't surprising."

"I had the impression it was her child."

Owen's head snapped up. "That's not possible. You must have misunderstood."

"I don't think so. She said something about how they were at her parents' and he doesn't sleep well outside his own bed."

He shrugged. "That could very well be one of Sandie's boys, Cass. Her sister was always dumping her kids on their mother. She's been doing it for years. Don't read any more into it than it was." He seemed to dismiss any other possibility by changing the subject. "So what do you say? Crabs at the Waterman?"

"Sure."

It was a perfect fall day, crystal-blue skies and deep blue water. They sat on the deck outside the restaurant and ate french fries and spicy crabs with their bare hands and watched other customers drive up on their boats to tie off on the dock.

"That's just the way I see the dock on the island being used," Cass told Owen, "only not this large. Just enough for a half dozen boats."

"Tell your dad to get his engineer out there to take care of business."

"I did. I think he said she'll be out this week."

"It shouldn't take long for the dock to be built. The construction should be in full swing before too much longer."

"That would be great." She toyed with a crab claw. "I can't wait to get started on my house."

"Did you decide on a lot yet?"

"I did. I want the lot that's sort of between the river and the bay. The one with the dune behind it." Her eyes lit up at the thought. "I'm enjoying my stay at the inn, but I'd rather be in a house."

"Really?" He munched a fry. "Alec's looking for a tenant for his house over on Lincoln Road since he and Lis have already moved their things into the cottage. Maybe you could rent it until your place is ready."

"Show me on the way home?"

"Sure. He left me the key, so we can go inside and you can take a look around."

They polished off a dozen jumbo crabs, and finally Cass begged off. She ordered coffee and drank it while she watched the swans across the inlet and Owen finished the last crab.

"This was fun. Of course, the tips of my fingers will forever smell like the seasoning they used, but it's a small price to pay for such deliciousness."

They stopped in the respective restrooms to wash off. When Cass came back out, Owen was standing at the end of the dock looking out at the bay. She came up behind him and her arms encircled his waist.

"Penny for them." She leaned into his back.

"I was just thinking about how, when I was a kid, I thought the bay was bigger than the ocean. Growing up practically on the beach the way we did, I couldn't imagine any body of water ever being bigger than the Chesapeake." His hands held on to hers. "I still feel that way sometimes."

"What? After diving all over the world, in just about every ocean?"

Owen nodded. "The Chesapeake still rules."

He drove leisurely on the way back to St. Dennis, taking side roads rather than the highway, pointing out small towns and historic markers, stopping a few times at Cass's urging so she could take a picture or two.

"I want to keep this day," she told him after getting back into the car, having photographed the marker for one of the houses on the Underground Railroad. "The whole weekend has been . . ." She searched for the right word.

"Life changing." He filled in the blank for her. "Best weekend ever."

She nodded. "Best weekend ever."

Thirty minutes later, Owen pulled into the driveway of a small white Victorian house with decorative trim on the porch and a tall black planter overflowing with vines and a few purple petunias that had somehow managed to hold on through September.

"This is it." Owen turned off the car. "Want to check out the inside?"

"Absolutely. It's so pretty. It looks like a wedding cake." She got out of the car and didn't bother to wait for him before she climbed the steps and peered through the glass window that comprised the top half of the door.

He came up behind her, key in hand, and unlocked the door.

"I can't wait to see— Oh, that fireplace." Cass stepped into the foyer, where a corner fireplace stood on one side of the small room and a desk on the other.

"There's another one in here." Owen went through an arched doorway into a sitting room that all but overflowed with furniture.

Cass followed, her eyes darting from one side of the room to the other, surveying the sofas and table and chairs that were crammed in. "Does Alec collect antiques?"

"He inherited some of the stuff when his uncle left him the house. Some of the other things belonged to his parents. He and Lis want to use some pieces in the cottage, and they'll leave some here for the tenant, but I think they'll still have too much."

"Maybe he'll decide to sell some things." Cass eyed a pair of Victorian side chairs. "I'd be interested in seeing what, once he decides."

"Let him know, and he'll probably bring you in before he calls one of the dealers in town. I know Nita, in the antiques shop two doors down from Bling, has been after him to let her come through the place."

Cass wandered into the dining room, which was also filled to capacity. The kitchen, on the other hand, was sparsely furnished, with just a table and two chairs.

"There were never more than two people living here at one time," Owen told her. "Alec's uncle lived here alone. Then he and Alec. Then Alec was by himself until he and Lis got together. Want to see the upstairs?"

Cass nodded, and they went up to the second floor, which had three bedrooms and one bath with an old-fashioned claw-foot tub.

"How sweet is that tub. I can just imagine taking a bubble bath in there." Cass smiled at the thought.

"How *small* is more like it. And for the record, no self-respecting guy takes a bubble bath in a girlie tub like that."

"It sounds like someone's masculinity is threatened," she teased.

"As if," he snorted, and led her into the next room. "I think this room was Lis and Alec's, and the one across the hall was his uncle's. Which means this room"—Owen turned her around to look into the room next door—"is ghost-free. Want to test my masculinity?"

"Ew. Don't you think it would be totally creepy to be in someone's house when they don't know you're there and have sex in one of their beds?"

"No."

"Seriously?"

"Most guys don't think any place is too creepy to have sex."

Cass rolled her eyes. "I really like the house. When Alec and Lis get back from their trip through New England, I'll ask him if he's serious about renting."

"Yeah, and I'll bet you won't think it's too creepy then."

"Well, no. Not if I'm living here."

"I don't see the difference, but okay." He stood at the top of the steps. "Seen enough?"

Cass nodded and started downstairs. "Enough to know I'd like to make this my interim home while I'm waiting for my own house to be built."

"That means you're staying."

"Yes. I'm staying." She paused on her way down the steps. "You?"

"I'm seriously considering it."

FOR THE FIRST time in a long time, Owen *was* in fact considering staying on the island. When he'd made the decision to return, he'd thought it would be for a few months while he worked with Jared. He'd told himself that would give him time to spend with Ruby, and time enough to figure out what had been whispering in his ear, insisting it was time to go home. Now he was starting to believe that whatever in the universe decided such things had been pulling him back to Cass. Even though they'd never met, even though he never believed in fate, somehow he knew that he was meant to be here, meant to meet her, to be with her. Meant to fall in love with her.

It hadn't taken much, and it hadn't taken long.

They began spending their nights in her room at the inn, and their days on or near the island—Owen diving with Jared, Cass working with the crews. Before the end of the week following Lis's wedding, Lee Stafford, Deiter's engineer, had the area for the new dock surveyed and had requested that a permit be rushed through, citing hardship and Deiter's willingness to suspend work on the river side of the island. Deiter's lawyers spelled out to the lawyers for the state that the construction company could have sued for access to the island via the dock, since the permits had been approved and not officially revoked. In consideration of Deiter's understanding of the state's situation, the state should offer the same courtesy to Deiter Construction. In the end, the new permits were issued, and it had cost less than three weeks' delay.

For Owen, life was as good as it could possibly be. He had work that he loved during the day, and the woman he'd fallen in love with at night. While he'd never thought he'd settle down for real, he found himself thinking about it at odd times.

He maintained his previous routine of cooking dinner at the store for Ruby, with Cass joining them most nights. When Lis and Alec returned from their honeymoon trip through the New England states, they popped in several times every week. Life began to take on a different look and feel, one Owen found suited him more than his wandering ever had. It was difficult for him to admit, even to himself, but he was pretty sure his adventuring days were behind him.

"I'm ready for an adventure of a different kind," he told Cass one night after they'd finished dinner and they sat together in a rocking chair on the back porch at Ruby's and watched the stars come out.

"Where do you think you'll go?" He caught the hesitation in her voice and realized she thought he'd be leaving.

"I'm not going anywhere. I'm staying here. Here, or wherever you are."

"I probably won't be swimming with sharks in the Indian Ocean." Her fingers wound around the dark curls that fell slightly forward onto his forehead. "Or flying small planes across the Gobi Desert. Or searching for yeti in the Himalayas."

"Been there, done all that." He pretended to yawn. "Ho hum. Like I said, an adventure of a different kind."

Later that night, when Cass lay spent and sleepy in his arms in her room at the inn, he lay awake thinking about the choices he was making.

"You'll miss the challenges."

"I thought you were asleep."

"You're thinking so loudly, it's keeping me awake." She turned in his arms and looked up at him. "You're thinking about that job Jared told you about. The one off the coast of Louisiana."

"I thought about it, yes. Jared's so hot to trot to get there. He's like a kid, you know? He has this job here, but suddenly something else looks newer, shinier. Sexier. So he can't wait to get to it."

"So what's he going to do?"

"He's going to go, and I'm going to stay and finish up what we started here. It's going to take a while to get everything sorted out. We're still bringing up artifacts from the merchant ship, but we have to be careful not to disturb the remnants of what could be an early settlement that lies beneath it. It's painstaking work, but it's interesting. To me, anyway. To Jared, not so much. I think he has serious commitment issues."

"Pot, meet kettle."

"What's that supposed to me?"

"What do you think it means?"

He knew exactly what she meant. He hated to put words to it, but she had asked and he should answer. "I admit that for the past few years I have done some moving around. I'm starting to feel like maybe that's overrated."

"So you're taking over Jared's job here, but after you've done all you can do here, then what?"

"I've been mulling that over. I can hire myself out as a consultant. I'm a good diver and I've had years of experience salvaging sensitive wrecks. That could take me away for a few days, maybe a week here and there, but I'd be back on the island. I can make my home here."

"That's a big change for you, Owen. You sure you're ready for it?"

"I never thought I would be, but yeah, I am. I just want to be wherever you are." He sat up and leaned against the headboard. Cass leaned against him. "Ruby always says you have to know where you belong. She always said I belonged on the island. I never thought I did until now." His fingers trailed gently on Cass's arm. "You know, there's a line between want and need. When we first got together, I wanted you. I was dizzy wanting you. Somehow over the past three weeks, I crossed that line. Wants turned into need. I need to be with you more than I want anything else." He rested his chin on the top of her head. "What about you?"

"You know I'm staying, I'm building a house."

"That's not what I'm asking you."

For a long moment, Owen thought she wasn't going to respond, and his heart dropped. He'd never put himself out there like this, and he was starting to remember why. He began to feel like the guy who saw the train coming but was too afraid to jump out of the way.

"What do you want, Cassie? What do you need?"

"I married someone who thought he could stay in one place, but when push came to shove, he couldn't do it. It hurt a great deal to face the fact that I wasn't enough for him."

"I'm not your ex-husband."

"True, but . . ." She went silent for a moment. "Did you ever ask yourself why you stayed away for long periods at a time, when you so obviously love this island and your family so much?"

"I've wondered about it."

"Ever do more than wonder?"

"Maybe."

"One might think you were running from something."

"Maybe."

"Want to talk about it?"

"I'm still thinking that through. Can we get back to that?"

"Sure." She sighed, and Owen heard resignation and maybe disappointment. If he was ever going to face himself, it should be now, while it mattered to her. It was time to put up or shut up.

He took a deep breath. "I think I was afraid that I'd turn into my father," Owen said softly.

"What?" She sat up so she could look him in the eye. "You're nothing like your father." He opened his mouth to say something, and she cut him off. "By your own admission, your father was a bitter man who drank rather than face his own shortcomings. He relied on his son to take care of his daughter because he couldn't be bothered. He hurt you and he hurt Lis and he probably hurt your mother most of all. Owen, you don't have a mean bone in your body. You'll never be like him."

Her unexpected defense of him caught him off guard and embarrassed him, and he tried to make light of it. "Wow. I sound like quite a guy."

"You are quite a guy. You're my guy. You'd

never turn your back on anyone you love, certainly not your wife or your kids. You're not a bitter person, and you don't drink yourself into a pity party." She paused as if watching her words sink in. "You're nothing like your father."

He pulled her to him so that she was resting against his chest. "So I'm your guy, eh?"

Cass smiled and raised up to kiss him. "Yes. You're my guy."

It wasn't quite everything he'd wanted to hear. It wasn't *I need you* or *I love you*. Or even *I want you*. But for now, he'd take it.

"I HOPE YOU'LL still make it back for afternoon tea, Cass." Grace had walked Cass and Owen from the bottom of the lobby steps to the double doors.

"Of course." Cass shifted the garment bag holding her clothes from one hand to the other. "You know how I love spending that hour every day with you and whoever else shows up."

"See you, Gracie. Cass, I'll meet you at the house," Owen said as he passed by, carrying her laptop and a briefcase full of files. He loaded everything into the backseat of his Jeep.

When Cass was ready to move from the inn to the house on Lincoln Road, she realized her sports car could carry only her clothes and personal items. There wasn't room for anything she'd used to set up a temporary office in her suite at the inn, and rather than her making a second trip, Owen had offered to move those items for her.

Alec had been delighted when Owen mentioned

that Cass was interested in renting the house. Aside from the rent—which Cass discovered was so much less each month than the suite at the inn—he was happy to have someone living in the house where he'd been taken in and raised after his parents died. He was especially pleased it was Cass, who had clearly become close to Lis's brother. Even though Alec'd been hoping for a long-term lease agreement, he was okay with Cass's having a month-to-month arrangement until her house was ready to move into. And who knew how long that might be? The construction hadn't even begun and probably wouldn't for a while.

Owen didn't care which house she was sleeping in, as long as he was sleeping there with her. He'd been reluctant to leave Ruby alone, though she'd reminded him that she'd been alone in the store for years.

"Don't recall anyone being excited over the fact I be alone back then," Ruby told him. "You go on and take care of your own business. I be fine."

Not until his cousin Chrissie mentioned that she'd decided to remain on the island for a while and that Ruby had offered her Lis's old room could Owen sleep in St. Dennis with a clear conscience.

"Not that Chrissie'd be any great help in a crisis," he'd complained to Cass. "She always was flighty and a little silly. She'll probably drive Gigi insane after about three days. I don't know anyone who could take more than that when it comes to Chrissie."

"She seemed perfectly normal at the wedding," Cass reminded him.

"She was on her best behavior."

"Well, it's nice that she's getting to have some time with Ruby. Did she say how long she's staying?"

"She said she wasn't sure. It's like good news, bad news. The good news is that someone's staying with Ruby so she won't be alone in the store at night. The bad news is that the *someone* is Chrissie."

"I'm sure she'll be fine, and if she gets to be too much of a pain, Ruby won't have a problem telling her to leave."

"You're right about that. I did say something to Ruby the other day, and she said something like 'The girl needs to be here. Go mind your own.' Which is pretty funny when you think about it because of all the great-grandkids, Lis and I always thought Gigi liked Chrissie the least."

"Maybe we should ask her if she'd like to go to the fall festival with us today."

"If she's anything like the old Chrissie, she'll talk us both to death. Let's leave well enough alone, okay?"

"She seemed pretty quiet at the wedding, but okay. I'm ready to go whenever you are."

"I just need to run upstairs and get my wallet. I left it on the table next to the bed."

While Owen went to get his wallet, Cass rinsed her coffee cup and set it in the dish drainer. The house had no dishwasher, but she didn't care, since it was just the two of them. They'd never spoken about a division of duties, but she figured if he cooked, she should clean up afterward, and there was something relaxing, almost enjoyable, about washing their few dishes in a sink full of soapy water while Owen drank a second cup of coffee and they continued whatever conversation they'd had over dinner.

The kitchen was definitely old-fashioned, with red Formica counters that had faded over the years and one light fixture in the center of the ceiling. The floor was an old black-and-white checkerboard pattern that was scuffed and worn, and the cabinets were painted the same dull shade of green as the walls. If she owned the place, she'd have done a job on this house beginning with the kitchen. But Alec had been content living with it the way it was, and it didn't seem to bother Owen. Cass couldn't help but think about at least painting the walls and the cabinets, and maybe even springing for new counters just because it would make her happy. She'd done what she could to brighten the room by taking down the curtain on the only window to let in more light—she was thinking about replacing it with a pull shade—and placing little pots of blue asters on the sill. A pretty painted vase she'd found in one of the cupboards held the dahlias she'd bought at Petals and Posies, the flower shop in St. Dennis, but she could do little else to make the kitchen seem more homey.

Still, it felt more like home than her condo in Baltimore ever had. She heard Owen's footfalls on the stairs, and she smiled. His presence in her life made this house feel like home. She was grateful every day she'd given him a chance to prove that he was so much more than the man she'd initially thought him to be.

"Ready, babe? Want to walk into town?" He appeared in the kitchen doorway and looked so adorable, so irresistible, that she had to kiss him.

"You look so sexy in plaid flannel." She kissed him again.

"So you go for that rugged he-man look, right?" He wrapped his arms around her.

Cass nodded. "Flannel shirts and cords. You could pass as a lumberjack."

"I actually worked for a lumber company in Oregon for a few months."

"Do tell." Cass grabbed her bag off the back of the kitchen chair and took his hand, tugging him to the front door.

"Good to know I still look the part."

"It's that almost-beard look you're sporting these days."

He locked the door behind them, and they went down the porch steps hand in hand. Cass had picked up some pumpkins at the Madison farm the day before and lined the steps, saving the largest to place next to the planter Lis had left next to the front door. The house needed a paint job and could use a few chairs on the porch, but the little bit of décor gave it life.

It seemed pumpkins, mums, tall cornstalks, and bales of hay in one configuration or another were on the front porch of just about every house they passed on their way to Charles Street. Trees had begun dropping their leaves, so the sidewalk was dotted here and there with yellow, orange, and green. None had yet dried, so there was no crunch beneath their feet, but Cass knew that in a few more weeks, there would be. She looked forward to it. Autumn always energized her.

Their walk took them down Hudson Street, past Cassidy House, with its wide front porch and pillars. On the front lawn was a FOR SALE sign that Cass hadn't noticed before. "Looks like the owners are moving. Any interest?"

"Are you crazy? That's the last house in the world I'd want to buy. When I was a kid, I had a friend who lived in that house, and I got to play there a few times after school until my father had to come pick me up one day because my mother was at work. When he realized where my friend lived, he went off like . . . man, it was ugly. It was the only time in my life that I honestly thought he was going to kill me." It seemed to Cass that Owen walked just a little faster as he spoke. "No, thank you. Any place but there."

They walked in silence to the center of town, where all the shops were dressed for fall and had special sales. A clown was painting kids' faces in front of Cupcake, the local bakery, and another was making balloon animals on the corner of Cherry and Charles Streets near the light. Later there'd be a band down by the marina and a pumpkin roll in the municipal parking lot near the police station, where Gabriel Beck, the chief of police, handed out toy police badges and bottles of water to kids who stopped by to meet the dogs rescued by Grant Wyler, the local vet. Grant ran a shelter and brought with him a selection of pups available for adoption. Grant's wife, Dallas MacGregor, had a film crew there to capture the moments when each prospective puppy parent found his or her new companion. The crowds were just gathering when Cass and Owen stopped to look at the dogs, who were on leashes held by the shelter's volunteers.

"Do we need a dog?" Owen asked when Cass knelt down to pet a sweet little dachshund wearing a pink rhinestone collar.

"Maybe. I wonder if Alec would mind if we brought one home." Cass heard *we* where once she'd heard *you* or *I* and knew in her heart she was exactly where she was meant to be.

"Mommy! Puppy!" A little boy broke free from the hand that had held his and raced to the pen of mixed-breed puppies where several volunteers stood by to show off the litter that had been born six weeks earlier at the shelter. "Puppy." The boy pointed a chubby finger at the pen.

"Yes, J.J. Those are puppies."

From the corner of her eye, Cass saw Cyndi pick up the child, who squirmed in her arms, fighting to get down.

His face had been painted in orange and white to look like a jack-o'-lantern, and some orange paint was stuck in his dark curls. He'd smeared something on the front of his tan corduroy overalls, and in his hands he held what remained of a Popsicle. He held the stick out toward the puppy pen as if wanting to share.

Cass held her breath.

"Oh. Owen." Cyndi turned absolutely white when she saw him. "Hi."

"Hey, Cyndi. I heard you were in the area. Nice time of the year to visit." Owen sounded perfectly cordial, perfectly okay that he'd unexpectedly run into his ex-wife in the midst of puppy mania. "How've you been? Who's this little guy? One of Sandie's boys?"

"Oh, man, this is awkward," someone said from behind them.

Owen turned to see Cyndi's sister, Sandie, with a child in a stroller. "What's awkward?"

Cyndi and her sister exchanged a long look. Finally, Sandie walked away. "I'm not sticking around for this, Cyndi. You're on your own. I'm outta here."

Owen turned back to his ex. "What's her problem?"

"Not her problem, Owen. Mine." Cyndi turned the boy around so that Owen could see his face.

Green eyes looked into green eyes, and it was Owen's turn to pale.

"What the hell . . . ?" he whispered.

Cyndi sighed. "We need to talk."

Owen stood stock-still as if suddenly paralyzed. He opened his mouth to speak, but no words came out. The depth of confusion on his face broke Cass's heart. They both knew who they were looking at, but Owen had been completely blindsided.

"Is that . . . ?" He swallowed hard. "Is he . . . ?"

Owen couldn't say the words, so Cyndi spoke them for him. "Yes. He is." She hadn't needed to say more than that.

Cass watched Owen's expression build from confusion to quiet rage. "You owe me an explanation." He grabbed his ex by the upper arm. "And you're going to give it to me now. Right. Now."

"Owen, this isn't the place . . ." Cass heard Cyndi whisper.

"You don't get to choose now. We could have had this conversation—*should* have had this conversation—a few years ago by the looks of things, but you chose not to, God only knows why. So now you don't get to choose."

"Lower your voice. You're going to scare him." Cyndi put a hand protectively over her son's head.

"We will discuss this calmly, but we're going to discuss it now."

"This isn't the place." Tears were in Cyndi's eyes and her voice was shaking.

"You're right." Owen appeared to think for a moment. "We're going to the island. To Ruby's."

"No. Not there. She hates me," Cyndi whispered.

"Tough. Come on. Let's go." He took her arm.

"Let me at least hand him over to my sister. . . ."

"No. He comes with us." Owen's face was stony and his voice harder than Cass could ever recall having heard it. "Did you drive?"

Cyndi nodded.

"Good. Let's go."

Owen started to steer his ex toward the parking lot. He'd taken ten steps away before he stopped and turned around to look at Cass in pure devastation, as if he'd just remembered she was there. He seemed to be trying to think of something to say.

She shook her head. "Go."

Cass stood where the unthinkable had begun to

unfold and watched the man and the woman and the child snake between the cars in the crowded parking lot. When the dark SUV passed by, Cyndi behind the wheel, Owen in the front passenger seat, he didn't even glance over to where he'd left Cass.

It was as if she didn't exist.

She stood in the hot October sun, anxiety causing her heart to pound unmercifully, until she realized he wasn't coming back anytime soon.

With tears in her eyes, Cass turned and walked back to the house on Lincoln Road alone.

Chapter Thirteen

It was almost dinnertime when Owen came through the front door of the house he and Cass shared. He went into the kitchen, still looking as shell-shocked as he had when he first looked into the eyes of the child who was so clearly his.

Cass was leaning against the counter when he came into the room and waited for him to say something. He merely looked at her and shook his head as he dropped into a chair. His eyes were rimmed with red, and he'd clearly been crying. She wanted to ask, but knew she had to wait until he could say whatever he was going to say.

She had never been so frightened in her life.

Finally he said, "I have a son, Cassie."

"I figured that out."

"I'm sorry I just left you. . . ." His voice was slow, hesitant, as if he'd used so much of it that afternoon there was little left.

"It's okay. I understand." *I understand, but I hate this and what it's doing to you.*

And what, she couldn't bring herself to ask, was this going to mean for them?

"I swear I didn't know, Cass. She didn't tell me. I swear. I wouldn't have lied to you."

"I know. It never occurred to me that you had." She pulled the other chair next to his and sat and took his hands. They were cold as ice despite the warmth of the room.

He sat and stared at her with empty eyes. "She wasn't going to tell me, can you imagine that? She never wanted to tell me."

"So why did she? I mean, obviously she should have, but why now?"

"Because she's engaged, and her fiancé won't marry her until she comes clean to me. He said it wasn't right that I didn't know." The only emotion in Owen's voice was disgust. "Can you get your head around that? If this guy hadn't had a stronger moral sense than she has, I still wouldn't know that I have a son."

"Why didn't she tell you back then? I don't understand. Why did she keep it from you all this time?"

Owen blew out a long breath. "Remember I told you we'd separated? And then I was back for a week or two and we tried again, but it was clear it wasn't going to work out?"

"I remember."

"Well, during that time—over those two weeks— we had sex more than once. She'd gone off the pill because we hadn't been together." He smacked his hands together. "Boom."

"So why didn't she tell you? I still don't under-stand."

"Frankly, neither do I." His hands were begin-ning to warm between hers, and his thumb rubbed her wrist as if to comfort both of them. "She said at first she was really pissed off at me."

"Because she was pregnant? Two to tango, right?"

"Right. But I'd left and gone back to Alaska. Then she said she didn't know where I was, though her lawyer didn't have a problem finding me to have me served with the divorce papers. She knew where to find Ruby. She could have found me if she'd wanted to."

"I heard her say Ruby hated her."

"With good reason. Ruby never wanted me to marry her, tried to talk me out of it."

"She could have written to you, she could have—"

"The bottom line? She didn't really want me to know. She wanted to hurt me."

"She wanted to hurt you, so she didn't tell you about the baby?"

He nodded slowly. "Is that the most messed-up, ass-backward, stupid thing you ever heard? 'I want to hurt you, so I'm never going to let you know you have a son'?" Owen shook his head. "What kind of a person does that?"

"So she wasn't ever going to tell you . . . ?"

"She says as time went on she realized how wrong she was, but at that point she didn't know how to make it right. The more time that passed, the older J.J. got—James Joseph, she named him. James Joseph Parker." Owen paused and swallowed hard. "Anyway, she said she kept thinking about it and knew she should tell me, but she didn't have the nerve, had less and less nerve the older he got. Everyone in her family had urged her to come clean, but she'd made them swear not to tell me. Said she kept saying she was going to do it. Well, finally, this guy she's in love with forced her hand." Another pause. "He must be a good guy because he wouldn't put a ring on her finger until she told me. Said he wouldn't feel right about raising someone else's son the way things were."

"Sounds like a nice guy who isn't above a bit of emotional blackmail." It was Cass's turn to pause. "You think he's just that good a guy, or do you think he wants to make sure you're in it for the child support?"

"Maybe a little of both, but the way she told it, I think he really was appalled that she'd kept this little secret to herself for the past eighteen months." Owen looked up at Cass, his lips twitching slightly. "That's how old he is. He's eighteen months old and I never even knew about him. He doesn't know me, Cass. It's like he hasn't had a father all this time. Well, except for her boyfriend, that is."

"Well, if it's any consolation, children that age don't know better. He doesn't know that he didn't have a—"

"But I know that I wasn't there for him, whether or not he realizes it yet. I know. And no, it's no consolation at all. I don't know how I kept from doing her bodily harm. I'm so angry I'm seeing stars. Keeping that in check for J.J.'s sake is killing me."

Owen got up and poured a glass of water, drank it, and left the glass on the counter. "I'm going to take a shower, and then I'm meeting Cyndi to talk about where we go from here."

Didn't you discuss that at all? she wanted to ask. *You were with her all afternoon. Surely you would have talked about custody?*

Or was he talking about something else. *Where we go from here* could mean a lot of things.

CASS STAYED UP past two, waiting for Owen, but when it became clear he wouldn't be back anytime soon, she curled up on the sofa under a throw and fell asleep. The dreams she had were torture, and when she awoke and found Monday to be dark and rainy at 6:00 a.m., she dragged herself upstairs and got into bed. It was another hour before she fell back to sleep, the fear growing inside her.

Maybe they've found each other again. Maybe they've discovered they still care, maybe they're talking about giving it another try. They have a son together. Maybe they're thinking they should try to be a family.

She woke up with tears still in her eyes, aware that Owen was tiptoeing around the room.

"When did you get back?" she asked quietly.

"A few minutes ago." He'd opened the dresser drawer where he'd been keeping some of his things and took out some clothes, though she couldn't tell what.

"I'm sorry." He didn't turn around. "I should have called you."

Where did you stay last night? she wanted to ask. *What's going on?*

As if he'd heard her or read her mind, he sat on the edge of the bed. "I stayed at Ruby's last night, in my old room. I was so exhausted from all this craziness, I was too tired to walk back here."

"Cyndi had her car, right? She could have dropped you off."

"I didn't think to ask her."

Or maybe he didn't want his ex to know he's practically living with you, that vicious little inner voice poked at her.

"Did you get to spend any time with . . . with your son?"

"A little. Cyndi called one of her brothers to come pick him up and take him back to their parents."

"Did you resolve anything?"

"Not really. I'm having a hard time with this, Cass."

"Of course you are. Anyone would." She sat up and put her arms around him, and he leaned against her. Cass stroked the side of his face, and he seemed to morph back into the man she knew.

"Why don't you get into bed? How much sleep did you get last night?"

"None."

She moved over to make room for him, but he shook his head.

"I'm going to meet Cyndi and J.J. for breakfast.

She thought it would be a good thing if he started to see me more. You know, so he could get used to me."

"Oh. Sure. I guess he's going to have to get to know you."

Owen leaned over and kissed the side of her face. "I'll see you later."

He went into the bathroom across the hall, and she heard the shower turn on. Cass got up and went downstairs, still in the clothes she'd worn the day before, and made coffee. It was going to be a very long day.

Monday led into an even longer Tuesday. It seemed that after almost two years of avoiding Owen, Cyndi couldn't spend enough time with him. Late that night, when he crawled into bed, he'd had little to say, and Cass hadn't pushed him because she hadn't been sure how. She was trying to be understanding, trying to feel what he felt after learning he'd had a child who'd been deliberately kept from him. She wished he'd talk to her about it, but his thoughts, his emotions, seemed tied up inside him.

On Wednesday morning, Owen was already in the shower when Cass awoke. She tossed on a short robe and went downstairs to make coffee. When he finally came into the kitchen, she handed him a mug of coffee fixed just the way he liked it.

"Thank you." He pulled a chair away from the table and sat for a moment. He looked tired and worn-out. Even his tan seemed to have faded.

"You okay?" she asked.

He shook his head. "Cassie, I'm sorry. I know I should talk this out but I don't know how I feel about any of this. I'm so out of my element. I don't know how to be a father. I don't know if I'm ready to take on this child—hell, I don't even know this little guy, but he's mine. I know I'm supposed to feel a certain way, but I don't know how." He ran a hand through his hair, wet strands falling onto his forehead.

Cass filled a mug for herself and sat across from him at the table, and let him talk.

"I've been pretty much on my own since I was eighteen and I left for college. I'm not used to having anyone depend on me. I've never had to be responsible for anyone but myself."

"You took care of Lis when she was little," Cass reminded him. "When your mom was at work and your father didn't bother. You made dinner for her and you read to her at night."

"That was different. I'd known Lis my whole life. We were really close back then. I knew what she liked to eat and what books she liked to read. I know absolutely nothing about my son. I don't have that emotional connection to him yet. What if I never do?"

"You must have learned something about him since you've been with him and Cyndi for the past couple of days." She tried to keep an accusatory edge from her voice, but she wasn't sure she'd succeeded.

"I'm sorry." He reached out for her hand. "I should have called or texted. I just lost track of time, I guess."

"Are you sure it was only time you lost track of?"

"If you mean us . . . no, I'm sure of us. I'm just not sure of anything else right now." His fingers locked with hers. "He's a cute little guy, isn't he?"

"Adorable. He looks so much like you. I look at him and I see what you must have looked like at that age." *I see the son I thought we'd have together one day.*

"Gigi said he looks a lot like me. And I'll give Cyndi credit. He doesn't whine or act up much. I mean, he doesn't seem bratty or anything. I just wish I knew . . ."

"Knew what?"

"Knew what to do about him. How do you learn how to be a father in a couple of days? He and I, we're total strangers. I don't even know how to talk to him. It's like he and Cyndi have their own language and I don't understand most of it."

"You'll catch on."

"When will I do that? She's going to take him back to Connecticut. How am I even supposed to get to know him? I swear, I'm wearing myself out from walking on eggshells around her. Like if I say the wrong thing, she's going to scoop him up and disappear with him and then whatever chance I might have had to try to be his dad will have disappeared."

"Do you want to ask for partial custody?"

"She'll never let me take him away, even for a weekend."

"That's not really her decision, is it? I mean, if you sue for custody and it goes before a judge, he gets to decide. I would think, under the circumstances, after you explain that J.J.'s very existence was deliberately kept from you, a judge might tend to lean toward you when it came to custody. What do you want, Owen? Deep down inside, what do you want?"

He was quiet for a very long moment.

"I want to know my son. I want to have a place in his life. I want him to know that I'm his father. I want to have a role in who he grows up to be."

"Then that's what you need to work out with Cyndi. And if I could make one suggestion? I'd tell her to get this guy she's marrying down here so you can check him out yourself. If he's going to be with your son on a day-to-day basis, you need to know firsthand what kind of a man he is. And the three of you are going to have to work out a custody agreement and make it legal."

Owen nodded slowly. "I should call Jesse Enright and talk to him. He's a lawyer in town."

"Sophie's brother. Yes, I've met him. That's a good start."

"I guess working out the custody thing is the right thing to do. But what if J.J. doesn't like me, doesn't want to be with me?" He rubbed a hand over his face. "And what if I'm no good at being a father? What if I never learn how? I am so confused right now, Cassie."

"Maybe you should stay at the store with Gigi until you figure things out." She hated to say the words but she could sense he needed some space.

He blew out a long breath, and Cass could tell he was conflicted.

"Maybe you're right. Maybe what I need is time to myself to think things through."

Cass could hear the reluctance in his voice, but they both knew she was right. She disengaged her hand slowly. "You left a few things in the dryer the other day. I'll get them for you. . . ."

CASS WAS ON-SITE at the island with the crews as they cleaned up one lot after another and the dock construction began. She couldn't help but wonder what Ruby thought of all this. On Thursday afternoon, Cass headed toward the store.

"Hi." Cass waved a greeting to Ruby, who sat at the table near the window.

"Hello, Cass." Ruby nodded but didn't lift her head from whatever she was reading. "Haven't seen you these past few days."

"I've been busy. You know, all the stuff going on here on the island. What do you think of the progress we're making?" Cass tried to sound casual, referring to the construction that had begun.

"I know all about what's going on here, and I know what I be thinking." Ruby turned to Cass. "What you be thinking?"

"I don't know." Cass felt the tears begin to flow down her cheeks. "I don't know what's going to happen, Ruby."

"Now, you come right on over here, girl, and you sit with me. . . . That's right, pull that chair closer."

"I don't know what I'm supposed to do."

"Do? Not for you to be doing. That be someone

else's burden." Ruby reached for Cass's hands and patted them as if to comfort her. "Choices be made, but not by you. Wait and see what those choices be."

"I'm not a very patient person, Ruby."

"Then maybe one of those choices be yours after all." Ruby patted Cass's hands again. "You just be you, Cass. That be all you can do. Just be Cass."

"I'm afraid, Ruby. What if that's not enough?"

"Fear be for the weak. And if you not be enough, then you be in the wrong place. Girls not as smart as you know that much. Uh-uh." Ruby stood and folded the newspaper she'd been reading. "If you not be enough, that be on that fool boy of mine, not on you." Ruby walked toward the counter shaking her head and muttering something under her breath.

Cass followed Ruby and got a bottle of water from the cooler. When she went to pay for it, Ruby waved her off. "No charge for family."

Cass's eyes filled with tears again. She had felt like part of this family, had wanted to be part of what held them all together, Ruby, Owen, Lis, and Alec. She'd started to feel as if she belonged here. Now she wasn't sure where she belonged.

"Thanks, Ruby. I'm going to head back to work."

"Your people be taking apart the old Collier house today. 'Bout time. That place been tilted on the foundation for the longest time. You think you be saving anything there?"

Cass nodded and brushed away her tears with the back of her hand. "There's some decent wood on the floors in the back of the house. The floors in the front are all water stained and soggy, I can't reuse them. The brickwork is good—I'll use that for the back patio. There's a piece of one of the door surrounds where someone marked off the height of a child as he or she grew. I'm going to try to save that, try to find a use for it. It's such a personal thing to that house."

"Alfie Collier. Only child that family had. Died when he was eleven or twelve." Ruby nodded slowly. "Had the leukemia. They took him all the way to Baltimore for the doctors there, but it didn't help. Didn't seem right for a child to suffer so and then die anyway."

"No, it doesn't." Cass turned to go.

"You have a good heart, Cassidy Logan. A good heart and true."

"Thank you." Cass watched Ruby's face, unable to read what she saw in the old woman's expression. "You know, don't you." It wasn't a question but a statement of fact. "You know what he's going to do."

"Can't say either way. Just have to wait and see."

CASS HADN'T BEEN kidding when she told Ruby she wasn't patient. By the end of the week, she was worn-out from worry and speculation. It was almost as if the time she and Owen had spent together before Cyndi came back into his life had been a dream.

And there was no question Cyndi was back in his life. Owen might have needed some space, but Cyndi was certainly occupying more than her share of it. So Cass was surprised when, on Saturday morning, he called her cell. "Would you come over to the island today?"

"Sure," she managed to say. "What's up?"

"I want you to meet J.J."

"I'd love to meet J.J. How are you getting along with him?"

"It's slow going. I've actually been spending these past two days working. Jared left me with his ship and two divers and a contract with the Maryland Historical Society that needs to be honored." He paused. "I'm sorry. I should have been in touch more."

"It's okay." She hadn't wanted to hear him say he was sorry. She'd wanted to hear him say, *I still want you. I love you. I choose you.*

"It's really not okay. I don't want you to think this changes things between us, Cass. But this is my mess and I have to find a way to make things right for everyone."

Cyndi created this situation when she decided not to tell you that you had a son. Why is it on you to clean it up? It's her mess.

Aloud, Cass said, "You will. You'll do what's best."

"I'm trying. Look, her fiancé is driving down from Connecticut today. He and Cyndi and J.J. will be at Ruby's by around noon. I'd really like you to be there, too."

"Okay. I'll see you there."

Cass disconnected the call, and for the first time in a week, she felt that maybe—just maybe—things could work out after all.

CASS PARKED HER car on the point and stopped at the cottage to give Alec an envelope containing her rent payment.

"Boy, what a mess," Lis complained when Cass walked into the cheery kitchen.

"Actually much less of a mess than the first time I saw this place. It's actually quite charming now."

"I wasn't talking about the house." Lis had been drying off a glass, which she then put into a cupboard.

"I know." Cass sighed. "I'm just trying to find a little levity where I can these days."

"I hear you. Honestly, I could smack that girl. I can't understand why Owen is being so nice to her." Lis dried another glass and put it away, her back to Cass. "Well, except for the fact that she has his son right now and she could make things tough for him if she thought he was pulling attitude with her."

"I guess there's that. They've been spending an awful lot of time together this week. I guess they're getting reacquainted."

Lis spun around to face Cass. "Do not go there. He'd be an absolute idiot to even think about getting back with her."

"Lis, they have a son together."

"No, they *made* a son together. *She's* had their son." Lis's anger flashed. "The son she kept my brother from knowing about. There's no *together* there." Lis slapped the counter with her dish towel. "I cannot forgive her for what she's doing to him. And you know, if it weren't for this fiancé of hers— who apparently has shown more heart and better sense than she has—Owen still wouldn't know about J.J."

Lis folded the towel and slid it onto a rack. "Have you seen him yet? J.J.?"

Cass nodded and told Lis about the first encounter with Cyndi in Bling.

"Holy crap, are you serious?"

"I had this feeling—the day after your wedding, Owen and I were in Cuppachino and she was in there—and I swear, I just knew. I told him about seeing the little boy and he was adamant that it must have been one of her sister's kids."

"She was bad for him back then, and she's even worse for him now. I told him to get a lawyer involved immediately. I don't know what she's up to. I don't know what she wants from him at this point, and what she's willing to give. I'm so angry I could spit." Lis growled. "I hate her for this. I used to think she was okay before, but now I hate her for what she is doing to my brother."

"Her fiancé is coming today, so maybe he'll help to get things resolved. At least maybe he can help work out some sort of custody agreement. I would think she'd need his input since she's going to marry him and he'll be J.J.'s stepfather."

Cass took the rent envelope from her bag and handed it to Lis to give to Alec. "I guess we'll see."

"You're liking the house?" Lis asked as she walked Cass to the door.

"I am. I love the house." She forced a smile. *At least I did when Owen and I were sharing it. Now . . . not as much.*

Cass headed to Ruby's, her heart in her mouth. She didn't have a good feeling about what was going to unfold, but she knew she had to put one foot in front of the other and see it through.

Cyndi and her fiancé had already arrived at the store and were sitting on the back porch with Owen when Cass drove up. J.J. sat on the floor between his mother and soon-to-be stepfather. When Cass joined them, Owen rose to kiss her cheek and offered her his chair, which she declined. Before he could begin to make introductions, Cyndi extended her hand to Cass.

"Owen's told me so much about you." Cyndi's smile appeared fixed, and Cass couldn't tell how sincere it really was.

"Likewise." Cass turned to the man on Cyndi's left. "You must be . . ."

"Kevin. Kevin Cook." He stood and shook Cass's hand. He was a nice-looking man in his early forties who was the same height as Cyndi.

"Cass Logan," Cass returned the greeting, then turned to Owen. "So what's on the agenda?"

"There's no agenda. We—that is, Cyndi and I—thought we should all get to know each other."

Cass sat on the top step, where she could observe the child, who played with two little cars and who had no idea that he was the heart of all the drama that had been going on around him for the past week.

Every once in a while J.J. looked up at his mother, or at Kevin, but not at Owen and certainly not at Cass. The situation was so awkward, Cass began to feel uncomfortable. She tried to engage Owen's son, but he totally ignored her. He'd obviously deemed her unimportant in his world.

Kevin and Owen were making small talk about the island and fishing and water-skiing. Cyndi tried to make conversation with Cass, but everything Cyndi said sounded to Cass like a challenge.

Finally J.J. got up and took himself down the steps and into Ruby's garden. Cyndi watched as he went from flower to flower, announcing each time, "Flower," which earned him the praise of his mother.

"Good, J.J. That's right. Flower." Cyndi beamed at his obvious brilliance.

"Bee," J.J. announced. "Bee." Then he screamed.

Cyndi and Owen were off the porch in a flash. Owen got to him first and picked him up. J.J. sobbed and reached for his mother, holding out his finger; he'd apparently gotten too close to the bee. They carried him, still sobbing, into the store, where Ruby could fix him up with one of her miracle salves.

Kevin and Cass chatted until Owen and Cyndi returned with J.J., who had stopped crying and held a Popsicle in both hands.

"I see he's been in Ruby's cooler," Cass said.

Owen nodded. "Nothing like an ice pop to make things all right with the world."

If only it were that easy, Cass thought.

J.J. toddled off onto the dune with his mother trailing behind. A minute later, she called to Owen to come identify a bug they'd found.

Owen sat on the sand and pointed to something on the ground, and J.J. leaned over to see, then sat next to his father, who held J.J.'s rapt attention. Soon Cyndi sat, too, and the three of them continued to look at whatever J.J. had found. Cass and Kevin sat on the porch watching the scene on the dune play out, and Cass wondered if Kevin felt as much like an outsider as she did. To Cass's eye, the three sitting together—talking and laughing together—appeared to be the perfect family. The image burned itself into her brain.

Finally, she could no longer deny the obvious. She wasn't blind.

Cass stood and turned to Kevin. "It was nice to meet you."

She picked up her bag where she'd dropped it on the porch and walked to her car. She knew she should have said good-bye to Owen, but she just couldn't bring herself to intrude on that perfect little family of three. She drove back to Lincoln Road, packed her bags, locked the door behind her, and headed to Baltimore.

CASS SAT IN front of her parents' home for several minutes trying to collect her thoughts. She tilted the rearview mirror and peered at her tired face, then searched her bag for the little jar of concealer she always had with her. She couldn't erase the dark circles completely, but maybe she could mask them just a little. She grabbed the suitcase she'd packed and the tote holding her laptop and swung her bag onto her shoulder. Straightening her back, she followed the cobbled walk to the big front door and knocked before she opened it. At that moment, she needed nothing more than a hug from her mother.

"Mom?" Cass called from the hall.

Her mother appeared in the living room doorway. "Cassie, I didn't know you were coming home today. Did you tell your father and he forgot to give me the message?"

"No, I just . . . I just . . ." Cass dropped her belongings and walked into her mother's arms. "I just wanted to come home." She burst into tears.

"Oh, sweetheart. What is it?" Linda embraced her daughter.

"Owen . . . Owen has a son and his ex-wife is back in the picture and they look so right together and they should probably get back together but I love him and I thought he loved me but now he's going to go back to her so they can be a family and—"

"Whoa! Stop! Come in here and sit down and start from the beginning." Linda led Cass into the sunroom and sat her down on the wicker sofa. "Start talking."

Cass talked. She told her mother about Owen and how she'd fallen in love with him. How they'd been together almost every night, sharing a sweet little house in St. Dennis. How it had felt like the most right thing that had ever happened to her. How, despite her resolve to never get involved with another adventure-loving man, she'd fallen hard for him. How she had believed him when he said he'd stay, how she'd trusted him.

Then she told her mother about Cyndi and her deception, about the child that had been hidden from Owen, about how the truth had come out. About how she'd watched them together and how much they looked like a family.

"Well, they are a family, Cass. They are parents to that child."

"No, I mean they looked like they really liked each other again, like they were mother and father and son."

"That's what they are. And they should appear to like each other, whether or not they really do. If for no other reason than to make that little boy feel comfortable with Owen so he can get to know his son."

"They looked like they were doing more than just trying to make J.J. comfortable."

"I think you're jumping to conclusions, Cass. I think you're reading something into this that may or may not be there."

"What if they decide to get back together and be a family for real?"

"Has Owen given you any reason to think that might happen?"

"Well, no, but I have eyes, Mom."

"And an active imagination. Unfortunately, I have to take the blame for that." Linda cleared her throat. "What did you tell Owen before you left St. Dennis?"

"Nothing. I just left."

"You just left? You didn't say, 'Good-bye, I think I'll go see my mom in Baltimore'? 'I need space, I need to think'? Nothing?"

Cass shook her head.

"Cassidy," Linda said softly. "I think that was a cowardly thing to do."

"Oh, thanks, Mom. I come home crying for some motherly advice and you call me a coward. Way to kick a girl when she's down."

Cass tried to get up but Linda pulled on her arm to make her sit back down.

"I said it was a cowardly thing to do, not that you're a coward."

"Same thing."

"No, it isn't, and you know it isn't. You have a relationship with this man that sounds very serious."

"I thought it was."

"And I'm sure he thought it was, too. He probably thinks it still is. But his whole world has been turned upside down, Cassie. Put yourself in his place. I'm sure he's going crazy trying to figure out the right thing to do for his son. I can't even imagine how conflicted and confused he must be."

Cass's phone buzzed in her pocket and she glanced at the screen. Owen.

"Is that him?"

Cass nodded.

"You should talk to him."

"I'm not ready to talk to him." Cass slid the phone back into her pocket.

"He might be worried about where you are."

"I don't think he's thinking about me these days." Cass stood and went into the hall and gathered up the things she'd left there. "I'm going back to my apartment. Thanks for the pep talk, Mom."

"Cassie . . ."

"I know you're trying to be rational and to see both sides. But that's not what I need just now." Cass fished in her pocket for her car keys. "Right now I need someone to just be on my side."

"I am always on your side, sweetheart."

"It doesn't feel like it." Cass kissed her mother on the cheek.

"Cass, you're giving me the impression that you've given up." Linda stopped her in the doorway.

"Maybe."

"You know, ever since you were little, you were my warrior girl. I never saw you give up on anything. You always fought for what you wanted. What happened to my little warrior?" Linda folded her arms over her chest and stared at her daughter. "Where's that fighter now?"

WHERE'S THAT FIGHTER now?

Cass was wondering that herself. Was she not fighting because she was afraid she'd lose? When, she wondered, had she started to become afraid of losing?

When had the stakes ever been this high?

Yes, she finally admitted to herself. She was afraid of losing Owen. More accurately, she was afraid he was already lost to her.

And maybe that was the right way for this to end. Maybe Owen and Cyndi owed it to themselves to try to be a family for their son. They'd looked happy together, hadn't they? Maybe she, not Cyndi, should bow out gracefully. Wouldn't that be best for J.J., better than being shipped back and forth between—where were they living now? Massachusetts? Rhode Island? Somewhere up there. It's a long way for weekend visits, Cass thought. But if Cyndi moved back to the Eastern Shore, maybe they could spend more time together. They'd cared about each other once. Maybe for the sake of their son, they should try again.

Maybe Cass was the one who should back away.

The thought of doing that was like a thorn in her heart.

It isn't fair, she thought as she unlocked the door to her apartment. *I love him and . . .*

She sighed and put her computer on the dining-room table.

And I never told him. Not in words, but I should have. What was I waiting for?

Her apartment was dark and she was too depressed to turn the lights on. The place was dusty, and something in the refrigerator smelled terrible and the odor had seeped into the entire kitchen and dining area. She opened the door to the fridge and found something unrecognizable wrapped in clear plastic wrap, which did nothing to contain the nasty smell. She dropped it into a plastic bag and took it outside to the trash.

She went back upstairs and into her bedroom and tossed her phone onto her bed. What she needed was sleep. She hadn't had a full night's sleep since the previous weekend, and she was mentally and physically exhausted. Not the time to make a major decision about Owen or anything else in her life. She'd ignored his last few calls, and a glance at the screen told her she'd missed yet another. Finally she broke down and listened to his voice mails:

"Babe, where are you? Where'd you go? Why'd you just disappear like that? Call me, would you please?"

"Cass, what's going on? Kevin said you just got up and left. Where are you?"

"Cass, please come back. Whatever it is, we'll work it out. Call me, please?"

"Okay, this is getting scary. I'm starting to think the worst. That something's happened to you. If you're okay, at least let me know. Otherwise, I'm going to be tempted to call the state police. Cassie . . ."

His frustration came through loud and clear in that last message. She sent him a text:

In Baltimore. Need to think things through. Will be in touch.

He'd texted back, When are you coming back?

I don't know was the most honest answer she could give him.

Almost immediately, her phone pinged.

I'll be waiting.

Chapter Fourteen

Owen paced the floor, wondering what had happened that had made Cass leave without a word. He realized he'd been caught up in his own drama all week, but it wasn't every day a man found out he had a son.

He had a son.

He, Owen Parker, had fathered a son, and the woman he'd been married to at the time had hidden that from him for almost two years just to spite him. And for what? he'd asked her that first night as they sat on the back porch of the store, J.J. asleep on his mother's lap.

"For being you," she'd said, keeping her voice low so as not to wake the child. "For not being who I wanted you to be."

"You always knew exactly who I was. How many times had we broken up over the fact that I couldn't be the guy you wanted?"

"I thought you'd change after we were married."

"When has that ever worked?"

"Well, it didn't work well for us, and please keep your voice down. I'm sorry, Owen. It was stupid and petty and I deserve for you to hate me forever for what I've done. But please don't let J.J. know how much you hate me. I don't want him to feel that, and I never want him to think he was an accident."

Then she started to cry, deep sobs that Owen thought she must have been holding inside since the day she found out she was pregnant.

"I'm engaged to a guy who is so wonderful," she said between sobs. "He loves me more than anyone's ever loved me. And he loves J.J. like he's his own. When Kevin and I were first dating and he'd ask about the baby's father, I'd give him some vague answer. When he asked me to marry him, he said he wanted to adopt J.J., so we'd need to get his birth father to sign something agreeing to that. I knew I was in trouble then. I knew there was no way you would ever sign over the rights to your son to another man."

"Well, thanks for getting that much right."

"I kept making excuses about why I hadn't gotten in touch with you. 'Oh, he's out of the country right now.' 'Oh, I don't know where he is.' Finally, Kevin figured out that something was up, and he asked me point-blank what the hell was going on and if I was going to ask you about the adoption. And I had to tell him the truth." Cyndi swallowed hard. "I didn't know Kevin had a temper. He was always so calm about things, so reasonable about everything. But not about this. He said either I came clean with you and gave you the opportunity to say yes or no, that he could adopt J.J. or not, or the wedding was off. I knew you'd never give up your parental rights once you found out about J.J. At the same time, Kevin insisted he wasn't going to steal another man's son. Well, I was trapped and knew I had to face up to both of you. I couldn't even begin to imagine what you would do. Kevin looked at me like I was the worst person who'd ever been born." She started to cry again, then waved Owen off when he started to say something. "Not that I didn't deserve it. I did. I know I did. It was the worst thing I've ever done in my life, and I wish to God I could go back and do things differently. I swear, Owen . . ." More tears. "Can you ever forgive me?"

"I don't know. You're asking me now, and right now, I don't think I can, but maybe someday that will change. In the meantime, where do we go from here? Obviously, I want to get to know my son. And no, you can tell Kevin I'm not giving permission for him to adopt J.J. I admire him for being willing to do that, but I won't permit it, even though I'm grateful to him for his pushing you. If not for him, would I ever know I had a son?"

Cyndi averted her eyes.

"That's what I thought. So how are we going to handle this? How can I spend time with J.J. if you're living in . . . ? Where are you going to be living?"

"We just moved to Hartford, Connecticut."

"That's a long way to drive for weekend visits." She was silent.

"I'll tell you up front, weekends alone are not

good enough. You've had him for almost two years. It's my turn."

"Uh-uh. If you think I'm going to hand him over to you, you are crazy. He doesn't even know you."

"Whose fault is that?"

"You could have called once in a while, Owen. If you had, I probably would have told you."

"I'm thinking probably not."

Cyndi went silent again. Then she picked up her bag and J.J. "This isn't going to be resolved in one night, or two. I don't know what the solution will be. But I'm not here to give him to you."

"No, you're here because you were shamed into it, and you're here because I bumped into you by accident. How long were you going to be in Ballard before you finally came to see me? Or were you going to tell your fiancé that I wasn't around and no one knew where I was so he could go ahead and petition the court for the adoption, and I would never have known because I didn't know J.J. existed?" Owen looked at the sweet child in her arms. "I didn't even get to throw my two cents in when it came time to name him."

"I can't do this anymore tonight, Owen. I'll talk to you tomorrow."

She'd left Owen standing on the back porch at the store, watching as she drove away with his son in the backseat of her car.

The whole thing had made Owen feel like the world's biggest loser. He had a son he hadn't even known about. Cyndi was right. If he'd so much as picked up the phone and called her once in a while to see how she was, maybe she would have told him. But he'd cut off that relationship just as he'd cut off every other one he'd been in. Done? Over? Move on, then.

Only this time, moving on had cost him.

He wanted his son, but he wasn't sure how to make that work. Cyndi and Kevin were going to be living three states away. Was he supposed to pick up and move?

Where did that leave his relationship with Cass? He might move on from the island, from the work he loved, but he was not willing to move on from Cass. He'd fallen in love with her, but could he ask her to accept another woman's child? What must she think of him now? And how could he get J.J. to understand that he, Owen, was his father, not Kevin?

He'd posed that to Ruby two nights after Cyndi and J.J. had left. They'd had dinner together and he'd made attempts to have his son warm up to him, but he had to acknowledge that was going to be slow going. For the most part, J.J. seemed a bit suspicious of Owen, which was compounded by the child's apparently being somewhat shy by nature.

"He acts like he's afraid of me," Owen had complained to Ruby.

"He doesn't know you. Give him time. Don't be expecting a baby to know you're his daddy when you never been around."

"That's not my fault."

"Not be talking fault, Owen. That kind of talk be folly. You want to be angry at Cyndi, you have every right to be. But don't let that show to your boy. He be picking that up, by and by, and all he be knowing is his mama and this man of hers."

"It's not fair," Owen grumbled.

"Oh, we be talkin' like a five-year-old now?" Ruby harrumphed. "I'll pretend I didn't hear you say that."

"I want to know my son, Gigi."

Her tone softened. "I know you do, boy. And you be right in that."

"I don't want him to ever think I didn't want him."

"You work this out the right way, he'll know who you are and what he is to you. Just don't be trying to steamroll over that ex-wife of yours."

"Seems I'm the one who got steamrolled," Owen mumbled.

"Yes, you did, but what did you expect from a girl like Cyndi? But would I be one to remind you that you were told way back when to stop messin' with her, that it was going to lead to a heap of trouble for you one day?"

"Yes, you would be one to remind me. You like to say, 'I told you so,' as much as the next guy."

"True enough, that."

Owen sighed. "I just want a chance to be his father, Gigi. He barely looks at me, and when I try to talk to him, he buries his face in his mother."

"He be a shy boy, that's all. Lots of young ones go through shy times."

"He didn't seem so shy when Kevin showed up."

"Don't you think that be natural? He be around

that man all the time, and from where I'm sitting, Cyndi's man be good to that boy. And to her, not that she be deserving."

Owen could feel Ruby's eyes on him. He was waiting for her to say whatever else was on her mind. He knew she wouldn't keep to herself something she wanted him to hear.

Finally she said, "And don't be resenting that man for being as good as he is. You be a stranger to the child, son. Not of your doing, but that be the fact. Give him time to know you. He'll know who his real daddy is, by and by."

"Not if I don't get to spend time with him."

"That'll work out." She sat back in her chair. "What is Cass thinking about all this?"

"I'm not sure."

Ruby smacked him with her newspaper. "That be the business you best be taking care of. You lose that woman, you lose your heart, boy. You lose yourself."

"Don't you think I know that?"

"Knowing and doing be two different things. Best you get that done."

"She left, Gigi."

Ruby harrumphed again. Twice in one conversation, Owen realized. Things were worse than he'd thought.

"That be on you. Why would she be staying, with you not talking, not telling her where her place be in all this?"

Owen looked at his great-grandmother. "You knew all along, didn't you? About J.J.? About Cyndi not telling me. About Cass coming into my life, and about Cass leaving me. You knew it all."

"What I know or don't know, when or if—some things not be mine to tell. But of all those things, only one you have control over. The rest of all that, none be in your hands. They be decisions you had no hand in. But that one thing . . . you can control what happens."

"You're not talking about J.J. You're talking about Cass."

"Maybe you're not as dumb as you look after all." Ruby left the newspaper on the chair and went inside. "Then again . . ."

THE FOLLOWING DAY, Owen and Cyndi spent the entire afternoon hashing out a plan to move forward. It hadn't been easy, but eventually, with Kevin's help, they'd managed to get on the same page. Owen drove back to Lincoln Road, rehearsing what he'd say to Cass when—if—she came back. He stopped at the local supermarket on the way and made a few purchases because he knew there was no food and nothing to drink at home. He went into the one liquor store in town and picked up a bottle of wine for her, a six-pack of beer for himself. He was almost out of the store when he spotted a bottle of Jack Daniel's. The only thing he knew about the whiskey is that his father drank it when he was feeling particularly mean and wanted to get rip-roaring drunk. Rip-roaring drunk sounded pretty good right about then. Owen picked up the bottle and returned to the cashier and paid for it. He refused to examine the reasons why.

Less than three minutes later he pulled into the driveway, hoping against hope that Cass's car would be there. It wasn't. He gathered his purchases and went into the dark, empty house. The air was still and his footsteps echoed on the old pine floors as he found his way into the kitchen. He hated the silence that hung in the room where he and Cass had laughed and talked every day they'd spent in this house together.

He put the groceries away, then popped open a bottle of beer. Sitting at the kitchen table, he tried to make sense of his life. For years, all he'd wanted was the freedom to come and go as he liked. He remembered all too well the feeling his father had given his children when he'd made it clear he'd rather be somewhere else, that he would be somewhere else if it weren't for them. As a child, Owen had felt guilty that he'd been responsible for having tied his father down. Wouldn't he have been happier if Owen had never been born? Wouldn't he have been free to leave, to go wherever he wanted?

Owen was never, ever going to make anyone feel responsible for his unhappiness. So for years he'd kept moving. The closest thing he'd ever come to settling in one place was his marriage to Cyndi. They all knew how that had worked out.

He finished off the beer and opened another.

Funny, but he hadn't felt tied down to Cass. He'd been happier than he'd ever been in his life. He'd not spent a minute with her when he wished he were somewhere else. With her, he'd felt more like himself than he ever had before. He'd felt loved. He'd felt anchored but not in a bad way. Right now he felt hollow. He wanted her to come back but didn't know how to make that happen. He'd been so focused on his son over the past week, he'd almost forgotten about the woman he loved.

Not true, he told himself. He hadn't forgotten her. He'd just . . . neglected her. Failed her. Had he even told her he loved her? He wasn't sure. How could he not know that?

He tossed the glass bottle into the recycling bin across the room, and it smashed into the side of the container with a crack. He threw the second one in for good measure. He opened another beer and went out onto the back porch and sat on the top step. It was a beautiful night, and he should be sitting here with Cass. They should be looking up at the stars together. Owen remembered the night before they found out about J.J. He had looked down into Cass's face and felt immense gratitude that she'd chosen him, that he was her guy.

"You're my guy," she'd told him.

Where was she now?

He brought out the rest of the six-pack and drank until they were gone. He sat for a while longer and listened to an owl in one of the pine trees at the back at the yard. From somewhere off to the left another owl answered the call, and he heard the chatter as the two birds flew closer to each other. It was almost mating season, he thought.

"Hope your luck's better than mine is," he muttered as he went back inside.

The whiskey was on the counter where he'd left

it. Owen stared at it for a long time before he took the bottle from the bag and opened it.

IF SHE'D HAD any sense, she would probably have called first, but Cass was having trouble getting her thoughts organized and figured she'd use the time in the car on her way back to St. Dennis to rehearse what she was going to say to Owen. She'd been unable to sleep and decided she'd just as well get up and start driving. It wasn't something that could— or should—be done by phone. She cared too much about the outcome of the conversation for anything but a face-to-face talk.

It seemed Linda's little warrior girl wasn't gone at all. Cass was ready to fight if there was any chance she could keep Owen in her life. If he was already lost to her, she'd leave with her head held high, but this time, she'd say good-bye.

It was still dark—half-past five in the morning— when she pulled up in front of the house. Owen's Jeep was at the end of the driveway, so she had to park on the street. She unlocked the front door and went inside the quiet house. She left her bag on the desk inside the door and noticed the kitchen light was still on. She went in and found the empty beer carrier on the table. On the counter was an empty bottle of Jack Daniel's.

"Oh, Owen." She sighed. "What have you done?"

She looked in the living room, half expecting to find him passed out on the sofa, but he wasn't there. She started up the steps, wondering how he'd managed to make it to the second floor after drinking a six-pack of beer and an entire bottle of whiskey.

She stood in the doorway of the bedroom she'd shared with him and looked down at the sleeping man. He was on her side of the bed, her pillow in his arms, and she almost wept. She sat down on the edge of the bed next to him and he stirred. She wanted to lie down beside him, but he hadn't left much room.

Owen turned over and opened his eyes.

"I knew you were here," he murmured. "I felt you here." He sounded amazingly lucid for someone who must have a horrendous hangover. "I'm sorry things got so screwed up this week."

"It's not your fault. I know you were blindsided and you were trying to make things work with Cyndi. I don't blame you for that."

"I think we've finally figured things out. She's going to move to Ballard to stay with her folks until the wedding. I'll be able to spend time with J.J., and maybe after a while he won't look at me as if I'm the bogeyman."

Cass's stomach turned into one big knot, her worst fears confirmed. So he and Cyndi were going to remarry and be a family after all. The truth took the fight out of her.

"I should have told you. I should have let you know what we were thinking. It just took a while for us to get on the same page, you know? Decisions like that shouldn't be made quickly."

"No, I understand. It's the right thing to do. I was thinking that when I saw you together with J.J., you looked like the perfect family. I'm not surprised that you decided to try again. I wish you all the luck this time around."

Owen sat up and scratched his head, consternation on his face. "You wish who luck? What are you talking about?"

"You and Cyndi. It's the right thing to do."

"What's the right thing to do?"

"Marrying Cyndi and being a family for J.J." The words burned her tongue as she spoke them.

"You think Cyndi and I . . ."

She nodded, and as difficult as it was for her, she remained calm. She'd known this was a possibility.

"Cassie, I'm not marrying Cyndi."

"You just said she's staying with her parents until the wedding—"

"Her wedding to *Kevin*. He's an accountant, and he's applying for a job with a firm in Chesapeake City. He's quite a guy, Cass. He's giving up his job to move down here so that I can be a father to my son. I told Cyndi she should thank God that she found a man like that." Owen took Cass's hand. "You didn't really think I was going to get back together with her, did you?"

"You looked so happy together, laughing and playing with J.J."

"We were happy. Kevin told us about the job right before you got to the store, and everyone was relieved, believe me. I didn't get the chance to have that conversation with you because you left without telling me you were going. Kevin has saved us a nasty custody battle, and we all recognized the biggest loser would have been J.J. Cyndi and I had decided we'd both do all we could to make this as painless as possible for him. I want to be a good dad, Cass." Owen seemed to think about that for a moment. "Actually, I want to be a great dad."

"You will be." Cass studied his face. "You're not in love with her?"

"I haven't been in love with her for years. Maybe I never was. But I am in love with you."

"I love you, too, Owen. I came back here to tell you that. I came back to fight for you if I had to, but then you were talking about doing the right thing for J.J., and it made me stop and think that maybe what was best for me wasn't right for you and for him."

"Whatever you were thinking, you were obviously wrong."

"I've never been this happy to be wrong." She took his face in her hands and kissed him, long and hard. Then she remembered what she'd seen in the kitchen. "Owen, was someone here with you last night?"

"No, why?"

"I saw the empty beer bottles and the empty whiskey bottle, and I thought maybe you had company." She hesitated. "I never saw you drink more than a few beers, or some champagne at the wedding, so it didn't seem possible that you drank all that stuff by yourself."

Owen groaned. "Do you know who I'd be if I drank a six-pack and an entire bottle of whiskey?"

"The man on a gurney in the ER with his head in a trash can?"

Owen laughed. "I'd have been my father. Actually, I was starting to feel like my father for reasons I can't explain. So when I stopped to pick up the six-pack, I saw the Jack Daniel's there, and something made me buy it. I was feeling sorry for myself because I thought I'd lost you. But I sat outside and thought things over, and after a while I started thinking I didn't have to be my dad, I could be myself. I could be a good husband to you and a good father to J.J. and whatever children we have someday. I had a choice to make. I opened the bottle and poured the whiskey down the drain."

"You thought you'd lost me?"

He nodded.

"I thought I'd lost you."

"That makes us both idiots." He gathered her close. "Look, this thing with J.J. is going to work out. I'm still angry with Cyndi for doing what she did, but at least when she learned she was pregnant and I was gone, she decided to go ahead and have the baby, and she kept him, so I'm giving her credit for that much. Not telling me still rankles, but I'm going to have to get over that. So I think it's time we decided what we want for ourselves, for each other."

She opened her mouth to speak, but he held a finger to her lips and smiled. "I'll go first. I want to marry you. I want the next baby in the family to be ours. I want to live happily ever after with you on

Cannonball Island in that little house you're planning on building." Owen sat back. "Now it's your turn. Go."

"What you said." She kicked off her shoes and pushed him over on the bed to make room. "I do want to marry you. I do want to live happily ever after with you on Cannonball Island. But that little house isn't going to have room for the two of us, J.J. when you have him, and another baby or two someday. I'm going to have to go back to the drawing board and see if there's any way I can expand that little house to accommodate that family you're talking about having someday. I may have to look at a different lot," she said thoughtfully. "The one I had in mind isn't going to be big enough to expand."

"There are more to choose from, right?" He pulled her down to lie beside him and turned on his side to face her. "You'll make the right choice."

"Hmmm. Funny you should say that." Cass rested both arms on Owen's chest and leaned against him. "Ruby was talking about choices not so long ago."

"Of course she was," Owen muttered. "What did she say?"

"Something like, there were going to be choices made but not by me, and I had to wait and see. I told her I wasn't a patient person, and she said maybe one of those choices would be mine after all."

"There were plenty of choices made these past few days. Cyndi chose to come clean about J.J., though it was a choice made under duress. Kevin has chosen to look for a job down here. I chose not to be my father. And I decided I was going to ask you to marry me, if you'll have me." He pulled her closer. "Will you, Cassie? Will you marry me?"

"Of course I will. I definitely will." She stroked the side of his face because she knew it comforted him.

"Ruby said you were my heart." Owen looked into the eyes of the woman he loved. "That if I lost you, I'd lose myself, and she was absolutely right. You're everything to me. My everything and my always. Somehow Ruby knew."

Cass smiled. "Doesn't she always?"

Epilogue

～

On Christmas Eve, the ballroom at the Inn at Sinclair's Point was the vision of winter. The bride had wanted an all-white wedding, which meant Lucy had to go deep into her most creative place and figure out how to transform the great room into something resembling a blizzard—and she only had six weeks to pull it all together.

"Most holiday weddings are relatively easy, compared to this one," Lucy had told her mother. "Lots of red and green, all those poinsettias and evergreens. But Cass had this idea of all white, and that's what she's getting. It took me a while to figure out all the components, but I think everyone—including Cass—will be wowed."

Everyone was. White birches in white pots were placed at the front of the room, their branches arching together to form the focal point where the happy couple would exchange their vows. The room twinkled with thousands of tiny white lights in the birches and on the live Christmas trees that had been sprayed with white flocking. The table linens were all-white, and at the center of each table was a cloud of baby's breath in a white terra-cotta pot. Even the favors—meringue kisses—were white, and were left at each place in a white box tied with white satin ribbon. The chairs were white, and the aisle—lined with smaller white trees—was marked with a white runner.

The bride's attendants wore white chiffon gowns and carried white roses. The bride wore a strapless lace dress with a train she'd fought her mother against having, but Linda Deiter was not to be denied. Cass gave in, but won the veil-or-no-veil argument. In her hair she wore white orchids, sans veil. She carried an all-white bouquet of orchids, roses, and stephanotis.

At first, Owen had balked at wearing a white dinner jacket, but Cass had talked him into trying one on, and even he had to admit he looked pretty good, so she caved on his choice of socks—dark navy blue with orange crabs. Owen's son, J.J., dressed in similar fashion right down to the socks, carried the rings in a fancy white box. He toddled his way up the aisle, taking his sweet time getting to where he was supposed to be, but eventually, he made it.

The parents of the bride escorted her down the aisle. Linda wore a sleek cocktail dress with a white cashmere wrap under which she hid a stash of tissues, and a wristlet of white orchids. The mother of the groom wore a long dress with white chiffon ruffles and her Arizona tan.

Lis and Cass insisted that Ruby, too, wear white, but since it was difficult for Ruby to get about in the cold weather brought by November, Vanessa took several dresses Lis thought might suit to the general store. The dress chosen by Ruby was white crinkled silk that had long sleeves and buttoned down the front. Because she was always chilled, a white cashmere cardigan completed her outfit. All went perfectly with her brand-new spotlessly white tennis shoes.

It being the evening of December 24, Christmas carols were played throughout the night, and later in the evening the band encouraged everyone to sing along. Most of the color in the room came from the food, a buffet prepared by the inn's chef, who was recognized as one of the masters on the Eastern Shore.

The bride and the groom danced their first dance to "From This Moment On," and much to the surprise of his sister, Owen did not step on Cass's toes nor did he make a spectacle of himself, so Lis assumed they must have been practicing. The dance floor was filled most of the night, and by the end of the evening, everyone was convinced this had been the best wedding ever.

The newly married couple spent a week in Costa Rica, where, during the day, Owen renewed friendships and indulged his passion for diving while his bride indulged herself on the beach with a stack of books and a comfy lounge chair. From time to time a waiter brought her a cool drink. At night they dined under the stars, danced in the moonlight to a song only they could hear, and indulged their passion for each other.

Every once in a while Cass took off the wide gold band he'd slipped on her finger and read the inscription:

My everything and my always. My Chesapeake bride.

Diary~

Sometimes things work out exactly as they're meant to. Oh, not always, but sometimes. I look back over the past few months and I can see where Fate has had her finger on the pulse in St. Dennis—in a good way.

My sweet Alec—my sweet nephew—married his Lisbeth back at the end of September. She was a beautiful bride, I must say. My darling sister would have been thrilled to have been there to dance with her son, but she was fine with me taking her place. Not that I ever could, but for that one dance, yes, that was lovely. I know she was there with us, I could feel her beside Alec and me as we danced, and I know she was smiling. Which of course was the reason I couldn't hold back the tears. Carole's been gone for so many years now, and I still miss her every day. That I could feel her presence at such a happy moment, well, who wouldn't have been overcome?

The houses on the island are starting to come together nicely. Brian Deiter was able to have his way, and the dock he wanted was built on the bay side with just enough room for six small to medium-size boats. They've started to advertise in newspapers and magazines, particularly in the DC area, so we'll see who shows up to buy a bit of the island. Cass has started building a home for her and Owen, not after all on one of the lots her father purchased. When she and Owen announced they were going to be married, Ruby would hear of nothing but that they rebuild her grandfather's place over on that spit of land next to the point. I know Owen wanted to be closer to Ruby, but she'll be fine. I understand Chrissie will be staying a little longer than she'd originally planned so she can spend some time getting in touch with her roots. About time, some would say.

The house Owen and Cass will live in won't be ready for them until early February, which is fine because they still have Alec's house in town. My brother Clifford's house has sheltered many a searching soul over the years—Clifford's included. Cass and Owen are only the latest, and I know there's another who'll be staying under its welcoming roof by and by.

I don't know that anyone was happier than Ruby at Owen and Cass's wedding. She'd been worried about her boy for so long—she'd confided in me once that she feared he'd be off on a jaunt when his destiny arrived on the island. It remains to be seen whether she had anything to do with his returning at just the right time to meet Cass. Let's face it—Ruby's not above occasionally taking matters into her own very capable hands. Not that I would ever ask, of course.

It's no secret that Cass is a favorite of mine. She's breathed new life into Cannonball Island, preserved much of what might have been lost in the not-too-distant future. That she is talented and beautiful and has such a sensitive heart—well, one must say Owen certainly hit the jackpot when he met her.

So for Ruby—and her Kathleen, of course—there were two weddings in the family, two joyous events last year. Within the next eighteen months there will be more good news to rejoice in when their family grows. I see—and I know Ruby does as well—and I could not be happier.

We had tea this afternoon in the conservatory—it's too cold to have it on the veranda—and Cass brought both Owen's cousin Chrissie, Cass's own cousin Jane, and a friend of Cass's from college.

One of them is destined to be the next Chesapeake bride, but that's all I have to say about that~

Grace~